Also by J.D.Missen

CW01498384

Fiction
Confessions From A Fractured Mind
Secrets From A Misty River (Detective Inspector Morgan Mystery)

Poetry
Love, Death and Madness

Childrens
The Little Spider
The Little Mole

Hartsmere Estate

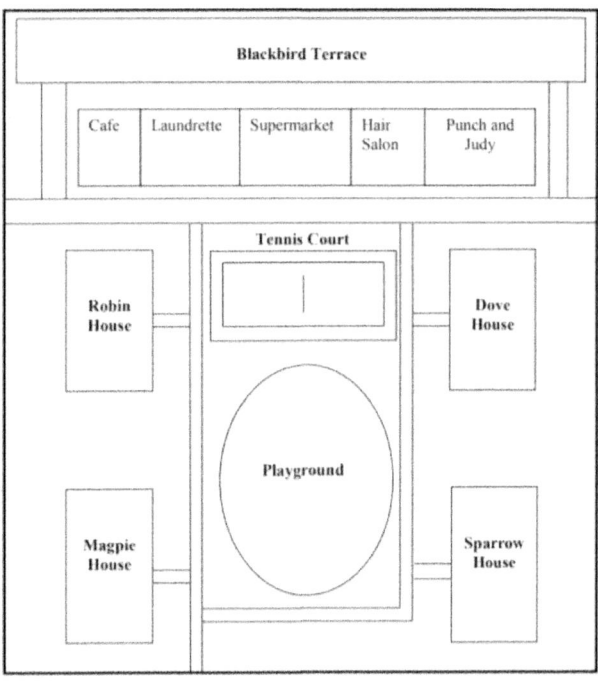

| Cafe | Laundrette | Supermarket | Hair Salon | Punch and Judy |

The Evil Within Us All

J.D.Missen

Published 2024 by Carrot Press
Book cover and image design by Carrot Publishing

ISBN: 978-1-7384353-88 (paperback)
ISBN: 978-1-7384353-95 (ebook)

Chapter 1

Detective Inspector James Morgan is sitting in a layby on the outskirts of town with his closest friend DCI Tom Cook. It is early Tuesday evening and Morgan, as is customary for him at the start of a late shift, is rapidly demolishing a greasy bacon bap. Cook, being slightly more health conscious, is finishing off the ploughman's sandwich that his wife made earlier using her home-made granary bread. Morgans own wife, Celia, would have happily made something similar but she knows her husband well enough to understand that he would never deign to eat something so healthy.

Morgan watches as fat droplets pelt down onto the windscreen, the weather reflecting his mood at the thought of the long shift ahead. He drums his fingers on the leather steering wheel in time to the music blaring out from the radio. Having never been blessed with much patience - a trait that seems to be worsening as Morgan gets older - he glares at Cook, who is still munching his last sandwich. Morgan clears his throat, ready to chivvy his friend into hurrying up, when the police radio crackles into life.

Morgan reaches across the dashboard to turn the down music, grateful for the excuse to do so - he has so far managed to keep up the pretence to his work colleagues that he enjoys the same music as they do, when in truth he really cannot bear it. Cook, who has preteen children to goad him into listening to all sorts of modern drivel, has taken to listening to all manner of tuneless noise, leaving Morgan feeling that he has little choice but to do the same to avoid being teased.

The two detectives concentrate intently on the monotonous voice coming over the radio waves from the control room, which is reporting the discovery of a body in one of the ground floor flats of Sparrow House. The Hartsmere estate is well known to Deben Quay Police Force and particularly Sparrow House, one of the older tower blocks. The building has been unoccupied for several years after the residents were moved out when it was earmarked for demolition. The derelict building is an ongoing source of grievance for both residents and the local police, who are frequently called out to deal with drug-related assaults, along with a multitude of burglaries in the occupied buildings and thefts from the shops. The fact that much of the petty crime involves basic items such as toilet rolls, bread and alcohol, is a sombre reminder of the dire situation that many of the Deben Quays most destitute residents have found themselves to be in.

The town's small fire service is also well-acquainted with both the estate and Sparrow House, which has been subjected to a steady onslaught of fires being set, accidently or otherwise, by the drug-users who still squat there despite knowing that the building could be pulled-down at any moment. It is a wonder that the building is still standing given the number incidents that continue to occur there, despite the councils recent decision to employ a security guard. Of course a simple resolution to the problem would be to carry out the original intention of demolishing the structure but the ongoing debate between potential developers and planning officers on its replacement, have left the residents of the estate caught up between an uncomfortable stand-off.

Shoving the remainder of his roll back into its torn plastic wrapper, Morgan throws the greasy object into the footwell, near to Cooks immaculately polished black shoes. Cook looks sideways at his friend sporting an expression of avid disgust at the flippant action by his friend, a sentiment that is promptly backed up by the senior detective pointedly moving his feet to the other side of the grubby plastic floor mat. Then, with a deep sigh of acceptance, Cook crumples up the foil wrapper from his home-made sandwich, moulds it into a ball and lobs into the footwell, where it comes to rest next to Morgans discarded food.

Morgan snorts with laughter, 'Well that didn't take long did it,' he says, amused that his usually tidy friend has succumbed so quickly to his slovenly ways.

Cook rolls his eyes, 'Come on, we'd better go and see what's happening on the estate.'

'Sure thing boss,' Morgan says cheekily as he switches on the engine. He swiftly pulls out into the road, ignoring the plethora of frustrated beeping that is immediately emitted from a van that has just been forced to swerve onto the other side to avoid colliding with the police car.

With the road clear of any other vehicles, Morgan puts his foot down and concentrates on the route ahead, which will take them directly to the estate. As they drive swiftly towards the Hartsmere estate, the control room continues to relay over the radio the sparse information they have received. Morgan decodes the usual abbreviations and acronyms, which would be unintelligible to anyone outside of the police force, to deduce that two teenagers, who decided it would be fun to poke about through Sparrow House, had found a body.

'Why anyone would think it's fun to rummage through that old building is beyond me.'

'I guess it's the thrill of finding something of value amongst all the rubbish and debris that's accumulated in there. I reckon a lot of stuff was left when the previous tenants moved out.'

'I can't imagine there's much of any use there now though, not with the squatters and junkies trashing the place,' Morgan snorts.

Cook produces a thin-lipped smile, he knows his friend is right, even if he chooses not to acknowledge it.

When they reach the outskirts of the estate, Morgan pulls the car up onto the footpath close to the parade of shops. Before he has even switched off the engine, Cook has taken off his seatbelt and is already reaching for the door handle.

'Looks like the news has already got out.' Morgan nods in the direction of a small group of residents, who are standing in front of the parade of shops, staring at them.

Cook snorts, unconcerned by the onlookers attempts at intimidation. The residents on the estate frequently make clear their feelings about the local police force, who in turn, are now immune to it. He shoves open the car door and leaps out before striding off at pace up the pavement. He passes closely by the group, who do not to move out of his way, forcing Cook to step up onto the grass verge to move around them.

Morgan slams the car door shut with a little more force than perhaps he intended, then presses the key fob and waits for the reassuring bleep to tell him the central locking is working. - the residents of this particular estate, need little excuse to pilfer, especially when the property is owned by the local police force. Quickly he walks up the narrow concrete path towards Sparrow House, then follows in Cooks footsteps to bypass the group. Once past them, Morgan speeds up to reach the outer door of Sparrow House at the same time as Cook.

In front of the main door to the building, which is encased by a metal grill, two teenagers are sitting on a low red-brick wall, talking animatedly to a police constable. As Cook and Morgan approach, they hear one of the lad's telling the tale of how he found the body with perhaps a little more embellishment than the last time he told it.

'We could smell something awful coming from number three - the door was unlocked so we thought we'd better take a look inside. I saw it as soon as I opened the door,' Turnip says, his voice wavering as he recalls the moment when his world had momentarily stood still, transfixed by the vision of a dead person in front of him. 'It was slumped against the back wall of the living room. I could see his eyes were glazed over, staring at the wall opposite him. I've not seen someone dead before but it was pretty obvious that he was gone'.

Turnip concludes his narration to his awaiting audience, which now comprises of Cook, Morgan and PC Barnes, whilst omitting to say that his first action upon seeing the corpse through the open door, was to promptly vomit onto the threadbare carpet, retching so violently that he needed to hold onto the decaying door frame.

It seems however that Turnip's friend Stevie, did not consider that these sort of details should be left out and, ignoring his friends obvious discomfort, decides that he should fill in

11

the missing details to the awaiting officers. 'I saw Turnip throw up and wondered what the hell was in there, so I went in and found out for myself. Never seen anything like it,' Stevie says, grimacing. 'Hope I never do again.'

PC Barnes nods sympathetically as he jots down a few notes. The two lads will need to make a proper statement later when they have recovered from the shock a little. 'What did you do after you found the body?'

'Phoned you lot of course, what else would I do?' Stevie snorts as if he has just been asked the most foolish question in the world.

Leaving Cook to continue listening to the two witnesses, Morgan steps over the low wall and onto the concrete path that leads to the main door of the building. He pulls open the heavy outer door, letting it bang shut behind him with a metallic clang that echoes through the empty space. Picking his way through the litter lining the dingy corridor, Morgan heads towards the door that has a number three in the centre of it, located on the far side of the now-defunct lift.

Morgan pulls open the door, instinctively putting his hand over his mouth as a stench of urine, mixed with the other noxious smells that usually arise from cooking up heroin, hits him. As he opens the boarded-up door wide enough for him to pass through, a jolt of anticipation surges though him; a mixture of reluctance to see what is beyond coupled with the possibility that for once, he might have something more interesting to investigate then yet another stolen dog.

Standing in the corridor, Morgan takes in a deep breath and immediately regrets his action as he is rewarded with an infill of damp, musty air, tinged with the acrid stench of death. Stepping over the fresh heap of drying vomit next to the threshold, Morgan makes his way through the mounds of rubbish and debris until he reaches the edge of a large room that was once the living area. From this position, he can see the body clearly without having to assault his nostrils any further by increasing his proximity to the corpse.

At the back of the room, almost hidden in the darkness, the on-call pathologist Dr Len Bootle is examining the body, without it seems, any regard for the pungent aroma that is pervading through the dank space. The pathologist swiftly steps around the body then stands back to stare at it, as if trying to decide if he has seen enough yet.

The cause of death is obvious. Even from the threshold of the room Morgan can clearly see that a hypodermic syringe is protruding from a vein on the inside of the man's pock-marked elbow; a foil wrap and charred spoon lay discarded beside him on the grimy patterned carpet. The cadaver's youthful face now adorns the grey-green pallor of death, which came to him only a few hours prior to being discovered.

The lack of blood to the upper part of the body gives the young man an almost ghostly appearance, made even more eerie by the shadows cast across him by the waning light that is peeping through cracks in the boarded-up window. Morgan has had enough experience of death not to require confirmation from the pathologist that the man died in the same position that he is still in - sitting propped up against the back wall of the room. Dr Bootle, who is now crouching down on his haunches next to the cadaver, however either does not know this, or is not interested in knowing it, as he begins to describe aloud in minute detail the scene before him, as if he teaching one of his first-year medical students.

The rather large sigh Morgan emits immediately elicits a raised eyebrow from the pathologist, who momentarily pauses his diatribe to look at the detective. 'As you can see from the mottled appearance of the upper body, the blood has almost completely drained from the upper circulatory system and has pooled into the lower half of the body.' Dr Bootle continues to look at Morgan, checking that he is listening then diverts his attention to the deceased, whom he pokes with the tip of his biro. 'Given the presence of drug-related paraphernalia, the cause of death is most probably linked to drug abuse. I will however conduct a postmortem this evening and let you know the results in a couple of days.'

Morgan nods, only partially listening as he is trying to imagine how shocking it must have been for the two boys to discover the body. It is certainly not something they are likely to forget in hurry. With his vision now having adjusted to the low level of light, Morgan begins to peruse the rest of the dingy room. The squat is filthy. Hardening mounds of excrement are strewn between plastic bottles half-filled with a yellow liquid that can only be deduced to be urine. Used needles lay dotted amongst the piles of empty cider bottles, plastic sandwich wrappers and empty crisp packets. A sleeping bag lies huddled in the cleanest corner of the room, its' thin navy material ripped with dark patches that are most probably saturated sweat and urine. A pair of well-worn trainers lay vacant nearby, their latest occupant no longer having a need for them. Morgan instinctively knows without checking that the rest of the flat will be in a similar state. It is obvious that the bedsit's most recent occupant had only been interested in obtaining and using the drug that seemingly finally consumed him.

The scene is depressingly familiar and Morgan is in no doubt that it will be one that he sees again. Of late it seems to have become a greater part of his routine to be called out to this part of Deben Quay; an area that is situated a lifetime away from the more affluent residential parts of the town that are located closest to the river. Reports of muggings, overdoses and burglaries draw the serious crime squad to the estate on an almost weekly basis, instilling in Morgan a sense of dread every time the call comes to summon him to the unloved, soulless place. Contrary to the belief of some residents, every case that arises from the estate is in fact investigated thoroughly by Deben Quay Police Force, albeit sometimes half-heartedly and often with little enthusiasm.

It has not always been this way though recalls Morgan, as he carefully picks his way back out of the derelict flat. One of the older residents had enthusiastically informed him on one of his visits, that the estate had been built in 1962 as a proactive reaction to the increasing number of homeless families who were unable to find sufficiently well-paid employment to afford the extortionate rates set by the profiteering private landlords that dominated the town's rental market. The estate had been designed by local architects, not only to provide sufficient housing for the growing needs of the post-war baby boomers but also to encourage a sense of community, by surrounding the stark, grey utilitarian concrete blocks of flats with communal grass areas and what was preposterously called 'a park'. At its conception, the estate was a place the residents had felt proud to call home, where those who lived there had a firm sense of belonging. It was a place where neighbours knew everything about each other and looked out for one another. Now, little evidence can be seen that this idealised sense of community still remains. Instead, the shabby, run down estate is ruled with a rod of fear by the gangs who live there.

Stepping back into the corridor then out though the door again, Morgan inhales deeply, grateful to breath in the fresh air. He begins to make his way through the small crowd that has gathered on the pavement – their usual apathetic curiosity having been peaked by the larger than usual police presence on the estate.

Cook, who is still standing with the two teenagers, spots Morgan and strides across the path towards him. 'What did Len Bootle say about the cause of death?' He asks, shoving his hands into his coat pockets to shield them against the biting wind.

'Probably drugs. He'll do a postmortem and let us know for definite in the next few days,' Morgan says, feeling slightly relieved. Even though it would have been a welcome change to be assigned to a more interesting case, a straightforward death such as a drug overdose, will not require the involvement of the serious crime squad and will mean less work for the already over-stretched team.

The two men make their way back through the estate towards the car, passing by a small tennis court and children's play area, which recently replaced the park. Morgan cannot help but wonder if this simple offering could ever provide sufficient entertainment for the increasingly disillusioned residents, who have perhaps by now realised that the purpose of situating the estate at the edge of the town, had more to do with keeping the riff raff away from the more desirable parts of Deben Quay frequented by tourists, then to provide poverty-stricken residents with a decent standard of housing.

Five minutes later the two men reach the parade of shops that are located at the far end of the estate. 'I see the obligatory group of youths are hanging about the shops,' grumbles Cook.

Morgan smiles tight-lipped as he gazes in the direction that Cook is looking in. This particular gang has become a real cause for concern for the local police, who are called out to investigate reports of assaults, which are invariably then retracted by the witnesses who suddenly decide that no crime took place after all. It seems that the sporadic rumours of kidnappings, beatings and torture that echo through the residential blocks are more than enough to keep a lid on the more lucrative goings-on that happen on the estate.

'It's so frustrating that we can't get any decent evidence on them.'

Cook stops to stare at the youths, who are blatantly glaring back at him, 'They'll slip up soon, I'm sure of it.'

Morgan looks at his friend for a moment then turns his attention to the low, squat building in front of him. Only one of the retail units on the estate is still in use. Unlike the smaller independent shops, the supermarket is part of a large commercial chain and is therefore able to afford the increasing insurance premiums stemming from frequent claims made for broken windows, damaged doors and stolen goods. The tiny supermarket is the only one within walking distance of the estate, though it is barely able to support the needs of most of the residents, who have learnt to exist frugally on the basic rations being made available to them. The shop provides all manner of budget and own-brand household goods as well as a limited selection of fresh produce and the ubiquitous nicotine and alcohol products. It fails however, to provide its customers with any products that are considered too luxurious to appeal to the lower classes, who are expected to exist only on cheap convenience foods of low nutritional value.

The parade of shops links the main part of the complex to the newest addition to the estate, through a series of footpaths and elevated concrete walkways. Morgan can just about recall when Blackbird Terrace was erected in the late nineteen seventies. It had aimed to provide additional homes to help cope with the ever-increasing housing waiting list that had grown exponentially after the Thatcher years and the controversial sale of council properties. Morgan ponders on how miserable it must be for the occupants to reside in such a soulless place, feeling very fortunate to live on the other side of the town.

'Even the café has given up,' Morgan remarks as they continue through the estate towards the inadequate car park that usually contains a number of burnt-out cars and pimped up rides that the Hartsmere dealers use to tout their business. The car park was the subject of debate at a recent meeting of the councils local planning department. The main topic of conversation had focused on how to best rejuvenate the area but with no majority decision forthcoming on how to tackle the ever-growing issue of the gangs, who confidence seems to be growing along with its numbers, the area has stayed exactly the same as when the Terrace had first been built.

'The laundrette as well,' Cook observes, pointing in the direction of the empty units. The laundrette had provided a place for residents to gossip as they waited for their clothes to be cleaned but the frequent bouts of vandalism and break-ins had caused it, along with the neighbouring café, to close three years ago.

As Morgan reaches into his trouser pocket to locate the car keys, he wonders what the original planners would think of their present-day creation. Over the years the idealistic dream that had been created by those optimistic, proud architects, has been gradually squeezed and finally crushed by the very residents it aimed to serve. The locals, having become disempowered by the regular free handouts from the Government, no longer care enough to even try to gain any sort of meaningful, lawful employment and have instead found other ways to while away the long hours spent milling around the estate. These new and largely illegal pastimes have sprung forth from the growing passivity seeping through the estate, as well as driving the need for some of the residents to supplement their cash reserves in the days preceding their government hand-outs in order to continue to feed the habits that are consuming them. In this most modern of estates, resident's income is being enhanced by stealing, mugging and burglarising the community they live in and there is widespread domination by the gangs who control not only the drugs trade but a large proportion of the criminal activity that is rife across the estate. This new culture of fear not only pervades the Hartsmere estate but is echoed across the rest of Deben Quay, effectively ensuring that few people from outside of the estate would dare to enter the alleged lawless place. On this estate, it is the youth who are in control.

Chapter 2

The next incident to occur on the Hartsmere estate comes in the form of a disturbance at Robin House - the most heavily populated tower block, situated next to the tennis court.

Lewis Smith, one of the elderly residents who resides on the first floor, was awoken from his habitual afternoon nap by the sounds of shouting and jeering. Lewis Smith, being far too frightened to investigate the disturbance for himself, immediately summoned for police assistance. The frail man has lived on the estate long enough to know when something serious has just occurred outside his front door.

By the time one of the local beat officers has traversed the rubbish-strewn staircase and reached the first-floor landing, an eerie silence has descended upon the building, yielding little sign of the earlier disturbance. PC Barnes officiates a cursory glance around the landing, just long enough to satisfy the paperwork he will need to complete once he returns to the station later. He heads back towards the stairwell, sighing deeply at the unwelcome interruption to his afternoon cigarette break. Just as the paunchy constable reaches the top step of the concrete stairway, he hears the feint sound of sobbing, which seems to be emanating from the far corner of the landing, beneath the boarded-up window. It is there, cowering in the darkness amongst the litter, that he discovers the girl.

Even in the fading autumnal afternoon light it is obvious to PC Barnes that the traumatised girl, who appears to be in her mid-teens, has been viciously beaten. Her right cheek is blotchy and swollen, stained by the tears that are now cascading involuntarily from her rapidly swelling eye. The shirt of her school uniform has been ripped open and is stained crimson from the large droplets dripping from her bloodied nose. The girls' shoulder-length chestnut hair has become loosened from its fastening and is partially covering her ghostly face, caressing her rounded shoulders, which are shaking violently. She is clutching tightly onto her school bag, placed in front of her pale legs that are drawn up protectively in front of her thin pubescent body.

'Hello,' PC Barnes says quietly as he approaches the frightened teen. 'Has something happened to you?' As soon as he speaks, the girl clamps her eyes firmly shut then places her trembling hands over her face. PC Barnes tries again to coax the teenager to speak to him before conceding that it would be best to request the presence of an officer from the serious crime squad and preferably one who might be better equipped to deal with this type of incident.

For once, Morgan is almost relieved to be summoned to the Hartsmere estate; grateful for the distraction from a planned afternoon of sifting through the seemingly endless pile of paperwork that need completing.

Within twenty minutes of leaving the office, having battled through rush-hour traffic and acquisitioned one of the few spaces available in the car park, Morgan reaches the main door to Robin House. His footsteps echo through the quietness of the stairwell as he makes his way up to the first floor landing, where PC Barnes is still ineffectually trying to coax the frightened girl away from the corner, where she is curled up tightly into a ball.

It would be obvious to anyone if they were watching that these futile attempts to communicate with the traumatised teenager were not having the desired effect and perhaps frightening her further.

'Thank you, I can take over from here,' Morgan says smoothly as he reaches the top step. 'Why don't you go and watch the front door and make sure no one enters or leaves.'

'Thanks, I will,' PC Barnes replies cheerfully, relieved by the opportunity to go and do something else.

Once alone, Morgan looks at the girl, who has taken her hands away from her face and appears to have been listening in to the conversation. Cautiously she opens her eyes and observes Morgan through her swollen lids, as if daring him to try to communicate with her.

Slowly Morgan moves towards the girl, stopping just before he reaches her. He crouches down to her level, his knees creaking in protest at the movement. 'There, there now, you're safe,' he says quietly.

The girl looks up at Morgan, tears of relief cascading down her cheeks.

By the time the paramedics arrive, Morgan has managed to extract the girl's name and address and the probable location of her mother, who is well known to both estate residents and police alike. Morgan wonders how Shania's mother will handle the news that her daughter has been assaulted. He does not relish telling her but it is a task that will fall to him as Cook is tied up investigating a robbery on the other side of town.

Shania clings to Morgan as he coaxes her away from the relative safety of the landing then escorts her to a waiting ambulance, which will take her to the local hospital. The girl even manages to produce a faint smile and wave goodbye to Morgan, as he leaves her in the safe hands of the paramedics.

The arrival of the emergency services acts as a signal to Lewis Smith, the elderly gentleman who first alerted the police to the incident, that it is now safe for him to emerge from his flat. Mr Smith, who was one of the first residents to be given a home on the Hartsmere estate, is now feeling so reassured by the presence of a police officer, that he is only too eager to relay to Morgan a multitude of tales relating to the numerous episodes of violence and intimidation that have been infiltrating through the once safe and friendly community.

'It's the parents fault of course,' grumbles Lewis Smith. 'No discipline these days, that's the problem. In my day we'd never have got away with this sort of behaviour. They seem to think its normal now to do this sort of thing.'

Morgan nods whilst scribbling diligently in his notebook. 'We'll need a statement from you please Mr Smith,' he says, taking down Lewis Smiths phone number.

Lewis Smith ignores Morgans request and instead, continues with his tirade. 'She won't press charges you know, they never do, too scared of what might happen. I don't want to get involved either, I'm too old to be worrying about stepping outside my own front door. Maybe she pissed them off, maybe she didn't know them and they just wanted a bit of fun. Who knows, there's nowt you can do about any of it except pull the whole place down and start again. Put them all in prison and give them hard labour I say. Not one of them has ever had a job or done an honest day's work in their life.'

'Now, in my day we had to work. No choice you see, we either worked or starved. We didn't have Government hand-outs in those days and we wouldn't have wanted them anyway. We would've felt ashamed to be out of work and living on hand-outs.'

Morgan suppress the smile that is forming as he tries to imagine how the elderly man justifies to himself, let alone to others, why he has been living in a council housing for the last forty years. The detective decides that it is time to interrupt the elderly man's flow before it becomes a full blown rant about the youth of today.

'I'm afraid I've got to go Mr Smith, I need to find the young girl's mother,' Morgan says, closing his notebook and shoving it into the back pocket of his trousers.

'She'll be pissed down the pub, like the rest of them around here,' Lewis Smith spits before shuffling back into his flat and firmly locking the door behind him.

Morgan trips back down the concrete staircase, gingerly stepping over the piles of rotting rubbish strewn down the sides of the stairwell. He passes by PC Barnes, who is still standing at the main entrance to the building, then hurries outside into the more fragrant but cooler autumnal air.

It only takes a few minutes to reach the Punch and Judy. The pub had been built with those residents in mind who could afford to, or perhaps needed to, escape into a drunken stupor without having to spend any of their dole money having to catch a bus into the town centre. Morgan has often wondered if the more cynical residents may have considered that perhaps this is yet another way for the council to ensure that the 'undesirables' are kept away from the more affluent parts of the town.

Somehow the pub has managed to survive, even in this hostile environment, providing a refuge for many of the residents to escape from their dreary, monotonous lives. Paradoxically though the pub is also a contributor to many of the estates problems and is known to be a source of fuel for the ever-growing levels of domestic violence that are openly becoming rife throughout the estate. Of course, it is likely that this has always been prevalent on the estate but previously it had been kept hidden behind closed doors.

As Morgan approaches the outside of the pub, he notices that the metal grills fixed to the large windows and front door, give the building an incarcerated appearance. The establishment certainly looks very unappealing to any newcomers, though perhaps that is the intention. Morgan pushes open the heavy outer door and strides through the entrance porch and into the main room of the pub, his shoes immediately sticking to the swirly carpet. A worn, dusty mahogany bar occupies the centre of the large room, where several customers are propped up on tall bar stools.

'I'm looking for Susie Smart, is she here?' Morgan asks the smooth-headed, muscular male who is serving a group of men at the other end of the bar.

'What do you want her for?' The barman responds gruffly, a sneer spreading across his face.

'Is she here?' Morgan repeats curtly, not wanting to divulge the reason for his visit.

The barman snorts and flashes Morgan a look of contempt before turning his back on him to serve another customer.

'I wouldn't want to arrest anyone for obstructing police business', Morgan murmurs.

The quiet words have their desired effect as the barman instantly swings back around. "How can I help officer?"

Morgan repeats his request whilst glaring at the insolent member of staff.

'She's over there in the corner', the barman says, as he continues to pull a pint of Stella for an awaiting customer.

Morgan follows the direction the man pointed in and immediately spots an emaciated blond, slouching into a worn leather sofa in the far corner of the room. She is flirting with her seedy-looking companion, who has one hand on his pint glass, the other firmly placed on her knee. Morgan is in no doubt that the slightly receding, paunch-bellied man is paying for Susie Smarts drinks in return for some kind of comfort and companionship.

The couple look up at Morgan with interest as he approaches their table. 'What do you want? Going to buy us a drink then?' The woman says cheekily. From the way she is slurring her words it is obvious that she has been in the pub for some time.

'Are you Susie Smart?' Morgan asks.

'Might be, depends whose asking?' She responds with a forced grin that reveals a row of stubby blackened teeth.

'I need to speak to you urgently,' Morgan replies, trying to keep some distance from the woman's rancid breath, which reeks of cigarettes and alcohol.

'Oh yeah, that sounds interesting,' she says, attempting to sound alluring. Her companion bristles at the sudden change in attention away from him and picks up his half-finished pint, pushes back the stool he has been occupying then stomps off towards the bar in defeat.

Morgan, growing tired of the charade, decides a blunter approach is needed in order to penetrate through the woman's drunken haze. 'Your daughter's been taken to hospital, or are you too drunk to care?'

Instantly a hush descends across the room. Morgan can feel everyone in the room staring at him as marches off towards the main door without waiting for a response from Susie Smart. It is quite obvious the woman is too drunk for a sensible conversation and in any case, he has no desire to discuss the details of Shania's assault in front of the other customers who are quite openly listening.

Susie Smart drains what little remains of her pint, whilst trying to comprehend what has had just happened. Slowly her saturated brain begins to piece together the information that has just been presented to her and she manages to deduce that something serious must have happened to Shania. Delicately she stands up, holding onto the back of her chair, then stoops down to pick up her leather jacket from the fabric-covered booth seat. With the item retrieved, she meanders her way past the bar stools as elegantly as she can muster, then heads towards the main door.

Morgan is waiting impatiently outside the pub in the hope that Susie Smart might appear. His level of irritation is worsening by the second as he paces up and down the pavement, stopping occasionally to exhale forcefully in an over-exaggerated show of annoyance. As soon as he hears the pub door creak open, he turns to watch as Susie stumbles out into the fading sunshine and attempts to walk towards him in a straight line, her hips sashaying as she totters about on her high heels.

'So, what's this about then? She slurs, fumbling about in her handbag for a cigarette. 'What's happened to my Shania?'

'Your daughter was attacked in Robin House this afternoon. She's been taken to Hemley Hospital to assess her injuries,' Morgan replies, rather more bluntly then intended.

'What do you mean, attacked? You don't mean…' Susie stops searching in her handbag momentarily to look at Morgan for some reassurance, her prematurely aging eyes filling with emotion. When Morgan does not respond, her search for nicotine resumes, eventually resulting in success as she locates a forgotten cigarette, hidden in a crumpled packet at the bottom of her bag. Susie sits down heavily on a nearby wooden bench, her fingers trembling as she struggles to light the stick. Eventually here hand stops shaking enough for her to light it and she sucks deeply on the cigarette to inhale as much nicotine as possible in the shortest time.

'We don't know yet what's happened to Shania,' Morgan says more gently this time, his earlier ill-temper beginning to wane. 'Shania was too traumatised to talk so she's been taken to hospital. She's in good hands though,' he adds, trying to placate the woman as she starts to wail loudly.

The loud noise attracts the attention of a group of youths who are lurking nearby. Intrigued by the noise, their conversation falters as one by one they all turn to stare at the odd pair. Their presence has the desired effect in making Morgan feel slightly unsettled, as he unsuccessfully tries again to placate the distressed woman.

To Morgan's relief, just at that moment a WPC appeared. The police officer places her arm around the distressed woman's shoulders. 'I know this is a shock to you but your daughter needs you. Why don't you go to the hospital and see her.'

Susie Smart nods then stares at the cigarette that is almost finished. She tosses the end onto the pavement and watches as it fizzles out in a puddle, then slowly stands up, as if the burden of what she has just learnt is too heavy to bear. 'Your right love, I'll go and see her. Can you give me a lift? I don't have any money for the bus?'

'I can take you,' the police officer says. 'Might be an idea to go and get washed first though and have some coffee.'

Susie Smart tilts her head to one side as if deciding if that was really necessary. After a moment she exhales deeply then turns around and heads towards Blackbird Terrace, the police officer following closely behind.

Chapter 3

Hemley Hospital was built on the outskirts of Deben Quay around the same time that the Hartsmere estate was constructed. The hospital was moved from its original location in the centre of town, under the pretext of allowing for the expansion of facilities in-line with the ever-growing community. Certainly, the hospital's new location is more convenient for emergency vehicles, being closer to the main trunk road that transports residents to and from the other nearby towns as well as in and out of the county. But to the cynic, it could be argued that it was by no means a mere coincidence that the site was also close to the Hartsmere and Walton estates; the areas of the town that house the lower income residents. Morgan remembers hearing rumours that the town planning committee decided the residents of these two estates were much more likely to need the services of the hospital than those living in more affluent areas. They were also less likely to complain about the increase in both noise levels and volume of traffic.

The early evening visiting session has already started by the time Morgan has battled his way through the heavy flow of peak hour traffic. The first thing he sees when he pulls into the car park, is the central high-rise tower block that dominates the site. He recalls being told that this was the first building to be constructed on this new site in the mid 1960's. The building rapidly became obsolete and is now surrounded by more modern, single-storey extensions, which house a first-class operating theatre and emergency department, along with several outpatient facilities and a restaurant that is highly subsidised for the numerous staff that work at the hospital.

The light is beginning to fade behind the tree-lined perimeter fence as Morgan circumnavigates the busy car park to find an empty parking bay. It takes almost twenty minutes before he finds a space at the far end of the visitor's car park close to the mortuary. Morgan switches off the engine and fishes around in his trouser pocket for some change, finding enough money for a couple of hours. After feeding the nearby machine, he returns to place the sticky ticket to his car window then makes his way towards the main entrance of the hospital.

When Shania had first arrived at the hospital, she was herded in through the busy emergency department, where they assessed and treated her physical injuries. With her assessment complete, she was then transferred to one of the mixed wards located in the vast tower block, which is now mainly utilised for in-patient treatment. The receptionist at the front desk explains to Morgan how to reach the ward, then ushers him towards the lift at the far end of the corridor. Having failed to find an alternative way to gain access to the upper floors, Morgan takes a deep breath and enters the lift, his hand trembling as he pushes the button for the second floor. He cannot remember when or even why he developed such a deep fear of elevators, but it is a phobia that seems to be worsening with age, along with his embarrassment of it. On this occasion he is grateful that there is no one else in the lift to witness him closing his eyes and taking in several deep breaths, trying desperately to think of something more pleasant as the lift judders its' way upwards.

By the time the lift doors re-open, a line of perspiration has formed across his lined brow and underneath his armpits. After what feels like an eternity, but in reality is only seconds, Morgan is out of the lift again and back onto solid ground. He walks through a long, brightly-lit corridor, his brogues clacking on the recently polished floor until he find Sproughton ward. Morgan pauses for a moment, trying to quell the nausea still lurking in the pit of his stomach, then he rounds the corner, arriving at the apex of several wards, which are fiercely guarded by a nurse. The nurse's badge reveals her name to be Senior General Nurse Sheila Berridge and her role, it seems, is largely to prevent anyone from entering the area without first disinfecting their hands.

'Make sure you use wash your hands,' Sheila Berridge barks as Morgan reaches the threshold of the ward. She points towards a liquid soap dispenser that is attached to the wall and watches carefully as Morgan rubs the sticky liquid onto his hands. 'Who are you visiting?'

'Shania Smart,' Morgan replies. 'I'm DI Morgan.' Morgan pulls his ID card from his wallet and holds it out for the nurse to inspect before returning the brown leather wallet back into his trouser pockets. When he looks up again, Nurse Berridge's rotund figure is towering over him. The nurse peers over her glasses at Morgan, trying to decide if the photo on the ID card correlates to the person standing in front of her. Eventually she grunts and waltzes off to the first ward on the right, clearly expecting Morgan to follow.

Shania's bed is near one of the large metal-framed windows that overlook the car park at the front of the hospital. From the doorway, Morgan can see the teenager lying propped up in bed, her head supported by three over-sized and firmly starched utilitarian pillows. Her school uniform has been replaced by a hospital gown that engulfs her tiny, underdeveloped frame. Her left arm is in a sling and she has several stitches adorning the right side of her face, where the worst of the bruising is now beginning to appear. The bruises on her nose and cheek have already deepened to a dark purple and the swollen tissue across the cheek bone gives her a hamster-like appearance.

Morgan walks purposefully across the room, ignoring the inquisitive glance from one of the other patients in a bed close to the door. He sits down on the grey leather chair next to Shania's bed and stares at the girl who is sleeping peacefully. He cannot help but wonder if

Shania sleeps that well at home, her mother certainly did not exude the air of competence that children need in order to feel secure.

Fifteen minutes later Shania opens her eyes. Her freckled nose wrinkles as if trying not to sneeze, then her eyebrows knit together, as she tries to recall where she is. It is only when she is fully awake that she realises someone is now sitting in the chair beside her bed.

Morgan is immediately struck by how calm Shania is, leaving him wondering if she has been given something to make her relax. According to the sister who carried out the ward round ten minutes earlier, Shania has said very little since she arrived and it is obvious that whatever has happened, the youth has been deeply traumatised by it.

Morgan clears his throat, unsure of how to begin what he knows will be a difficult conversation. Talking to teenagers is not his strong point, especially when they had just been brutally attacked. 'Hello Shania, do you remember me? I was in Robin House this afternoon.'

Shania nods, biting her bottom lip as if willing herself not to speak.

'I know this is hard Shania but I need to talk to you about what happened to you today.'

The girl shifts her attention away from Morgan, her eyes focusing instead on the elderly woman lying propped up in the bed opposite, being fed somewhat unsuccessfully by a care assistant.

Morgan tries again to engage her in conversation. 'Your mum is on her way over here. I thought perhaps you might like to talk to me before she arrives?'

Shania turns to look at him, her eyes wide with fear. 'I don't know anything. Just leave me alone.'

'I know something has happened to you Shania and we want to catch whoever did this but we can't do it without your help,' Morgan says gently.

Shania shrugs her rounded shoulders, her lips forming into a sulky pout then she turns to gaze at the bed she is lying on, pulling at a loose thread on the crisp white sheet.

'Please Shania, tell me what happened. Do you know who did this to you?'

Before the girl can respond, Susie Smart breezes onto the ward and plonks herself into the vacant chair next to her daughter's bed. She stares at Morgan, her eyes portraying the disgust she clearly feels at finding the presence of a police detective at her daughter's bedside.

Morgan is slightly taken aback by the change in both Susie's demeanour and appearance. The vivid transformation is only explained to him later, when he learns that she had first been persuaded to shower and change and then to visit the hospital café, where she downed three double espressos before making her way up to the ward.

'Perhaps I should leave you two to talk. I'll come and see you again tomorrow,' Morgan says, stiffly rising from his chair.

Both mother and daughter stare at the detective in silence, making it obvious that they are waiting for him to move out of earshot. Morgan lingers for a moment outside the entrance to the ward, trying to catch snippets of their conversation but hears little that he does not already know. Finally, he gives up and walks back down the ward in search of the Ward Sister.

A short walk through the maze of identical iridescent corridors takes Morgan to a cramped office, where he finds a petite woman hunched over a desk that is overflowing with paperwork, coffee cups and empty chocolate wrappers. Quietly he knocks on the open door, then enters without waiting for an invitation.

The woman raises her eyebrows in surprise at the unexpected intrusion. 'Can I help you?

'I'm DI Morgan,' he says, reaching forward to shake the nurses' outstretched hand. 'I'm investigating an incident involving one of the patients on your ward, Shania Smart. I wondered if she's said anything about what's happened to her?'

'Lisa Jennings,' the woman replies. 'They never do. I expect she knows who assaulted her but I doubt she will tell us what happened. She was raped as well, you know'. Sister Jennings exhales deeply, her eyes closing briefly as an image of the girl forms in her mind.

'I don't suppose you were able to get any samples from her?' Morgan asks.

'They're too clever for that. They know when to use protection. It's just a pity they don't use it all the time, we'd have a lot fewer pregnant teenagers blocking up our beds'. Lisa Jennings reaches down into her desk drawer to pull out a plastic bag containing Shania's clothes, which she hands to Morgan. They will need to be sent off to the forensics lab to check for fibres, hairs or anything else that might link to the perpetrators. Morgan feels a faint flicker of hope that perhaps some DNA evidence could be found, though of course finding out who they are is another matter unless they are already on the Police National Database.

The middle-aged nurse clasps her hands in front of her voluptuous chest, her elbows resting on the beech-coloured desk. 'We think she was raped more than once. The tissue damage around the vaginal area is extensive and she also has bruising to her upper arms, which could have been caused by someone holding her from behind.'

'We're certain there was more than one person present, the witness who called us said he heard several voices.'

Lisa Jennings shakes her head. 'I don't know how anyone could do such a thing, to someone so young as well. She'll never be the same again.'

Morgan nods, feeling a mixture of anger and despair. No matter what they do to help this young girl, it will not prevent it from happening again to someone else. He doubts Shania will make a statement against them, or if she does, she will be bullied into silence again by one of the gangs on the estate. He has seen it happen all too often. Morgan wonders if Shania is one of the few girls on the estate who keeps away from the gangs or if she too is part of one of them, giving herself freely to whoever wants her, whenever they want. Whichever is the case, Shania Smart will never go back to being the young girl she was the previous day.

Chapter 4

The first task for the serious crime squad is to carry out a door-to-door enquiry in Robin House. Despite the well-founded feeling that the search for witnesses on the attack of Shania will be futile, the officers keep any misgivings to themselves as the wander through the building in an organised fashion.

Depressingly but as expected, the resident's reaction to a police officer knocking on their front door is less than favourable. Door after door is slammed in their faces, snarling residents barking at them to leave them alone. The more vulnerable occupants refuse to take the security chains off their doors, leaving the officers no choice but to talk through the few inches of space revealed between the door and it's frame. After a couple of hours of fruitless questioning, it is clear that little progress is going to be made using this particular approach, so Morgan dismisses the team from the task.

Morgan decides to re-visit Lewis Smith, the elderly resident who originally alerted the police to the incident. He lifts the lid of the tarnished brass letterbox in the centre of the peeling front door and listens as it clangs against the metal casing, the sound reverberating through the empty corridor. Taking a step back across the tacky concrete floor, Morgan paces the length of the corridor as he waits. Eventually, footsteps can be heard shuffling towards the door, then the sound of a chain being slotted into place. The door is opened as far as the chain will allow and through the gap, a wizened face appears. As soon as Lewis Smith realises that it is Morgan on the other side, he pushes the door shut again to unhook the security chain, then pulls it open, motioning for Morgan to come in.

The flat is small in comparison to many of the other dwellings on the estate, having been designed to house a single occupant. Morgan follows the elderly man down the dimly lit corridor to a large, airy room at the far end of the flat that overlooks the front of the building. An old, mustard-coloured leather sofa occupies a third of the space with a portable TV set up at the other end of the room on top of a teak coffee table. On the TV, a presenter of a home improvement programme is informing his listeners that today they would be transforming yet another tired house.

Lewis Smith switches off the TV, leaving in its place, an almost deafening silence. In the distance, Morgan can hear the rhythmic thumping of music start up in another flat. He wonders if Lewis Smith would ever dare to complain about the noise. It seems very unlikely.

'How is she? The girl I mean,' Lewis Smith asks as he shuffles across the room.

Morgan is slightly taken aback by the question, having been left with the impression from their previous conversation that the elderly man wanted little to do with the problem that was unwittingly brought to his front door.

'She's recovering in hospital,' Morgan says, his eyes combing through the room, noting the elderly man's sparse possessions. 'She hasn't said much though, that's why I am here. I'm hoping you might have remembered something else that could help us?'

'Sorry, no, you know how it is around here. I know I'm getting on a bit, but I'd like to live a bit longer,' Lewis Smith smiles apologetically.

'So, you don't know who they were then?'

'I can't help you,' Lewis Smith says, throwing his arms up in exasperation. 'I didn't actually see anything, just heard the commotion outside, so called you lot to sort it out. I wasn't going to see for myself what was going on, I'm an old man you know.' He carefully sits down at one end of the ripped sofa and begins stroking the elderly ginger cat who is lying on the arm of the sofa, purring softly.

Morgan, who does not want to risk sitting down in case the ancient furniture is infested with fleas, ambles over towards the window. 'You've got a good view of the estate from here, don't you? I imagine you must see a lot?' Morgan places both hands on the metal window casing and peers out of the window at the dilapidated tennis court.

'I suppose so, I don't really look out that much,' Lewis Smith replies, still stroking the contented feline who is now stretching out his

45

back legs, his paws moving rhythmically as he purrs.

'The last time we spoke you said that there was a gang here on the estate?' Morgan turns around, returning his focus to the room.

'Yeah, well I might've been a bit hasty telling you that.' The old man continues to pet the cat, whilst deftly avoiding looking at Morgan.

'So, you don't know who any of the gang members are or where we can find them?'

'No. I would've thought you would know all about that anyway, you've been here enough times,' Lewis Smith snaps.

'That's a different team from mine. I deal with serious crimes such as rapes and murders,'

'She was raped then? Poor bugger. I suppose it doesn't make any difference really. They're all at it round here like bloody rabbits, out on the playground at night, in the doorways.' Lewis Smith stops stroking the cat, his hand resting on its soft fur and looks up at Morgan. 'I hear them you know. Those young men think nothing of it as long as they get their own way. They don't care who they hurt and the girls are too scared or too stupid to stop them. They'll do anything to be part of that gang, god knows why. What's going to happen if another gang comes onto the estate? Anarchy, that's what. Gang warfare. It's all about control you know. They control this estate and everyone in it one way or another. You're either with them or forever watching your back.'

46

The old man stops talking to splutter into a grey handkerchief that Morgan assumes had once been white. Lewis Smith picks up a glass from the coffee table and gulps down some of the clear liquid, stopping periodically to take in shallow breaths. As the coughing episode subsides, the elderly resident seemingly decides that he has had enough of talking and walks off towards the front door.

Morgan finds himself back in the brightly lit stairwell, listening to the metallic sound of a mortice lock being clicked into place, followed by a bolt being drawn across the door. His conversation with Lewis Smith is clearly over, leaving him little choice but to leave. It is almost impossible to avoid standing on the detritus littering the stairs, but Morgan manages to step over the worst of it, whilst holding his breath long enough to avoid the worst of the stench of urine that seems to be ever-present in each of the buildings on the estate.

It is nearly dark by the time he leaves Robin House. The nights are drawing in and the few trees that have survived from before the emergence of the estate, have begun dropping their golden, red leaves, littering the path in front of him. The wind, which has cooled considerably since Morgan arrived on the estate, is now whistling between the tower blocks, roughly tussling the discarded leaves lying on the path near to the main entrance of Robin House. Sporadically, when a gust is blowing in the right direction, the leaves float through the main door to the building, which as usual has been propped open.

Morgan zips up his jacket to the top, grateful that he remembered to bring it with him. He stands in the doorway and pulls up the collar to shield his exposed ears from the worst of the chill then marches up the cracked concrete pathway, which will lead him away from the tower block and back across the estate. A tense stillness has descended across the estate now that daylight has faded. The only audible noise penetrating through the turgid atmosphere comes from the broken leaves crunching underneath Morgans heavy boots. The noise seems vast as it ricochets through the concrete buildings that dominate the pedestrianised zone that is eerily absent of people.

Morgan quickly reaches the main path that runs along the length of the estate. As he strides at pace, he glances up towards the parade of shops at the far end, instantly regretting his actions as the bitter wind blows straight into his eyes, making them water. Even near the shops there are few people walking about, which is surprising for the time of evening. Morgan spies a group of youths who are congregating around a wooden bench in front of the supermarket. The young males are swigging out of cheap cans of beer, blowing smoke rings and shouting loudly at anyone who walks past. Morgan can faintly hear three teenage girls, who are sitting on the bench, giggling at the boy's antics. He wonders if the girls feel safe, perhaps even superior to the others in their class at school, with their protectors around them. One of the girls looks up at him, then quickly looks away again. Now is not the time, but Morgan knows that he might need to speak to them soon. If Shania ever finds the courage to speak out about who assaulted her.

It is early morning when Shania is released from hospital. Her bruises and dislocated shoulder will heal with time but recovering mentally from the experiences of the last twenty-four hours will take much longer.

Morgan decides to wait until mid-morning before returning to the estate to talk to Shania, to allow her a little time to settle back into her flat. This time he is accompanied by Detective Constable Fallow, a relative newcomer to both the team and to the police force. Fallow, a pale, lanky individual, had decided before he even left school that he wanted to become a police officer; a decision that greatly pleased his doting parents who wished for nothing more than for their son to be like his uncle, Chief Superintendent Bennett. Bennett, a stickler for family loyalty, had voraciously taken Fallow under his protection and made it his personal business to support and encourage the boy, even though he had his doubts that the quiet, shy lad was really cut out for this type of a career. It was Bennett who had ordered his nephew to be assigned to the Serious

Crime team and it was Cook, on behalf of his superior, who made sure that Morgan involved the inexperienced detective in as many cases as possible as part of his fast-track training. Morgan also has doubts over Fallow's suitability as a detective, especially working on serious crimes when he clearly has a sensitive disposition, but orders must be followed and he has no choice but to take the lad along with him.

Shania and her mum live in Blackbird Terrace, safely tucked away from the rest of the estate, behind the parade of shops. The terrace is linked to the shopping precinct by raised concrete walkways built either side of the retail outlets. The low-rise building is divided into ten, two-bedroomed flats on the upper two floors. The wooden-clad maisonettes that straddle the ground and first floors, contain four bedrooms and even the luxury of a tiny garden, so that residents can hang out their washing and on occasion, encourage their children to stop playing their computers for long enough to absorb some vitamin D.

Morgan and Fallow stroll to the main entrance at the back of the Blackbird Terrace, where a line of concrete outbuildings house rubbish bins and an area for recyclable materials. The introduction of this most recent scheme has become a constant headache for local council staff, who have received numerous complaints from residents who do not wish to bother recycling their rubbish and also from the fire service, who have now become accustomed to dousing out fires that have been started in the bins.

'Did you hear that the fire brigade found four of those bins in the middle of the tennis court?' Morgan nods his head towards the line of green wheelie bins that are now locked behind a trellis-fence area, with only the occupants of Blackbird Terrace being issued with a key. 'The original padlock for the gate to the tennis court was cut off. The little gits put a new padlock put on and locked it to stop the fire from being put out.' Morgan stops to look at Fallow, who seems confused at the concept of such obtuse vandalism. With no response forthcoming, Morgan sighs audibly. It is clear that Fallow still has a lot to learn about the behaviour of criminals.

Morgan decides not to bother retelling the remainder of the story, in that the blaze had become so intense, that the plastic bins had melted into the tarmac surface, rendering the tennis court unusable for the few residents who wanted to do something other than watch TV or dull their brains with alcohol and drugs. The council subsequently refused to spend any more of their already stretched budget repairing the damaged tennis court so it has now been left at the mercy of the residents.

Belatedly Fallow tuts in response but deigns to be drawn further into conversation. The pair walk on in silence as they make their way across the concrete area that leads to a heavy outer fire-resistant door. Morgan trips up the low step then pulls open the door, its hinges complaining loudly at the movement. He steps inside the echoey hallway, his shoes clacking loudly on the floor. His first thought is one of relief when he notices that there is no lift to contend with, which quickly turns to one of deep disgust as the familiar stomach-churning aroma of urine and vomit assaults his senses. The sound of the outer door slamming shut, tells the detective that Fallow is still behind him so he strides across the corridor towards the open metal staircase.

The Smart's live at number eleven, one of the middle floor flats. Morgan supposes that they do not need or perhaps had not wanted a garden, so had been placed in the less popular part of the building, where the waiting list was shorter. There are only four doors on the third floor and the two men quickly locate number eleven on the left side of the staircase.

Morgan stares momentarily at the blue front door, adorned by graffiti and peeling paintwork, then indicates to Fallow that he should knock on it.

'This one?' Fallow asks, pointing at the door to flat number eleven.

Morgan breaks out in a tight-lipped smile, wondering how someone with such low self-confidence will make a decent police officer. The two men wait in an uncomfortable silence that is echoed by the stillness of the building.

The door is opened by Shania's mother, who is presumably still in shock from the attack on her daughter as she has not yet left for the pub in order to satisfy her craving for cheap alcohol. Susie Smart is even dressed more appropriately for the role of a concerned mother; adorning a faded pair of jeans and a blue woollen jumper rather than the mini skirt and the leather jacket she had worn the previous day. Her blond hair has been swept back into a ponytail, revealing a recent love bite at the base of her neck. Morgan stares at it, wondering if it was made by Susie Smarts drinking companion in the Punch and Judy.

'What do you lot want?' Susie Smart snarls.

'We wanted to see how Shania is,' Morgan replies. 'We also need to talk to her again, see if she's remembered anything else that can help us catch whoever attacked her.'

Susie Smart sighs heavily, her red lips forming into a pout. Her low-cut camisole top reveals more than Morgan ideally wanted to see at any hour and certainly not at this time of the day. With an over-exaggerated show of displeasure, Susie huffs loudly then pulls open the heavy front door a little further to allow the two men in. She flattens herself against the hallway wall so that Morgan and Fallow can squeeze past her, leaving Morgan wondering if she deliberately thrust out her over-sized cleavage as he passes her to reach the living room at the far end of the corridor. Morgan blinks as he steps into the bright room, which is a complete contrast to the dingy hallway that is now behind him.

'I suppose you'll be wanting a cup of tea then?' Susie Smart offers, much to the surprise of the two detectives.

'Yes please,' Fallow responds, before Morgan can refuse. The senior detective's dislike of conforming to social norms was well known at the station.

When their preferences for milk and sugar have been given, Susie scuttles off into the kitchen. Morgan returns his attention to the large living room, which has recently been painted in the ubiquitous magnolia that is ever-present in local authority owned properties. On one wall, a colourful tapestry has been hung. Close by is a small beech table with two chairs, conveniently positioned next to the small kitchenette, where Susie Smart is now hurriedly washing up two mugs. Opposite the kitchenette, the wall is almost completely filled by an enormous metal-framed window that looks out over a small garden belonging to the ground-floor maisonette. Morgans eyes follows the window across the length of the room, towards the far end, where Shania is lying on a faded brown leather sofa, staring at the TV, which is showing a documentary on volcanoes.

'I've got nothing to say to you. I can't remember anything,' Shania mutters, her gaze still fixed on the TV. Suddenly she sits up and pulls out a packet of chewing gum from her jeans pocket. She selects one and unwraps it, throwing the plastic wrapper onto the swirly brown carpet. Pushing the malleable stick into her small, pouty mouth, the teenager begins to chew rhythmically, reminding Morgan of a cow munching on a handful of lush grass.

'You must be able to give us some description of the people who did this to you?' Morgan asks as he approaches the teenager.

'Nope. Can't tell you anything,' Shania says, her attention focused again on the TV.

'Well, how about where you were yesterday? What time did you leave school?'

Shania stops chewing for a moment, tilts her head to one side and stares at Morgan, trying to recall the events of the previous day. 'Usual time, three-thirty.'

'Did you come straight back to the estate after school?' Mogan asks, already becoming frustrated by the teens uncooperative attitude.

'Of course, don't I always?' Shania looks up at her mother, who has returned from the kitchen holding three steaming mugs of tea.

'Yeah,' Susie Smart automatically replies, despite having no idea what time her daughter usually returns from school as she is seldom around to greet her.

Susie clumsily places the mugs onto a small table next to the sofa, causing the contents of one of them to slop over, the resulting puddle of beige liquid adding to the existing stains. Swearing quietly, Susie selects one mug of watery tea to pass to Morgan, then hands the other to Fallow. She picks up her own chipped mug and sits down next to her daughter.

'Where did you first see the people who attacked you?' Morgan says, looking down in disgust at the vessel of scalding liquid he is holding. A sticky meniscus has already formed at the top of the tepid-brown liquid, which fails to hide the stains that have become ingrained in the porcelain from years of being hastily cleaned. Morgan takes one last look at the blue-striped mug and sets it down onto the nearby windowsill. There is no way on this earth he is going to drink that cup of tea.

'I walked past a gang in the playground, it might have been them,' Shania whispers, still focused on the TV in front of her.

'What happened after you saw them?'

Shania looks up at Morgan, blinking away the tears that are forming in her swollen eyes, 'I don't remember.'

'You're upsetting the girl, can't you see she doesn't want to talk about it,' Susie Smart snaps, her brief dalliance of acting the concerned mother clearly over as she reverts back to form. 'There's no point keep asking her, she don't know nothing and even if she did it won't do any good. We all know the police won't do nothing about it.' Susie grabs her mobile phone from the coffee table then pointedly looks at the clock on the home page.

'Did you walk home from school with anyone yesterday?' Morgan persists, ignoring Susie's very loud, exaggerated sigh.

'My mate Jade,' Shania replies confidently, relieved at the change in topic. 'We walked back to the estate together then she went home.'

'Where does Jade live?' Morgan asks, pulling out a notebook and biro from his inner coat pocket.

'Magpie House. Number fifty-seven. I don't remember anything after that though,' Shania says quickly.

'Well thanks for your time,' Morgan says, as he moves towards the door. Shania is clearly not ready yet to talk about what happened. Perhaps she never will.

Magpie House is one of the tower blocks that dwarfs the dilapidated play area, both equally in desperate need of modernisation. Morgan stands on the path that circumvents the building and gazes up at the building, which must be at least fifteen stories high. Behind him is the playground, consisting of two broken swings and a decrepit roundabout, which probably sees more usage from the bored teenagers on the estate rather than the toddlers for which it had been intended. Morgan looks across the estate, noting how overlooked the playground is. It is quite possible that someone saw the gang lurking there the previous day - finding someone who has the courage to come forward though will another matter entirely. Next to Magpie House is Robin House, where Shania was assaulted. Morgan wonders if there is a reason for the location of the attack, or if it was somewhere convenient to take the girl where they would not be disturbed.

Jade Thompson lives on the fifth floor. Morgan's heart sinks as he steps inside the cold, echoey entrance and is immediately faced with the choice of walking up ten flights of stairs or risking the urine-stained lift, which was prone to malfunction at any moment. Not wishing to reveal his phobia to Fallow, Morgan decides to risk the lift. It is a decision he instantly regrets as the stench of urea becomes more and more overpowering the longer they are incarcerated in the confined space. As they judder their way up to the fifth floor, Morgan tries to quell the feeling of nausea that is rising up from the pit of his stomach. He concentrates on breathing slowly and rhythmically, ignoring the almost overwhelming urge to vomit.

By the time they arrive on the fifth floor, Morgans hands are clammy and he is certain he must look pale but Fallow either does not notice or is too polite to comment. To add to his annoyance, when they reach number fifty-seven and knock on the door, there is no answer and Morgan is forced to repeat the experience of the lift far sooner than he would have wished.

Chapter 5

Celia Morgan feels as if she will literally burst with happiness as she enthusiastically dusts the bookcase in the living room, humming to herself as the cerise feather duster flicks over the tomes. Her husband has promised that they will visit a dog breeder this evening so that she can pick out a puppy at long last. Having gradually come to accept over the last three years that there is no possibility of them ever having children of their own, Celia decided she needed something else in her life other than her largely absent husband. After much persuasion, Morgan eventually conceded, perhaps even warmed to the idea by the time he finally agreed to purchase a small dog.

In anticipation of the new arrival, Celia has already enrolled the new pup onto a beginners training class and made an appointment at the vets to book him or her in for their vaccinations. A trip to a local pet shop has provided all the equipment they will need for the new arrival. She hadn't realised how much care a young pup would need but she is relishing her new role as a dog owner.

With the housework finished, Celia sits on the sofa to wait for her husband, her right leg rhythmically pumping up and down on the recently vacuumed shag-pile rug. She watches as the hands on the mantle clock tick towards six o'clock. Six o-clock arrives and passes, with no sign of Morgan. As the minutes slip by with no sign of her husband returning, Celias anxiety levels begin to creep up. She paces across the lounge carpet, stopping occasionally to try her husband's mobile again. By six forty-five she can wait no longer and in desperation, phones Tom Cook.

'Hello Tom, I don't suppose you know where my husband is, do you? We were supposed to be getting the puppy tonight and I can't get hold of him,' Celia explains, her voice wavering, unable to hide her disappointment.

'Sorry Celia, he's caught up with a new case on the Hartsmere estate'. Cook, unable to endure to Celias disappointment any longer, duly asks his wife to accompany Celia to the breeders house. It took some persuasion and a promise of a meal at her favourite Indian restaurant, the Bombay Potato, to persuade Sarah to undertake the task but eventually she agrees to it.

The weak autumnal sunlight is rapidly fading into darkness by the time Sarah has collected Celia and set off towards the Walton estate. Mr Holt lives close to the Hartsmere estate, a location neither woman feels particularly comfortable visiting at this late hour. Of course, had Celia known that her husband was not going to be accompanying her, she would have arranged the appointment during the daytime.

After making three wrong turns down the cramped estate roads that all look the same, the two women finds themselves parked opposite a small semi-detached house situated in the middle of a large, seedy-looking cul-de-sac. With more than a slight feeling of reservation about getting out of the car, the two women check the street is absent of anyone who looks furtive, then leave the safety of the vehicle, locking it carefully behind them.

Celia tentatively knocks on the door of number twelve, whilst smoothing down her thin, cerise cardigan with her slightly sweaty palms. After a few minutes, the door opens to reveal a stunted beer-bellied creature, adorned with short black curly hair and a small amount of greying stubble on his face. Celia delicately wrinkles her nose, her senses protesting at the stench that is now assaulting them.

Mr Holt's unshaven face stretches into a grin as he realises that the two women are here to see his puppies. 'Come in ladies,' he says.

Sarah just about manages to stop herself from pulling Celia away from the house. She desperately wants to tell her that this man is clearly only interested in their money but she cannot bring herself to upset her friend, knowing the heartache she has gone through over the last few years with learning that she is unable to have children.

Mr Holt squashes his rotund figure against the staircase to allow Celia and Sarah through the door and into the narrow hallway. The two women step into the front living room, where their senses are overwhelmed by the sights and sounds of a multitude of puppies, crawling over chewed furniture. The stench of urine and canine faeces is almost overpowering.

Celia carefully picks her way across the minefield of toys and excrement until she reaches the centre of the room. 'Aren't they adorable,' she says, turning to look at Sarah, who smiles thinly are her. She picks up the puppy nearest to her, a chocolate brown Cocker Spaniel, who is desperately trying to clamber up her legs. Celia looks into the puppy's soft green eyes and is immediately smitten. 'How much is this one?'

Mr Holt barely contains a smirk as he names his astronomical price, stressing that the puppy is a pure pedigree and has a family tree to prove it. He might be poor and uneducated but he can tell a money-making opportunity when he sees one.

Sarah, who quietly thinks it is a ridiculous amount to pay for something that will destroy their home and garden in a matter of months, if not weeks, politely keeps her thoughts to herself.

Celia is so enraptured by the dog that she does not notice her friends lack of enthusiasm, which she would normally pick up on. Her mind however was already made up before they entered the property and nothing is going to deter her from adopting the dog she has been longing for. Celia opens up her handbag and pulls out an envelope containing a wad of cash. She takes out the right amount and hands it to Mr Holt. Still holding the puppy, Celia carefully picks her way back across the sitting room again and out into the hallway.

It is only at this point that Sarah realises they have not brought a blanket to cover up the seats of her new car. She will just have to hope that the dog does not do too much damage. With the thought of the puppy and getting it out of her car as quickly as possible still uppermost on Sarahs mind, she manoeuvres her precious car back out of the road.

This time they manage not to get lost, which is a relief to both woman as it is now dark and some of the roads they are travelling down are not safe places to stop, even temporarily.

'Do you remember when these estates were built?' Sarah asks, still focusing on the road ahead.

'It was such a lovely area, lush green fields that grew barley and wheat. There was a small wooded area at the back there, where the Walton estate now is, we used to play in the stream in the summer and go back home covered in mud. I can't imagine the kids who live there now go out and play. They'd probably go home with a spliff and a debt to the dealers.'

'Sad really but I guess the houses were needed and they had to put them somewhere.'

Celia does not respond as she stares out of the window at the tower blocks that now fill the space where she once played as a child. If this was progress then it is a bad thing.

Sarah's fears are unfounded as the puppy remains well behaved throughout the journey back to Celia's house. She helps Celia and the puppy into the house before politely making her excuses. As she gets back into her car again, Sarah silently wishes Morgan the luck she is sure he will need through the weeks of sleepless nights and the frustration of toilet training.

Morgan arrives home from a long and exasperating day to find his wife sitting in the middle of the kitchen floor, feeding a puppy. He barely manages to hide his surprise at the sight of the new addition to the household, having completely forgotten about the promise he had made earlier in the week.

'I thought we could call him Bailey,' Celia says, stroking the puppy's soft fur. 'Or what about Cookie, seeing as he's a chocolate colour?'

'I think I prefer Bailey but he's your dog so you should decide,' Morgan says diplomatically. He watches in amazement as the young dog wolfs down a whole bowl of meat, then promptly squats on the kitchen floor. He never knew that such a large quantity of urine could be emitted from an animal of such a small size.

Celia quickly clears up the mess before transferring the puppy to the lounge where she plonks him onto her husband's lap so that she can go and prepare dinner. Morgan is not quite sure what to do with the dog and is relieved when it decides to curl up and go to sleep. The weary detective relaxes back into the soft cushions of the sofa, listening to his wife chattering away in the kitchen as she relays to him the tale of where the dog came from and how much it cost. Morgan is doubtful that the dog is indeed the pedigree stated on the certificate, but none-the-less has to admit that the dog is cute and more importantly, has made his wife smile for the first time in a long while.

Morgan is less pleased however with his wife's purchase when it begins whining and howling at two hourly intervals throughout the night. By five o'clock, Celia gives in and the dog is brought upstairs to their bedroom. As soon as the pup is placed on the duvet, it closes his eyes and sleeps through until morning without so much as a whimper.

Chapter 6

It is still early when Morgan leaves the house. The sun has not yet emerged and there is a light dusting of frost on the ground beneath his feet, a gentle reminder that winter is on its way. Morgan hates the winter months, despising the long dark days and freezing temperatures that always seem to penetrate through however many layers he wore. The thought of the impending cold weather does nothing to ease the gloomy mood Morgan has found himself in after a restless night that was predominantly caused by Bailey whining.

The car starts easily for once and the air conditioning quickly clears the condensation from the windscreen. Less than twenty minutes after getting out of bed, Morgan is pulling out of the driveway and heading towards the centre of Deben Quay to collect Fallow.

There are few cars on the road as Morgan makes his way through the streets, passing by asphalt pathways that glisten with frost. He clicks on his indicator then makes a left turn into Western Way. Half-way down the cul-de-sac is a stubby block of flats that were purpose-built in the late 1980's to infill a vacant plot that once contained a large Edwardian villa that was destroyed by a doodlebug during the second world war. A narrow track leads off the main road, circumnavigating the back of the building, where a small car park fills the space where a walled garden used to be. Morgan squeezes into an empty parking space that is lit by a security light that has been left switched on from the previous night. Picking up his phone from the passenger seat, Morgan messages Fallow to tell him that he has arrived.

As he waits for Fallow to appear, Morgan cranks up the heating and closes his tired eyes He listens to a gentle tune being played over the radio and the music begins to sooth his tired mind.

By the time Fallow emerges from the building, Morgan is fast asleep and softly snoring. The sound of a car door being opened, abruptly jolts Morgan from his slumber. He pushes his thumbs into his eyelids, willing himself to wake up.

Fallow coughs gently to announce his arrival, giving Morgan a moment more to fully awaken. 'Morning Sir,' Fallow says cheerfully, as he eases himself into the front seat of the car and clips on the seat belt. Fallow immediately senses Morgans low mood and falls into an abrupt silence, having learnt from prior experience when his colleague is not in the mood for making small talk.

Morgan pulls himself up straight, pushing his lower back into the seat. He looks at Fallow to check that his seat belt has been fastened then pulls out of the small car park and back onto Western Way.

The traffic has become much heavier and slows their journey to the Hartsmere estate. Morgan feels a spark of anxiety in the pit of his stomach - they need to reach Shania's friend Jade before she leaves for school otherwise they will need to come back yet again to talk to her.

By the time they have found somewhere to park at the edge of the pedestrianised zone, it is close to seven-thirty. The impenetrable darkness is beginning to recede as the two men walk across the estate, providing them with a clearer glimpse of the bleak concrete greyness which, even at this hour of the day, seems to exude a mixture of tension and despair.

There are few people about at this time of the morning; the walkway instead being inhabited by a large flock of pigeons that have congregated around the overflowing rubbish bins. Morgan and Fallow pick their way past the rubbish strewn across the path as they make their way towards the main entrance of Magpie House.

'Maybe they should've called it pigeon house,' Fallow says, trying to ease the tension, which is not perhaps the wisest of moves given Morgans current mood.

Morgan ignores the comment, concentrating instead on stepping over a fresh pile of crushed beer cans that have been dumped on the path sometime during the night. He pushes open the heavy fire-resistant door and steps inside, trying not to shiver in the damp corridor. From the pungent stench being emitted from the lift, which is for once working, it is clear that the inside of the building has also seen visitors overnight. Morgan exhales slowly, relieved that he now has an excuse to avoid the lift and heads towards the stairs without bothering to explain to Fallow.

Fifteen minutes later the two men reach the fifth floor, with Morgan still breathing heavily from the exertion. He makes a mental note that he really should take up jogging again, perhaps in the springtime, when the weather improves and the air is not so damp and chilly.

Morgan raps loudly on the door to number fifty-seven and this time the detective's perseverance is rewarded. The door tentatively opens to reveal a young girl behind it, who peers around the door to stare at the two men. Morgan judges the girl to be about nine, her chestnut hair fastened in two neat braids, cascades down the shoulders of her strawberry-coloured pyjamas.

The girl tugs at one of the braids then pulls it into her mouth and begins sucking on it. Her forehead wrinkles as she tries to decide if the two men are people she is allowed to invite in or not. In the end, she decides it's best to leave them where they are and skips back inside the flat, leaving the door slightly ajar. After a short pause, the girl can be heard shouting to her mum to 'go and look at the strange men' who are at their front door.

A few moments later a tall chunky woman appears at the door, clutching a bottle of milk in her left hand. 'What do you want? She asks sharply.

'Sorry to disturb you so early but my name's Detective Inspector Morgan and this is my colleague Detective Constable Fallow. We need to talk to your daughter Jade about her friend Shania Smart.'

'I know who you are, I can spot a copper a mile off. Is this about her getting roughed up?' The woman says, holding onto the door with her right hand to prevent them from entering the flat.

'Shania was seriously assaulted and if you don't mind, we'd like to talk to your daughter as she could be a valuable witness,' Morgan says, incensed at the woman's blasé attitude.

Zoe Thompson reluctantly pulls open the door, allowing the men to enter the grubby flat. They follow her through the dark, windowless hallway that runs through the centre of the flat. The once white walls are now stained with a yellow tinge from years of tobacco smoke infiltrating the textured wallpaper. At the far end of the hallway, they find themselves in a living area, with a small kitchenette tucked away in the far corner. Morgan notes that the layout is similar to the Smarts flat and ponders momentarily on the architect's lack of creativity. No doubt it was cheaper to simply replicate the same design over and over again.

The girl in the pink pyjamas is now sitting in front of a large TV. She stares at the ancient box, transfixed by it, whilst attempting to eat a bowl of cheap cereal, which keeps dropping off the spoon onto the floor. On seeing the mess, Zoe Thompson snatches the bowl from her daughter then storms back out of the room.

Morgan smiles tentatively at the youngster who is chewing one of her plaits again. Sitting crossed legged on the cheap laminate flooring, she stares wide-eyed at the two strangers who are standing in her living room.

Ten more minutes pass before the teenager finally appears. Jade is wearing a school uniform that is two sizes too big, drowning her slight frame. Her dark hair, which is pulled tightly back away from her face, makes her look much younger than her fourteen years. Morgan notices large hoop earnings threaded through both ears and a small stud adorning her left nostril that surely cannot be allowed in school.

'Mum said you wanted to talk to me about Shania?'

'That's right,' Morgan says. 'You know that she was attacked?'

Jade nods, her gaze falling to the TV screen where a local news programme has just started.

'Shania said you walked home from school together, is that right?'

'We always walk home together. She drops me off here then she goes home.' Jade moves over to the TV and sits down next to her sister, her eyes drawn to the image of a female newscaster.

'Did you go out again that evening?' Morgan asks.

'No,' Shania says. 'Sometimes in the summer we get changed and go out again, hang around the shops or the playground.'

'But you didn't on Wednesday? You stayed in the whole evening after school?' Morgan reiterates, surprised any teenager on this estate would stay in by herself whilst her friends are hanging out.

'I just told you, didn't I? I had homework to do.' Jade rolls her eyes, her gaze moving from the TV to the window.

'So, you didn't see Shania again that day?'

Jade sighs heavily, looking directly at Morgan. She folds her arms across her thin, flat-chested body, scuffing her feet against the laminate floor.

'Just one more question, as I can see you're keen to get to school. Did you see anyone else when you walked back from school?'

'Didn't notice anyone,' Jade mumbles, her eyes downcast.

Morgan tries to hide his annoyance at the teens lack of cooperation by forcing his mouth into a smile as best he can. Before they leave though, he gives Jade his card, just in case she remembers anything else. He knows its not likely to ever happen but perhaps one day Jade might need someone to help her and now she has someone she can call.

As they leave Magpie House, Morgan notices that the front of the tower block overlooks the playground; Jade would have a clear view of the estate from her living room window.

'She wasn't very helpful given that her best friend has just been assaulted,' Fallow says, stating the obvious.

'No, she wasn't. I expect she knows more than she's letting on. Everyone knows everything around here and if she hangs around with the other kids on the estate, I'm betting she knows who raped her friend. I wonder if she's been to see Shania yet?' Morgan wonders out aloud. 'Seeing as we're on the estate we might as well go and visit Shania again.'

The two men walk back down the path that cross-links all the buildings on the estate. It is close to eight-thirty and the estate is starting to come alive; young children are walking in groups towards the school; pockets of adults are making their way to the bus stop to catch a lift to work.

There is still an atmosphere of anticipation, as if something is waiting to happen. Morgan wonders how anyone copes with living in such a place, always being afraid to step outside their front door, never knowing when they might get mugged or their pitiful flat burgled. It is hardly surprising the residents look so downtrodden and forlorn. There seems so little hope that they could ever escape from it, trapped in a vicious cycle of crime and poverty.

By the time they reach the elevated walkway that leads to Blackbird Terrace, it has started to rain. Large droplets pelt down onto the worn concrete path, bouncing back up onto their shoes and soaking the bottom of their trousers. The weather seems to suit the mood of the place ponders Morgan, as he zips up his coat, wishing that he'd had the sense to bring an umbrella with him.

The rain becomes torrential just as the two men reach the main entrance to Blackbird Terrace. They make their way up the stairs to the flat where Shania and her mother live. Morgan raps loudly on the door and they wait a few minutes for a response. Just as they are about to leave, a voice quietly calls out from behind the door. Morgan responds and is surprised when the door is cautiously opened and a small face, peeks out to check on the identity of the caller. The face disappears again and light footsteps can be heard tripping up the hallway.

Predictably Shania's mother is absent. Morgan wonders if she has been out all night given the early hour of their visit and the fact that Shania is still in her pyjamas and dressing gown. It always surprises him how anyone could treat a child in this way but perhaps Susie Smart had not wanted children and so is determined to live her life the way she wants, no matter who she hurts in the process.

The door opens again and another face appears. 'Hello Shania. We were on the estate so thought we'd drop in and see how you are,' Morgan explains cheerfully.

The teenager shrugs her shoulders, opening the door a touch wider to allow them in. Morgan watches the figure move off towards the living area as he follows closely behind. Shania heads straight to the sofa and curls up onto it. Fallow immediately sits down on the remaining unoccupied chair, leaving Morgan perplexed that a junior officer would leave someone more senior to stand up. Clearly the younger detective needs some further education on etiquette.

'We wondered if you might have remembered anything else that would help us catch whoever hurt you?' Morgan says, hoping to engage the teenager into conversation.

'No,' Shania whispers, pulling at a loose thread on the seam of her pink dressing gown.

'Have any of your friends been to see you? We went to see Jade this morning.'

Shania looks up sharply. 'No. No-one's been here. I haven't even had a text from her,' she says, her bottom lip trembling as she fights back the tears that refuse to be contained.

'Perhaps she doesn't know what to say. Sometimes people find it difficult to talk about this sort of situation and so avoid talking to them at all,' Morgan explains diplomatically.

'That's stupid. Me and Jade have been friends for years, ever since primary school.'

'Ok, well we'll leave you to rest now. You've got my phone number if you remember anything you want to tell me,' Morgan says as the two men retrace their steps back out of the flat.

Chapter 7

Jade cannot concentrate. Her phone has been bleeping in her pocket most of the day, reminding her that she still has thirty unread text messages. She pulls the phone out of her pocket and glances at it, flicking through the list of messages from school friends who mainly want to know what has happened to Shania. There are also three messages from Shania, wondering why her best friend has abandoned her.

School drags by. She misses the whole point of the history lesson on the start of World War One and later cannot recall what they learnt in English Literature. At lunchtime Jade sits alone in the canteen, not wanting to talk to anyone. Even Mrs Jenkins notices she is not her usual cheeky self in Art. By the time lessons are over, Jade has managed to utter only three sentences and even then they are short and uninformative.

As it has stopped raining, Jade decides not to go straight home. Instead she heads for the playground, where she pulls herself up onto one of the swings, kicking her legs up in the air to lever herself up higher. She likes the swings, the feeling of the breeze tussling through her hair and the sense of freedom that the movement gives her. She closes her eyes, letting her mind drift, dreaming that she is somewhere else, somewhere warm. Somewhere safe.

When she opens her eyes again, she immediately spots a group of teenagers heading towards her. She puts her feet down onto the ground, stopping the swing abruptly. Her heart pounds as she watches the group coming closer.

One of the taller teenage boys breaks free from the group and quickens his step to reach her first. 'Where've you been all day? I've been trying to get hold of you,' the lad shouts, reaching over and grabbing hold of one arm of the swing.

'I've been at school,' Jade mumbles, her eyes downcast. She jumps down from the swing and pushes the lad out of her way so that she can get past him. Jade picks up her school bag that lies discarded at the side of the swings. Levering the bag onto her shoulder, she turns her back on the boy, her heart thumping, wondering how she is daring to be so defiant. Wondering what that defiance will cost her.

Almost immediately she regrets her actions as the boy grabs hold of her, squeezing his fingernails into the flesh of her upper arms. 'Get off me Marlon, you're hurting me,' Jade cries, gulping back the tears.

'You're my girlfriend, I'll do what I want,' he replies, smirking at the rest of the group, who have by now caught up with them. They surround Jade, imprisoning her inside the playground.

'Don't you want to be my girl anymore? Is that why you've been ignoring me?' Marlon spits. 'You can't just leave us when it gets rough you know. You're one of us now. We give you everything you need, look after you and in turn you look out for us. You know what happens when people try to leave us don't you, or maybe you'd like a taste of what your friend had the other night.'

Jade looks up at Marlon, her pupils dilating with fear. She is sure that the others must be able to hear her heart thumping as it beats violently against her rib cage.

'Sorry Marlon,' Jade whispers. 'Of course I still want to be your girlfriend.'

'Good girl, now you know what I want. Let's go.'

Jade meekly follows Marlon into the deserted Sparrow House with the rest of the gang following closely behind them. Marlon pushes open the door to one of the abandoned ground floor flats, holding it open for Jade to enter. Her shoulders drop, her school bag falling onto the grubby concrete floor as she reluctantly walks inside the room. The rest of the gang stand in a circle around the doorway and watch as the teenager crouches down and unzips Marlons jeans.

Morgan has spent the afternoon at the police station, catching up on paperwork for another case that is now drawing to a close. With the last file updated, Morgan logs off from his computer, remembering in time to switch off the monitor – he could do without having another lecture on saving energy. Just as he is about to leave, the phone rings. It is Lewis Smith, asking him to drop in on his way home. Intrigued, Morgan collects his coat and leaves before he gets caught up with any other work.

Morgan drives uncharacteristically carefully through the rush hour traffic, dodging irritable commuters who are returning home from their more lucrative jobs outside of the town. He makes his way slowly through the busy roads towards the Hartsmere estate. It irritates him every time that he goes to the estate that there are so few parking spaces. He often wonders if perhaps the architects who designed the estate had simply assumed the residents the buildings had been aimed at would not be able to afford the luxury of a car. This time though the detective is in luck as he squeezes into an empty space behind Blackbird Terrace.

After double checking that the car is locked, Morgan clambers over the grassy knoll and onto the damp long grass, immediately cursing his impatience in taking the short-cut, as the bottom of his trousers are completely soaked by the time he reaches the concrete walkway that bisects across the front of the building.

It is the busiest Morgan has ever seen the estate. Teenagers are milling about in front of the parade of shops, whilst scrawny women make their way towards the Punch and Judy for the start of the evening session. Despite the chill in the air, there appears to be a collective and determined ambivalence to the temperature, as warm coats have been shunned for more favoured short skirts and tight tops. The younger residents seem to have slightly more common sense than their peers, as they perch on the concrete benches outside the shops with their padded hooded jackets pulled up tightly around them.

Morgan marches past the tennis courts, which are as always, empty. A myriad of richly-coloured autumnal leaves blow across his path, following him through the heavy outer door into the stairwell of Robin House. This time he avoids the lift, justifying to himself that he needs the extra exercise by taking the stairs.

Little has changed on the first-floor landing since his last visit, though it did seem as if there might be slightly less rubbish cluttering the stairwell. The police incident tape is still drawn across the corner of the landing where Shania was found. It's unlikely that any useful evidence will be found in such a well-trodden walkway but of course procedures must always be followed, however futile they might seem.

Morgan knocks loudly on the worn front door. From somewhere inside, he can hear the noise of a television blaring out, leaving him wondering if the old man can hear him above the noise. He raps again on the door, this time a little louder. A few moments pass before Lewis Smith appears at the door. With the visitor having been identified, the door is flung open and Morgan is almost pulled inside the flat.

'Don't lurk out there, I don't want anyone to see you, do I? You never know what they might do around here and I for one don't want to be burnt alive in my bed,' he says anxiously before coughing into the used tissue that he is holding in his right hand.

'Sorry,' Morgan replies, without quite understanding why he is apologising. 'You said on the phone that you've got something to tell me about the attack on Shania?'

'That's right, I remembered after I had a kip this afternoon. I did recognise the lads who attacked that young girl. They live here, on the estate.'

Morgan raises an eyebrow, looking closely at the elderly man with renewed interest.

Lewis Smith motions for the detective to continue through the dingy corridor to the living area. 'Sit down lad, take the weight off your feet,' he says, pointing towards a floral armchair.

Morgan looks at the worn, stained piece of furniture and decides instead to walk over to the window, where he rests his arm on the sill. The flat directly overlooks the tennis court.

'That's what I wanted to tell you,' Lewis Smith says excitedly. 'I was stood here at the window and saw a group of lads walk from the playground towards this building.'

'What time was this?'

'I'd had my afternoon nap but it was before tea, so must've been about four o'clock,' Lewis Smith says. 'There were about six of them. I saw her as well, the girl, she was sitting on the roundabout. The next time I looked out the window she was walking with them towards this building. I went into the kitchen to make a cup of tea and after the kettle boiled, I heard a commotion going on outside the front door. Well, I knew what was going on didn't I. They're all at it these days, especially around here. Those girls go with anyone don't they. I didn't realise she was hurt or anything'.

'So why did you phone to report it?'

'I don't know, instinct I guess. They were making a lot of noise. I thought maybe she'd bitten off more than she could chew, if you get my meaning.'

'I don't suppose you can identify any of them?'

'I'm not sure. Ask anyone, they're always hanging around the playground. One's got his hair in dreadlocks, looks a bit like that rapper, the one that got shot last week. That's all I'm saying.' Lewis Smith turns his face away from Morgan, his jaw set hard, a glint of defiance in his eyes.

It is obvious to Morgan that little more will be forthcoming from the elderly man. 'Well, thank you for your time, Mr Smith, you've been really helpful.'

Lewis Smith grunts as he follows Morgan back up the corridor and shows the detective out of the flat, locking it securely behind him.

As Morgan leaves the building, the sun has begun to set behind Sparrow House, making the dilapidated building seem eerier than ever. He wonders what they will do with the estate in the long-term. How long will they continue to try to make it work before they pull it all down and start over again.

Chapter 8

Twenty years experience as a local beat officer puts PC Colin Barnes in the ideal position to interview the wayward youth who reside on the Hartsmere estate. It is something he enjoys in a perverse way, the power of authority coupled by the knowledge that he could make their lives very difficult if he wished. In truth, although a good proportion of the teenagers who live on the estate could do with a shock to their system and PC Barnes would joyfully enact on that, he is unwilling to do something that might jeopardise his job. Having grown up on a similar type of estate in the east end of London, Colin Barnes knows when he is onto a good thing.

They start early on Saturday morning, sweeping their way first through Magpie House then onto Robin House, interviewing every young male who lives on the estate. PC Barnes thinks back to his wayward youth as he traipses across the playground towards Dove House. It saddens him to think that gang culture has infiltrated this once quiet town in rural Suffolk, spreading outwards from London just as the plague had once done. At least though on this occasion, Lewis Smith has narrowed down the number of possible suspects to one of the boys who lives on the estate, rather than a rival gang from another area. It is one of Deben Quay Police Forces unspoken fears that rivalry from a gang outside of the town, could spark an even greater problem then they already have.

The moment PC Barnes knocks on number twenty-seven, he knows that he is in luck. The door is opened by a young girl, her hair pulled back into braids that caress her shoulders. Standing behind her in the dimly lit hallway, someone else is lurking in the shadows; someone who is waiting to see who is knocking at their door. As soon as he realises that the caller is a police officer, the young man barges past PC Barnes and runs off towards the musty stairwell. The youth clearly did not anticipate that PC Barnes was working as part of a team. The two officers, who were knocking on doors on the floor below, having caught sight of a young male running down the stairs, promptly trip him up before he can reach the main entrance to the building. There is no other reason why anyone would be running on the Hartsmere estate, except to get away from either the dealers or the cops, or both.

From his position at the top of the stairs, PC Barnes, who hears a tirade of swearing being emitted from the suspect, makes his way down the concrete steps two at a time to the lower floor. When he reaches the bottom step, a gleeful smirk erupts on his face as he sees that the suspect has been firmly apprehended by his colleagues.

The young man stares back at PC Barnes, a steely look of hatred in his eyes. The attitude does not bother the officer, he is too distracted by the appearance of the male; it is his first opportunity to get a good look at the youth. He takes in the youthful face, still sporting teenage acne on his chin that hardly yet needs a razor. It is not the young man's face though that holds PC Barnes' attention - it is the long braids that run down the back of his head. This is the person they have been searching for.

Morgan feels a slight tinge of displeasure about being called into work on a Saturday morning but it quickly dissipates when he finds out the reason for it.

'Hallo Morgan, what brings you in today?' asks PC Thomas, who is manning the front desk.

'Apparently there's someone I need to interview,' Morgan replies, shrugging his shoulders.

'Well, you'd best go and find out who it is then,' PC Thomas laughs, knowing full well why Morgan has been called in. One of the best parts of the job is getting to interview suspects that you know are guilty and with some luck, charging them with whatever misdemeanour they have carried out. There were some cases that really got to them and the rape of a young woman is one of them. PC Thomas knows full well that Morgan will be ecstatic when he finds out who is waiting for him in the interview room.

Morgan swipes his ID card across the door that leads into the back of the station. PC Thomas follows swiftly behind, wanting to see

Morgans reaction when he finds out who is in the interview room. Morgan peeks inside the room and catches a glimpse of a teenager, sitting astride one of the orange plastic chairs. The teenagers relaxed demeanour showing not only open ambivalence to his temporary incarceration but even perhaps annoyance at the early morning intrusion.

Morgan smirks then closes the door again. 'Well, that's made my day.'

'I thought it might,' PC Thomas says, 'Cook will be in soon, why don't you grab a coffee while you wait for him.'

There is a coffee machine in a small kitchen area between the interview rooms and the front desk where staff and visitors can obtain a quick, though usually unpalatable, caffeine fix. Morgan pours himself a large measure of the stewed liquid, just as Cook lollops up the corridor towards him.

'Right, lets go then,' Cook grins, patting his friend on the shoulder.

Morgan follows Cook into the interview room, where they introduce themselves and inform the teen of his legal rights.

'What would I need a solicitor for, I ain't done nothing you can charge me with,' he says confidently.

Morgan sits down opposite the suspect, feeling the teenager's eyes boring into him. 'Well, you'd better start with telling us your name then.'

'Why, don't you know it?'

Cook glares at the young man. 'You need to say it for the recording.'

The teen looks up towards the corner of the room and noticing the camera for the first time, waves at it. 'My name's Marlon Turner.'

'Why did you run when PC Barnes knocked on your door?' Morgan asks. Leaning back into the chair, the cold hard plastic pressing into his spine.

'I dunno, guess I don't like cops,' Marlon responds, the corner of his lips twitching into a slight smirk.

'Where were you on Wednesday afternoon?' Cook asks before taking a sip of the takeaway coffee that he bought on the way to the station.

'Dunno, I guess I was at home,' the youth replies, flicking a long braid across his shoulder.

'You don't seem to know very much, do you? Well shall I tell you what I think? I think you were in Robin house on Wednesday afternoon, where you and your friends raped a terrified young girl,' Cook says, throwing a pen onto the table and watching it as it rolls towards Marlon Turner.

'Prove it, can you? Marlon challenges, raising a pierced eyebrow at the senior officer.

'We have a witness who saw you walking from the playground towards Robin House about 4 PM on Wednesday afternoon,' Morgan says, leaning forward and placing his forearms on the table.

'No crime against walking is there?' The young man also shifts forward, clasping his fingers together. He stares at both Cook and Morgan in turn.

'That depends on whether or not you were walking up to the first floor stairwell where a teenage girl was assaulted. We know it was you,' bluffs Morgan.

'Prove it. You can't keep me here, I know my rights. You got no proof so you got to let me go.'

'You seem to have misunderstood the reason why you are here Marlon,' says Morgan. 'You're here to help us with our enquiries, just like your friends.'

A flash of insecurity crosses his face. 'I was with a girl Wednesday afternoon, I don't need to spell out what we were doing, been seeing her for a while.'

'She'll be able to corroborate this? Cook asks.

'Course, she's my girlfriend. We're always together. We do everything together her and me. And I mean everything,' Marlon smirks.

'You won't mind telling us her name then?' Cook says.

Marlon Turner relaxes back into his chair, the smirk deepening into a wide smile. 'Her name is Jade Thompson.'

Morgan tries not to react to the unexpected revelation. 'We will be talking to you again

Marlon,' he says, pushing back his chair to stand up, his jaw clenched in anger.

'Do I get a ride back to the estate then?' Marlon Turner asks cheekily.

Morgan does not respond but instead opens the door and ushers the young man down the corridor. 'We'll see you again soon.'

Marlon strides off towards the front door of the station. 'Whatever,' he says, slamming the door shut behind him.

Cook is already upstairs in his office when Morgan walks in, sporting a look of annoyance on his tired face. 'Little bastard, I'd like to slap him,' he says, leaning on the table, the palm of his hand cupped underneath his chin.

'He's right though. We haven't got any proof he raped Shania, or even that he was in the building, just that he was in the area. I bet Jade will give him an alibi,' Cook says evenly.

'They're too bloody clever these days, fancy carrying condoms about with you in case you might rape someone. Any luck with his friends?' Morgan asks.

'No, they're all keeping quiet.'

'No surprise there then. I think we need to make another visit to the estate,' Morgan says glumly, collecting his jacket and marching out of the door, leaving Cook dejectedly following behind.

Chapter 9

Jade is listening to music in her bedroom when she hears a loud knock on the front door. She is alone as usual - her mum is in the Punch and Judy and her younger sister has been left with a neighbour who has three kids of her own and barely notices an extra child.

The teenager sighs in annoyance when she opens the door. Reluctantly she pulls the door open wider to let the two men in.

'I still don't know nothing,' Jade says before either detective can speak.

'You know Marlon Turner though, don't you?' Morgan says, carefully sitting down on the worn brown leather sofa, whilst trying to avoid the ripped edge, which has been badly repaired with packing tape.

'So what? Yeah, I know him,' she replies, her lips pushed out to form a pout.

'Did you see Marlon the day Shania was attacked? Morgan asks, looking straight at Jade.

'I can't remember, I might have done.' Jade starts to chew her bottom lip, unsure of how she should respond.

'Either you were with him or you weren't,' snaps Morgan.

'Yeah, I was with him on Wednesday. Can you go now, I've got stuff to do'.

'So, you lied to us about where you were on Wednesday the first time we spoke?' Morgan asks, standing up and moving away from the sofa.

Jade shrugs her shoulders, 'I must have forgot.'

Cook snorts from his position, standing in the doorway. Morgan is a little taken aback by his friend's unusual lack of professionalism and wonders if the pressures of leading the team are becoming too overwhelming for him.

'Thanks for your help Jade. I'm sure Shania will be glad to know that it wasn't her best friend's boyfriend who raped her. By the way, have you been to see her yet? I'm sure she could do with a friend at the moment,' Morgan says, walking back up the hallway towards the front door.

I've been busy haven't I, with school and all that'. Jade follows the two men to the front door, waits for them to go into the corridor then slams it shut behind them.

Cook says, 'Well that was enlightening, I wonder if Shania knows that her best friend has given the person who attacked her an alibi.'

'I expect she's guessed by now. It certainly explains why Jade hasn't been to see Shania yet.'

'I reckon she feels guilty about something and so she should, given she's just stopped her best friend from getting justice for what's happened to her.' Morgan shakes his head as he makes his way back down the pungent stairwell towards the main entrance.

'We might as well go and see Shania again seeing as we're here,' Cook says as he reaches the door.

Morgan smiles thinly, pushing away all thoughts of getting back to his warm house where his wife is preparing a beef casserole, then strides off in the direction of Blackbird Terrace.

Shania is also alone in her flat, with her mum at the Punch and Judy as usual, though this time she is with Zoe Thompson. The teenager lets the two men into the flat and leads them into the living room. She sits down on the sofa, drawing her legs up underneath.

'How are you feeling Shania?' Cook asks after introducing himself - it is the first time he has met the teenager.

'It still hurts a lot, especially my face but my shoulders a lot better now.' Shania thrusts her arm out in front of her and wiggles it.

Cook smiles warmly at the teenager as he sits down at the other end of the sofa. Morgan takes a careful look at the only unoccupied seat in the room and decides to stay standing as the ancient piece of furniture looks as if it has not been cleaned for decades.

'Do you know Marlon Turner?' Morgan says rather bluntly, the thought of being back in his clean warm home uppermost in his mind.

Shania's head jerks upwards. She looks up at Morgan, her eyes widening. 'He's Jades boyfriend,' she whispers.

'A witness has come forward and identified Marlon as being with the group of lads who attacked you,' Cook says.

Morgan walks over to the back of the room and picks up a dining chair, then places it next to the sofa. 'Was Marlon one of the lads who attacked you Shania?' he asks, brushing the seat with his hand before tentatively sitting down.

Shania turns her head away from them, tears prickling at the corner of her eyes.

'If you won't tell us then we can't help you. Do you want them to get away with it and do this to someone else?' Morgan snaps.

Shania refuses to look at him, her gaze falling to her lap. She removes a stick of chewing gum from the front pocket of her jeans, tears open the packet and selects one.

Morgan turns to face Cook. 'We might as well go then. There's not much we can do if Shania won't tell us what happened. We'll be back on the estate though when they do it to another young girl.'

Shania stops chewing and closes her eyes. A knock on the front door interrupts the uncomfortable silence that has descended on the room. Shania shuffles to the front door in her fluffy pink slippers, clutching a small teddy bear in her right hand, which was lying on the arm of the sofa.

The caller is a district nurse who has come to check on Shania's injuries. Her shoulder injury is healing well but it will be many months before the cut on her face fades and even longer for any mental scars to start to recede.

Morgan sees the nurse's arrival as an opportunity to leave, if they go now they will have enough time to stop in at the Eels Foot. The pub is close to both men's homes and they need some respite from the stress of the last few days. It takes little to persuade Cook that what he needs now is a well-deserved pint of local Suffolk ale. In any case, the conversation with Shania is over with for now. There is not much else they can do unless either Shania or Jade decide to start telling the truth.

The pub is busy for a Saturday afternoon. The building, which was built in the late nineteenth century, consists of a large central room with two smaller snugs at either end. Morgan and Cook make their way through the crowd of customers to the bar, where a group of men are sitting on stools, chatting about their dreary jobs and moaning about their wives. Cook orders two pints of bitter, leaving Morgan to find them a seat in a quieter part of the pub. With a suitable table chosen, Morgan removes his coat and hangs it up on a nearby coat stand, before settling into the armchair that is nearest to the log fire. He picks up a poker and stirs the dying embers back into life, watching as the flames leap up the chimney. For a moment he is reminded of another time when he had sat watching the flames of a log fire, a time when he was not alone. Morgan pushes the memory aside, it is a part of his past that he does not wish to think about.

'Not much else we can do then?' Morgan says as Cook approaches the table holding a pint in either hand.

'No not really, silly girl.' Cook sets the drinks down on to the table, spilling a little of the creamy froth down the side of the glass in the process.

'I suppose she's scared they will come after her again if she squeals on them,' Morgan replies, feeling uncharacteristically empathetic. He picks up the pint nearest to him and drinks deeply from the glass of sweet honey ale.

When they have finished their drinks, Morgan picks up the empty glasses and takes them to the bar for a refill. Whilst he waits for their drinks to be poured, he listens in on the other patron's conversations. The gaggle of men who are still commandeering the bar area have now turned their attention to discussing the Hartsmere estate - one of the younger members of the group seemingly visits the estate as part of his job as a bus driver.

'They're a rough lot up there. I wouldn't go there if I didn't have to. They're always shouting and throwing things at my bus, it's a wonder I haven't had an accident yet.'

'Don't the police do anything?' One of the other men says between taking sips from his glass.

'Don't suppose they can do much, or maybe they don't want to. There's a gang of young lads on that estate, they run it don't they. Got some stupid name, "The Bloods", something like that. They're the ones that cause all the trouble. I reckon it was them that raped that poor young girl earlier in the week.'

'What rape? There wasn't anything about a rape in the papers?' Another man pipes up.

'Wouldn't be would there. The police don't want anyone to know how incompetent they are.' The men laugh then change the topic of conversation back to moaning about their wives. They do not notice Morgan staring at them, boring a hole into the backs of their heads as he picks up the now replenished glasses and carries them back to the other side of the pub.

'Those men at the bar were just talking about Shania,' Morgan says, still fuming. He hands an over-filled glass to Cook, trying not to spill any droplets onto his trousers.

'Men like to gossip as much as women do, especially after a few drinks,' Cook replies. 'What were they saying then?'

'They reckon the gang are called "The Bloods". Who the hell do they think they are, "The Cripps?"' Morgan snorts. He sits down again next to the fire, feeling the heat from the flames against his thigh.

'Did they say much about the attack?' Cook asks as he waits for the ale to settle.

'Just that they were surprised it hasn't been in the paper yet. Do you think we should do a press release, see if any more witnesses come forward?'

'We could do, though I doubt most of the people on the estate would have the intellect to read a newspaper and even less likely to come forward for something like that.' Cook peers at his glass and having decided that the drink has had long enough to settle, drinks deeply.

'It might be worth trying. We're clearly not going to get much out of Shania. If we could find some witnesses, we might be able to charge them without Shania's help.'

'Might as well try I suppose,' Cook says dejectedly, leaving Morgan wondering yet again how it is that his friend was promoted to the rank above him with such a negative attitude. He has to admit though that Cook is better at schmoozing with his peers then he is, something that holds little interest for him. He prefers to concentrate his energies into actually solving crimes rather than pushing paper and networking with peers.

The two men finish their drinks and leave the warmth of the pub, parting company at the end of the road to walk the short distance back to their homes alone. The walk gives both men time to reflect on the case. Morgan's thought as ever are for the young girls who live on the estate and what will happen to them. Cook's thoughts turn to the annual crime targets which, as the head of a newly formed task team, has become to burden him already. Both detectives know that they are unlikely to solve this crime and that Shania Smart will just become another statistic of the environment in which she lives.

Chapter 10

Celia is sitting on the sofa with Bailey, waiting for her husband to return so that she can re-heat the beef casserole she made earlier. As always, she had hoped that Morgan might have been able to return in time to have the casserole after an afternoon of slow-cooking but as Celia has come to expect with her husband's job, plans for dinner often go awry. Still, at least this time she has cooked something that can easily be reheated or if need be, can be put in the freezer for another day.

The moment she hears a key in the front door, she places the puppy onto the floor and races into the kitchen to switch on the oven, then opens a bottle of chardonnay that has been chilling in the fridge. Bailey, who has also been eagerly awaiting his master's return, greets Morgan as if he has not seen him for weeks instead of hours, his tail wagging furiously as he leaps up at his owner's legs.

Morgan firmly extracts himself from the over-excited puppy and walks into the kitchen just as Celia is pouring out the pale oaky liquid into two oversized glasses. Holding a glass of wine in one hand, he reaches down with the other to pull off his shoes, flinging them carelessly into the porch then quickly shutting the door again to prevent the puppy from reaching the discarded items. Gently pushing the over-eager dog to one-side, Morgan strides back into the kitchen and kisses Celia on the cheek.

'How did it go?' She asks, switching on the gas hob to heat up a large saucepan of potatoes and two smaller pans of vegetables.

Morgan shrugs his shoulders. Celia has known her husband for long enough not to enquire any further, he has obviously had a bad day.

Whilst the dinner is cooking, Morgan grabs a squeaky toy from the windowsill to play with Bailey, placing the object just in front of his nose before snatching it away again. The puppy barks in frustration until Morgan eventually concedes and throws the toy just within his reach, watching gleefully as the puppy bounces around the room with it in his mouth. The squeaky toy is quickly returned so that it can be thrown over and over again until both dog and master tire of the game.

Celia stands at the threshold of the kitchen and watches Morgan and Bailey curl up on the sofa and immediately fall asleep. Fifteen minutes later the food is ready and Celia deftly serves up the potatoes, cabbage and runner beans onto plates that have already been warmed, then carefully removes the bubbling casserole from the oven. As has become her habit, she quickly slams the over door shut again in case Bailey decides to stick his curious nose into the hot cooker. With the food assembled onto warm plates, Celia picks her way through the minefield of dog toys towards the large glass table that dwarfs the small dining room. Celia watches her husband and beloved dog for a moment as they sleep peacefully together but her rumbling stomach soon prompts her to awaken the pair. However cruel she feels at waking them both up, she knows that the food will soon go cold.

The couple eat in a comfortable silence, their every move observed by Bailey, who watches the couple intensely. Eventually the pup realises that no food will fall his way so he retreats to the kitchen, where he curls up in his wicker basket, his soft-padded paws twitching as he sleeps.

An adaptation of an Agatha Christie book has been scheduled on the television that evening. As soon as Morgan has delivered the dirty plates back to the kitchen and re-filled their wine glasses, he joins Celia in the lounge where she has already settled onto the sofa. Sensing his master's presence, Bailey wakes from his nap and quickly curls up on Morgan's lap, having clearly deciding that it is arguably the most comfortable seat in the house.

Halfway through the film it starts to rain. Even above the noise of the television, Morgan can make out the sleety droplets bashing against the double-glazed panes of the living room window. The rain is falling even harder by the time the credits roll up, with partially frozen droplets being thrown against the front of the house by the wind. Morgan is glad that the young pup is not yet able to go out for a walk. On the flip side, there is more than one reason to walk a dog - a plethora of stains have already appeared on the living room carpet and Morgan has no doubt that even more will appear before the pup is trained to go to the toilet on his walks. He's also noticed that the dog has started pulling at the corners of the carpet, shredding the coarse beige fibres to reveal the underlay beneath. It is just as well that they have not yet purchased the new lounge carpet Celia has been pleading to buy.

The sound of the telephone ringing startles them all. Bailey jumps down onto the carpet, barking furiously at the unwelcome interruption to his nap. Morgan shakes himself awake then reaches over to pick up the phone on the small table next to the sofa.

'Thank goodness I caught you,' Cook says breathlessly.

Morgan sits bolt upright, recognising the urgency in his friend voice. 'What's happened?'

'There's been a fire at one of the flats on the Hartsmere estate. It's in Robin House.'

Morgan's stomach flips. 'Which flat?' he asks reluctantly, not really wishing to know the answer.

'I don't know. All I know is it's on the first floor. I think we should go and take a look,' Cook replies. 'I'll pick you up in five minutes.'

Morgan replaces the phone then switches on the lounge light just in time to catch Bailey peeing on the carpet next to the TV. Celia leaps into action, scooping the puppy up into her arms before dropping him onto the kitchen floor so that she can grab some kitchen roll and disinfectant to clear up the mess.

By the time Morgan has pulled on a warm coat and laced up his boots, Cook is already waiting outside, his car headlights shining through the glass porch door, lighting up the carpet beneath Morgans feet.

The short drive to the estate seems to take far longer than usual as they race as quickly as they dare through the narrow streets, conscious of the slippery road conditions left by the sudden downpour. When they reach the estate, they find that the road is blocked by two fire appliances and an ambulance. Cook elects to park in the nearby bus stop, rather than trying to pick his way through the chaos in front of them.

Morgan pushes open the car door, then pulls up the collar of his coat to cover his neck in a futile attempt to keep out a little more of the bitterly cold rain. Without waiting for Cook, he strides off across the grass towards the centre of the estate.

The area in front of Robin House is alive with firefighters and police officers, their outlines lit up by the blue flashing lights of the fire engines. Two paramedics are waiting nearby in case any casualties need treating. A group of residents, who have already been evacuated from the building, are standing huddled together underneath the overhang of nearby Magpie House. Morgan spots three young lads standing in the shadows, watching as the flames leap out from two first floor windows that overlook the tennis court. He does not need to ask which flat is on fire, he can see for himself.

Cook catches up with Morgan then overtakes him to march over to the lead fire officer and find out the latest information on the situation. There is little Morgan can do as he tries to shelter as best he can from the harsh weather but wait nervously for any news. As time passes, his heart begins to thump harder and the bile in his stomach makes him feel sick. He knows from experience that the longer they wait, the more likely it is that it is bad news. If the occupant of the flat had been injured, he would have been brought out by now. Morgans worst fears are soon confirmed when the lifeless body of a man is brought out from the building.

Morgan rushes over to the ambulance and even in his blackened, charred state, can easily recognise the body of Lewis Smith. A torrent of guilt overwhelms him as he realises too late that the ramblings of a frightened old man have served to prophesize his own demise. Feeling crushed at his own ineptitude as a police officer, Morgan stands in the pouring rain, chastising himself over and over again, until Cook gently places a hand on his shoulder.

'I know what you're thinking James and it isn't your fault,' Cook says.

Morgan shrugs. It does not matter what other people think, he knows that he failed to protect the elderly witness.

The two detectives wait outside until the fire has been put out and some of the chaos has died down, with the majority of the onlookers having grown tired of the scene and returned to their homes. As soon as the all clear to enter is given by the firefighters, the police are able to enter the building.

Morgan is first into the building. He coughs a little from the lingering acrid smoke as he makes his way up the blackened stairs. As he reaches the first-floor landing, he hesitates, wondering what awaits him when he turns the corner. Part of him desperately wants to know what has happened, the other part wishes to never know. It is one of the worst experiences that can befall a police officer's - to have to investigate the death of someone they know. Lewis Smith might have been a bit of an enigma but somehow Morgan had grown to like the old man.

Morgans heart thumps as he approaches the flat. Even from the other side of the corridor, he can see the extent of the smoke damage inside the flat. The origin of the fire is immediately obvious. The front door to Lewis Smiths flat has been almost destroyed beyond recognition. The misshapen letterbox gapes open and there is an overwhelming smell of petrol fumes, making

Morgan cough as he breathes in the poisonous air.

The front door has been left ajar by the fire fighters. From his position in the corridor, Morgan can see much of the devastation caused by the flames. The blaze was intense and even with his amateur eye, Morgan can tell that some type of accelerant must have been used to start it.

'Let's hope that the smoke killed the old man before the flames reached him,' Morgan says to Cook who is following closely behind him.

'It normally does,' replies Cook gently. 'Come on let's get out of here. We won't be able to go into the flat for a while so we might as well go home for a few hours.'

Morgan nods before turning away from the scene of devastation, retracing his steps back out of the building where he can breathe in the fresh air again.

Cook overtakes him and begins to bark orders to a group of officers nearby, chastising them for not securing the area, which is now a crime scene. There is another group of officers talking to the few bystanders who are still standing in the freezing cold, some of them still wearing their night clothes.

'When can we go back to our homes then?' One elderly resident asks as she shivers in a pale green dressing gown.

'Which floor are you on?' Cook asks.

'The ninth floor.'

Cook inwardly groans. 'Well, you can go back in but you can't use the lifts yet so you'll have to use the stairs I'm afraid.'

'You're joking right? I'm seventy-three, I can't walk up all those stairs.'

A resident from one of the lower floor flats promptly offers to take the elderly lady back to her flat until the lift is operational again.

Cook wonders at the sense of housing elderly residents on upper floors, with the lifts out of action on the case of a fire and some of them being physically unable to walk down that many flights of stairs, they simply would not be able to get out of the building. In such a bleak scenario, you would just have to hope that the architects who designed the buildings had factored in adequate fire containment measures.

Morgan approaches to see if there is anything he can do to help but there is nothing until they are allowed into Lewis Smiths flat. The flat will first need to be assessed by the firefighters to be deemed safe to enter, before being investigated by the forensics team.

Fortunately, a police constable who has just turned up to help out on his night off, offers to give Morgan a lift home again, which he gratefully accepts as Cook will need to remain on the estate for now. For once Morgan is appreciative not to be in charge, instead he gets to go home to his wife and contemplate the life that has just ended.

Chapter 11

By the time Dr Bootle arrives at Hemley Hospital's mortuary suite, the body has already been laid out on a slab. The pathologist parks his new Jaguar in the space reserved for him, closest to the entrance to the mortuary. Len Bootle glances wistfully at the sun, which is promising a pleasant morning ahead, before heading towards the combination lock on the secure door, where he carefully punches in his passcode. A satisfying click tells the aging pathologist that his has correctly remembered the passcode and he pulls open the door and steps into the darkness of the building.

The idea of being called into work on a Sunday once again, coupled with the distasteful task ahead, has affected the pathologist's usual cheery disposition. Dr Bootle recently passed his sixtieth birthday and is beginning to consider more pleasant ways to spend his weekends, particularly ones that involve golf courses rather than the inside of a cold morgue. Especially when the body in question is in the condition that this one is in.

Thoughts of retirement are still uppermost in Dr Bootle's mind when Cook and Morgan arrive to witness the postmortem. The detectives settle into the hard plastic chairs in the viewing gallery, where a wall of glass isolates them from the stench of burnt flesh and the sounds of cremated tissue crackling under touch.

Even after thirty years of working in the field, handling such badly burnt bodies is something Dr Bootle refuses to grow used to. The smell of charred flesh penetrates through every pore of his body, an odour that always lingers far longer than the usual clinical odour of the hospital.

The pathologist quickly examines the outside of the body, which yields little of interest until Dr Bootle opens Lewis Smiths mouth to peer inside his throat. 'As I would expect,' Dr Bootle says, looking directly up at the viewing gallery, 'the delicate tissues show signs of smoke damage and the microscopic cilia that line the oesophagus have shrivelled under the intense heat of the fire.'

He then opens up the chest cavity, 'Can you see here there's a cherry-red appearance to the internal organs?' Again, Dr Bootle looks towards the two detectives on the other side of the glass. 'That tells me that the level of carbon monoxide in the body is high enough to be a potential cause of death. I'm certain that blood samples will confirm this.'

Next, the pathologist removes and weighs the heavy lungs. He slices open the spongy lung tissue, revealing a thick layer of blackened soot that has settled in the tiny alveoli; the presence of soot confirms that Lewis Smith was alive when the fire started and that he had breathed in the dense toxic fumes. The left lung has also been infiltrated by a large, calciferous tumour. 'I'll take some samples of the diseased tissue for closer analysis but it is likely that given the size of the tumour, death would have occurred within weeks.'

'So, you're saying that Mr Smith would have died anyway?' Cook says, using the intercom that connects the two rooms.

'Certainly. Of course, death by smoke inhalation is not a nice way to die but it's better than dying from cancer.' Dr Bootle states, as he opens up the lower abdomen. 'Can you see the shrunken, ulcerated stomach and there are some further lesions on the liver, indicating the presence of secondary tumours. He was a very sick man indeed'.

Dr Bootle closes up the body again before calling his assistant Harry to wheel the body back into the cold storage room. The pathologist then removes his gloves and gown, placing them in the hazardous waste bin, then makes his way out into the corridor that leads to the viewing room.

'Well, there's no doubt that the cause of death was smoke inhalation. Not a nice way to go but perhaps better than what awaited him. He would have been in a lot of pain,' explains Dr Bootle. 'I'll let you know when all the test results are in.'

'What about time of death?' Cook asks.

Well, from the amount rigour mortis I would say he died about twelve hours ago, so consistent with the time of the fire. He had smoke in his lungs so he was alive when the fire started, if that's what you were wondering,' Dr Bootle adds. 'If there's nothing else you need, I have other things to do.'

Cook and Morgan make a hasty retreat from the room to avoid irking the pathologist any further. They walk back down the dimly lit corridor towards the car park. The morgue is fortunate in that as well as having a separate entrance from the remainder of the hospital, it has its own, albeit small, car park for the few living visitors who need to visit this part of the complex.

'I think it's time to do a press release,' Cook says as he opens the car door. As soon as he has settled into the driver's seat, he pulls out his phone from his jacket pocket and instructs Fallow to organise a press release.

The two detectives make their way through the traffic and find a parking space in the overcrowded car park behind the main police building. Cook makes a mental note to bring up the subject of the lack of car parking during his next monthly meeting with Bennett. Whilst he understands that the budget is tight, something needs to be done about the lack of parking, especially when the new electric cars are adopted and will need specific spaces for charging.

Fallow is waiting for them in the incident room, eager to assist with the press release. Much to Morgans annoyance, the inexperienced detective has done a good job or organising it and the journalists are already waiting restlessly in the conference room. Fallows patronage by his Uncle, Chief Superintendent Bennett is enough to irritate Morgan on the best of days. The compliant and ever-helpful attitude of the young detective is enough to push his patience to its limit.

Morgan hides the flutter of nerves that he is feeling in the pit of his stomach as he enters the raucous room. It seems ridiculous to him that he can cope with arresting a murderer but when it comes to addressing a room full of journalists, he gets nervous to the point of wanting to run out of the room again. It is fortunate that Cook is normally the one to address the press but there is always a chance that one day he will need to take his place.

A short statement has already been quickly prepared by the Communications office, leaving Cook with just the task of relaying the message to the press.

Press Release – November 12th, 2008

Last night a flat was set on fire on the Hartsmere estate. Unfortunately a man who was living on the first floor of Robin House died as a result of the fire. We would like to appeal for any witnesses to come forward who may have information about how the fire started.

We would also like to urge anyone to come forward with information about a serious assault that occurred on the Hartsmere Estate at around 4 pm last Wednesday. The attack on a young female, also took place in Robin House.

Amongst the gaggle of journalists is the editor of The Suffolk Times, Phil Wattle. Cook has known Phil Wattle on a professional basis for many years and respects his keen nose and sharp intellect, which has made him one of the best journalists in the county. Of course, it is always helpful to keep the press on side and their mutual love of local ales has helped to cement their symbiotic relationship.

As soon as Cook has read out the formal statement and questions from the journalists, he makes his escape from the front of the room to go in search of Phil Wattle.

'Hello Phil, fancy coming to my office for a drink?' Cook asks the journalist who is sitting at the back of the room.

'That would be lovely, thanks,' Wattle replies cheerfully, collecting his coat from the back of the chair.

Morgan, who is still sitting at the top table, trying to extract himself from three eager journalists who are still asking questions, watches as the two men head for Cook's office to chat in private. He has no doubt that their conversation will be well oiled by the sampling of an unopened bottle of brandy that is kept in one of Cook's lockable filing cabinets.

The remaining journalists gradually dissipate, so Morgan traipses back to the team office to begin writing up the report on Lewis Smith's death. It is an unwelcome task at the best of times - most police officers would prefer to spend their time catching criminals rather than dealing with ever-increasing amounts of paperwork. On this occasion though the task is particularly odious given the circumstances. Morgan pours himself a mug of strong, black coffee from the jug in the corner of the office, then settles down resolved to complete the task as quickly as possible.

Two hours later with the paperwork complete, Morgan decides he should find Fallow and ask him to accompany him back to the estate so they can start interviewing Lewis Smith's neighbours. He feels certain that Bennett assigned training of his nephew to Morgan just to irk him. Regardless, he is determined to do a good job of it even if he is continually suppressing a trickle of irritation that is bubbling just below the surface.

At this early stage of the investigation, Marlon Turner and his friends are top of the list of suspects but they need the evidence to this. It seems doubtful they will find any witnesses brave enough to come forward but if they can just get the angle they need, the weaker members of the gang might just confess – the threat of spending time in prison for murder often had a long lasting effect on youngsters, especially when it is likely that at least some of the gang will have thought that the purpose of the fire was only to scare the elderly man. It may not have occurred to them that someone would actually die.

Morgan finds Fallow in the staff canteen, where he is devouring a sticky Danish pastry, washing it down with a large mug of coffee. Morgan feels an uncharacteristic flicker of sympathy for the young detective, who is still unused to working such long hours.

Having seen Morgan approach, Fallow jumps up from his chair and buys another coffee and pastry. Morgan cannot quite decide if he should be grateful for the lad's thoughtfulness or irked by his constant need for approval.

'I need you to come back to the Hartsmere estate with me,' Morgan says, munching on a pastry.

Fallow nods eagerly the drains the last remnants of coffee from his mug. Morgan watches as Fallow pushes back his chair, pulls on his coat and stands by the back door. The young man is beginning to remind him of Bailey - very eager and more than slightly annoying.

Having replenished their waning energy levels with the quick sugar fix, the two men head back to the Hartsmere Estate, feeling a little more refreshed.

'Our first task will be to take a look at Lewis Smiths flat. I know that this will be the first time you've been to the scene of a fatal fire, so I will warn you now that this won't be very pleasant. It's vital though that we try and find out as much as we can about what happened. We need to find out who did this horrific crime.'

'Don't worry, I know it will be difficult,' Fallows cheerfully.

He has no idea how difficult it will be, Morgan mutters quietly to himself as they make their way towards Robin House. No idea at all.

Chapter 12

Outside the main entrance to Robin House, a police officer has been posted to prevent journalists and nosy onlookers from making their way inside the building. It is a sombre symptom of modern society that part of a police officer's role now includes the management of the public's ghoulish and seemingly insatiable need for information.

When they reach the door to Lewis Smiths flat, Morgan pulls on protective overalls and shoe covers then waits for Fallow to do the same. He stoops under the crime scene tape that is pulled tightly across the boarded-up door. Morgan pushes open the front door, which creaks in protest, its hinges severely damaged by the firefighters levering it open the previous night.

The source of the fire is immediately obvious. A black v shaped stain of soot spreads upwards from the bottom of the door, just below the letterbox. The charred doormat is peppered with shards of glass, which Morgan steps over as he passes by the remnants of a glass bottle lying in the hallway. Carefully he picks his way through now unrecognisable debris scattered across the thread-bare carpet, that leads away from the front door.

From its origin on the inside of the front door, the fire had spread along the ceiling, its flames fed by the polystyrene tiles installed when the building was first furnished. Morgans eyes narrow, puzzled as to why the tiles were not replaced as part of the regular refurbishments that should be undertaken in council-owned accommodation. He makes a mental note to check up on this as the flammable material may have contributed to the ferocity of the fire as well as adding to the toxicity of the fumes. Something else that needs to be checked is why it took so long for the fire service to be notified. The smoke alarm in the hallway should have sent an automated alarm to the fire service control room, something that Morgan is well aware of from a recent departmental email that had raised awareness of the increasing number of times these alarms are activated inappropriately. The article went on to explain that one of the reasons why Suffolks fire service is overstretched is from the sheer volume of unwanted fire alarms, which all needed to be investigated just in case.

Morgan peers out into the corridor and the answer to his question is immediately answered - the cover of the fire alarm is dangling down from the ceiling, the wires have been cut and the space for the batteries is empty.

'Fallow, can you ask SOCO to come back and check if that fire alarm has any fingerprints,' Morgan says, indicating towards the alarm in the corridor.

Fallow diligently writes down the request in his notebook then carefully steps over the remains of the cremated carpet to inch his way down the hallway, where he takes notes on the condition of the flat. Photographs have of course been taken but they cannot record the smells, sounds and feelings that you experience from actually being at a crime scene. The young officer seems to be showing some promise of becoming a decent detective.

Morgan bends down to avoid the debris that is hanging down from the ceiling in the hallway, where the tiles have melted and peeled downwards like an orange, dripping onto the charred, damp carpet. He turns into the room nearest the front door - the bedroom where the old man died. Scorch marks show where the flames had licked their way underneath the door, spreading quickly through the chipboard and into the room. A path of destruction is clearly visible across the room from the door to the window, where the fire has eaten up everything in its path.

The bedroom is almost un-recognisable as somewhere that was once lived in. Singed curtains are being tussled by the breeze that is coming through the open window and below them, Morgan can just make out the outline of the bed. A pile of charred remains that loosely resembles bed covers are piled up on top of the metal structure and in the centre, blackened ginger fur can be seen. Morgan hopes that Lewis Smith took some comfort in having his feline friend with him in his hour of death.

A mahogany wardrobe stands in one corner of the room with it's doors shut, protecting the contents inside. Morgan opens one door and peers in, poking his way through the few clothes the elderly man had owned. There is little else in the room and the sparseness of it makes Morgan feel depressed. Poverty is not a place where anyone wishes to end up, particularly not in their final years.

Morgan walks back into the hallway, squeezing past Fallow who is looking closely at the scorch marks on the inside of the front door. At the far end of the flat, the living area has also suffered smoke and water damage. The adjoining small kitchen area has escaped the worst of the effects of the fire, its cluttered worktops and stained cooker revealing its former occupant's apparent lack of regard for cleanliness. The bathroom too has escaped the flames, though smoke still managed to creep in through the gap beneath the door, blackening the once avocado coloured suite to a dusty charcoal. The entire flat will need to be gutted and refurbished before any new occupants can be found, not only from the damage caused by the fire but from the poor state it was left in by its former resident.

Morgan and Fallow complete their search of the flat then head back out to the corridor towards number six, Lewis Smith's closest neighbour. The elderly occupant who has lived in the flat for almost twenty years, has now put in an urgent request to be re-housed away from the estate. The fear of becoming the next victim is uppermost in the mind of Audrey Bickham, who is busy packing away her many belongings when she is unexpectedly interrupted by a knock at her front door.

After peering around the door at the two men with intense suspicion, Audrey Bickham feverishly inspects the ID cards that are duly presented to her, before allowing the two detectives into her flat. Once inside, the elderly woman shuffles back into the living area, turning her withered back to the two strangers so that she can continue with her packing.

Morgan watches as the elderly resident carefully picks up a brightly coloured ornament of a young girl, wraps it up in sheets of newspaper, before adding it to the box in front of her. When the task is complete, she pulls out a chair and eases herself down onto it.

'I'm Detective Inspector Morgan and this is Detective Constable Fallow,' Morgan says.

The old woman stares at him intensely. 'I suppose you're here about the fire. Not a surprise really is it given that he talked to you the day before. We all know who it was, that's why I'm getting out of here. I've had enough of those toe rags running this place. I hope you're pleased with yourself,' she spits.

'We're all very upset at the death of Lewis Smith, Mrs Bickham. We will catch whoever is responsible for his death and those who attacked Shania Smart.'

Audrey Bickham snorts, turning her wrinkled face towards the window. A group of youths are standing in the tennis court below and seem to be staring right up into the flat. The elderly resident stands up and moves further away from the window.

'Well, you won't get nothing from me. I don't move into the sheltered housing for another week and I want to leave this flat alive,' she says as she resumes packing up the ornaments from the windowsill.

It is obvious that the woman is too frightened to say anything that might help so Morgan thanks her for her time and leaves. The two men continue knocking on the other doors on the first floor. None of the other residents are at home, or if they are, they do not wish to open their doors. The same thing happens on the upper floors and the two officers decide to head back to the station.

As they are leaving Robin House, Morgan notices the group of youths who are lurking the playground. As soon as the teenagers see the police officers, their conversation halts and instead they all stare at the detectives. Morgan notices that Jade is amongst them, standing sheepishly behind Marlon Turner. He can still feel them watching them as they walk past the playground and onwards towards the centre of the estate. Morgan resists the urge to stare back at them. They will be brought in soon enough and he will enjoy every moment of it. They will just have to hope they can find enough evidence to actually charge them this time.

A few minutes later Fallow and Morgan reach the edge of the estate and the road where Morgan parked the car. As they draw closer, Morgan can see a teenage girl pacing up and down on the path next to his car. Even from this distance Morgan instantly recognises the lonely figure as Shania. Surprised by her presence, Morgan quickens his pace to reach her before she decides to leave again.

'Hello Shania, are you looking for me?' Morgan calls out as he approaches the young girl.

'No, course not. I just didn't have anywhere else to hang around now that my friends won't talk to me.'

'I'm sorry to hear that. Do you want to go and get a drink somewhere so we can talk?'

'There's nowhere around here is there. Nothing stay open very long as they keep getting broken into.'

Shania stops pacing for a moment and stands still, her hands tucked into the pockets of her jacket. 'Got nothing to say anyway. You got no evidence, that's what the lady said who came round yesterday, so there's no point is there. I don't want to end up like Lewis Smith.'

'Ok well you've got my phone number if you need anything or want to tell me anything,' Morgan replies, pulling open the car door.

Shania begins to walk away from them but only goes a few yards before stopping and turning back to look at them. Morgan waits for the girl to speak, hoping she can find the courage to talk to him but Shania turns around again and slowly walks back up over the grassy slope in the direction of the shops.

'Do you think she's ok?' Fallow asks.

Morgan snorts, 'Well of course not. She's been raped and beaten up and I bet you anything her friend Jade has something to do with it all.'

'I meant to walk back home by herself,' Fallow says quietly.

Morgan looks back towards the estate and watches as Shania walks into the supermarket. 'I don't think she'd appreciate two police officers following her into a supermarket, do you?' He replies sarcastically.

As soon as Shania's slight figure disappears from view, Morgan clambers into the car and starts the engine. He steers the vehicle along the main road towards the town centre, driving at speeds that are far too fast for such a built-up area.

Fallow almost bites through his tongue when Morgan nearly knocks over a cyclist who is wobbling precariously into their path. In the end he resorts to closing his eyes to quell his rising fear.

The ten minutes it takes to reach Fallows flat are passed in silence with the younger policeman not wishing to distract the senior officer and Morgan not wishing to expend any further energy on chatting to someone who he finds exasperating. Eventually they come to an abrupt halt outside Glebe Court. Morgan stares straight ahead, drumming his fingers on the steering wheel, waiting for Fallow to climb out of the passenger seat. Fallow, seemingly also tired of the company, does not make his usual customary goodbyes before shutting the car door. He strides off up the path, quickly disappearing through the secure entrance to the flats.

It takes a further fifteen minutes of erratic driving through the convoluted estate roads, for Morgan to reach home. As soon as he unlocks the front door, a feeling of calm descends as he picks up the delicious aroma of a pork loin joint that Celia roasted earlier in the afternoon. Morgan pads through to the kitchen, where three large saucepans are waiting on the hob, containing sliced carrots, new potatoes and Savoy cabbage. The house is quiet. Morgan looks out of the kitchen window which overlooks the back garden. He smiles as he watches Celia throw a ball for Bailey, who promptly returns it and waits for it to be thrown again.

Celia's intuition tells her before she even looks up that her husband is home. She waves at Morgan then strides across the lawn to the kitchen door, the over-excited puppy following behind, leaving a trail of muddy footprints all over the newly washed floor.

Celia kisses her husband on the cheek with some difficulty given that Bailey is jumping up and down in between them. 'How was your day?'

'Bloody awful to be honest. I'd rather not talk about it, if you don't mind,' Morgan replies, leaning over to kiss his wife on the cheek before returning to the porch to remove his boots and coat.

Celia flicks on the kettle then turns her attention to feeding the ravenous puppy. After Bailey has been fed, she pulls two mugs out from a cupboard and adds tea bags and milk to them, then turns her attention to the task of cooking dinner.

It is only when Morgan has showered, changed and come back down stairs, that he notices the table in the dining room has been set for four people.

'I invited Tom and Sarah for dinner,' Celia reluctantly confesses. 'I thought we should thank them for their help with getting Bailey.'

Morgan suspects it is more likely that Celia wants to show off her new purchase but keeps his thoughts to himself as he steels himself against what could be a tiring evening and one that he could have done without. He is still feeling somewhat irked at the thought of his evening being hijacked when his guests arrive. Although he has been close friends with Cook since they joined the police force, his friend's recent promotion above him has driven a wedge between them, though neither would care to admit it.

'Hello, come in,' Morgan says, more cheerfully than he feels.

Cook steps into the porch laden with wine and flowers for their hosts. Sarah, who has dressed casually in anticipation of the dog shedding hair over her clothes, immediately makes a beeline for Bailey, scooping him up in her arms, leaving her husband to hand over the gifts.

Morgan ushers Cook into the lounge so that they can discuss work before they sit down to dinner. It can be difficult socialising with work colleagues as the job ends up creeping into their conversation, so the two friends made an agreement to allow themselves fifteen minutes of shop talk at the start of the evening, after which the very notion of work was banned.

'I hope you're looking forward to the raid tonight? Guess who you'll be interviewing?' Cook says smugly.

Morgan shakes his head.

'Marlon Turner,' Cook grins, knowing full well that Morgan will relish the opportunity to grill the teenager again. 'There's a rumour going around that one of the other gang members has a soft spot for Shania, so I'm going to interview Callum Woods. Rumours have also come back via the estate beat officer PC Barnes, that Marlon Turner was seen hanging around the tennis court when Lewis Smiths flat was set alight.'

'I remember seeing some lads lurking in the shadows of Magpie House, but I couldn't see who they were,' Morgan admits.

The two men finish their conversation and return to their wives, who are still entertaining the puppy. The remainder of the evening passes quickly and by the time the Cook's go back out into the dark, damp night, they are all grateful for Celia's home cooking, which has left a warm glow in their bellies. Celia has fed them enough food to keep them going through the long night ahead and even packed them up some sandwiches and home-made Victoria sponge for when their energy levels drop in the early hours. Neither man will be involved in the actual arrests but will be waiting impatiently at the station.

It is a little before midnight when the police officer return to the station with four members of the Hartsmere estate gang. As soon as they heard that the suspects had been apprehended and were on their way in, Cook had headed towards one of the vacant interview rooms to wait for Callum Woods to be processed by the custody sergeant. Morgan collected Fallow from the incident room, where he was diligently catching up with paperwork, before they too made their way back down the stairs to another of the interview rooms to wait for Marlon Turner to arrive.

Chapter 13

Marlon Turner is showing few signs of being concerned by the unexpected interruption to his nocturnal activities. He is by now very familiar with the inside of Deben Quay police station - his criminal record started when he was just nine years old. Numerous cautions for shoplifting and petty thefts have made him a well-known character to the local police force. His most recent arrest, the previous summer, was for common assault against another lad who attended the same local school. The complaint did not result in a conviction; the case was dropped as the witness changed their statement three days before the case was due to be heard at court. Unfortunately, victimisation of key witnesses was a frequent phenomenon on the Hartsmere estate and certainly occurred far more often than the police would like to admit.

Morgan watches as Marlon swaggers into the interview room, flicking one of his long braids over his shoulder. The teenager sits down heavily onto a plastic chair, resting his left leg across his knee.

'What have I supposed to have done this time then?' Marlon asks, breaking the silence.

'I'd have thought you would know that, a clever lad like you,' Morgan responds.

Marlon's dark brown eyes narrow, the corner of his lips pulling back into a slight smirk.

Morgan leans forward, shifting closer to Marlon. 'The reason why we've brought you in for questioning is that you were seen in the area of Robin House on Saturday night.'

'Yeah, so what. I know a lot of people who live there,' Marlon snorts, clearly unconcerned by the line of questioning. 'Or is it a crime now to know people? I ain't done nothing wrong. Nothing that you can prove in any case.'

'Did you know Lewis Smith?' Morgan asks, placing his forearms on the table in front of him.

'Who's that then?' Marlon replies, raising his left eyebrow, the smirk deepening.

'Lewis Smith lived on the first floor of Robin House, which also happens to be where Shania Smart was raped last Wednesday and also happens to be where a fire was started on Saturday night. You must have heard by now that someone died as a result of that fire?' Morgan leans in closer towards the suspect, closing the gap between them that has been enforced by the battered teak table.

'Do you mean that miserable old git who used to watch the young girls playing on the swings?' Marlon snorts.

Morgan inhales sharply, trying to hide the deep level of contempt that he feels towards the young man.

'How's that Shania then? Last time I saw her we had a nice chat as she hadn't been feeling too good,' Marlon sniggers. 'She's hot stuff that girl. Now she's been broken in she'll make a classy bird.'

Morgan cannot contain his irritation any longer. He stands up and pushes back his chair, hitting it on the wall behind him. 'I'm suspending this interview'.

A few hours alone in a cold cell might make the arrogant teenager think more seriously about the situation, Morgan decides as he follows Marlon Turner back down to the custody suite and watches as the cell door slams shut.

Cook is faring little better in his interview with Callum Woods. The youngster is far less confident than the other older gang members, especially now that he has been separated from them, but for now, he is still toeing the line by refusing to admit to anything.

'Why don't you tell me what happened Callum? We all know that the fire was just meant to frighten the old man,' Cook says quietly.

'I don't know anything about a fire,' Callum replies defiantly, his right foot tapping as he speaks.

'Come on, we know you were there and once we get the results back from SOCO, we will be able to prove it.'

Callum shifts uncomfortably in his seat. 'I wasn't there. I'm sorry but I can't help you.'

'Do you want to be arrested for murder? Because that's what's going to happen. I know it was an accident but someone died and the CPS will treat it as murder,' Cook says, picking up the cup in front of him and sipping the tepid, sludge-coloured coffee.

Despite Callum's obvious concern, the words do not have their desired effect and Cook is left with little choice but to call a halt to the interview. He finds Morgan upstairs in the team office, sitting at his desk looking as exhausted and dejected as he feels.

'Any luck?' Morgan asks hopefully when he sees Cook enter the room.

'Not yet but I think he might crack eventually. The problem is that if we don't get a confession soon, we're going to have to let them go.'

Morgan expels several expletives before stomping across the room to switch on the kettle. He pulls out two mugs and spoons some powdered coffee into them, before adding a little long-life milk to the unappealing concoction.

'What do you reckon then?' Morgan asks, stirring each of the mugs in turn.

'I don't think we're going to get anywhere. We need to find some evidence and I can't see SOCO finding much of that. Maybe we'll get lucky and find a witness.'

'Yeah and maybe that witness will suffer the same fate as Lewis Smith,' Morgan says, throwing his hands up in the air, exasperated by the entire situation. He plonks himself down on the chair behind his desk and takes a sip of the coffee, scalding his tongue in his haste for another caffeine fix.

'I just wish I could wipe that smug grin off Marlon Turners face. He's more clever than I had given him credit for.' Cook also tests out the temperature of the coffee and immediately winces as the bitter liquid scalds him. 'Let's leave them to stew in the cells overnight and try again tomorrow. You never know, we might get lucky.'

Morgan nods in agreement. He finishes his coffee and pulls on his coat. He waits for Cook to turn off the lights and lock the door, then they both head for home.

Bailey greets his master with his usual enthusiasm as soon as hears him creeping through the front door. Morgan is beginning to warm to the puppy and is almost glad that his wife insisted on buying him. He is however looking forward to the day when he can be walked outside as he is now chewing everything in sight. It will not be long before they will need to get a new carpet, not to mention a coffee table and several pairs of shoes.

Given the late hour and that Celia is already asleep, Morgan decides to sleep in the spare room so as not to wake her. He lies in bed for what seems like an eternity, milling over the day, trying to work out how they could find some evidence that would put the two lads behind bars. Perhaps he should visit Jade again and see if she has changed her mind about speaking out?

The thoughts churn around and around his mind, preventing him from the sleep he so desperately needs. Eventually he gives up, goes downstairs and switches on the TV, grateful for the company of Bailey who soon falls asleep on his lap.

Jade is also wide awake, lying on the thin, lumpy mattress in the small bedroom that she shares with her younger sister. Jade is lying on her back, staring at the powder pink curtains as they sway back and forth, tussled by the chilly draft that is coming from a deep crack in the plaster underneath the bottom of the metal window frame. On the small bedside table next to her bed, her mobile bleeps again. It will be another text from Shania, Jade decides. Either way, she does not want to find out. Instead, she pulls the duvet up underneath her chin and closes her eyes. All she can see though are flames coming out of the first floor flat in Robin House. All she could think about is how an old man who was not yet ready to die is now no longer alive. Jade knows that if Marlon found out she had followed them that night, watched them pour petrol onto some material and set it alight before stuffing it through Lewis Smith's letterbox, that her life too would be in danger.

A long night in a police cell has not had much effect on Marlon Turner's attitude. His friend Callum however looks pale and shaky as he is led back into the interview room. Cook almost feels sorry for him as notices the young man's hand shaking as he clutches tightly onto a polystyrene cup of weak tea.

'Do you know Shania Smart?' Cook asks as he soon as he has settled into the chair opposite Callum.

Callum is surprised at the change in line of questioning. 'Yeah, I know Shania, we're in the same class at school.'

'Were you there when she was raped and beaten?' Cook says bluntly.

Callum swallows nervously, his gaze shifting away from Cook. 'No, I wasn't there.'

'But you know who was there.' Cook allows an uncomfortable silence to descend. 'Come on Callum, do you want them to get away with it, blaming you for what they did to Shania? I know you're not like them. It's not too late for you, you know. You can have a better life than this.'

The conversation halts when there is a knock on the door. Morgan, who is standing alone in the corridor, asks Cook to step outside so that they can talk in private.

'The CPS are insisting that we let them go. We haven't got any evidence to charge them and they don't want the press finding out we've been holding two juveniles overnight.'

'Bugger,' Cook says, walking off towards the back door of the station, where he pulls a cigarette out from his emergency packet.

When he returns, Cooks seems more determined than ever that they will find the evidence they need to charge Marlon and Callum. 'Let them go, send them back to their drunken whore mothers and we'll go and find some evidence.'

Morgan smiles, relieved at the return of Cook's steely inner determination, which has been largely absent since his recent promotion. It is good to see his friend back on form again.

Chapter 14

It is almost lunchtime by the time Deben Quay police station has rid itself of its' overnight guests. As soon as the juveniles have been dispatched, Cook and Morgan stroll to a nearby café to grab a cooked breakfast. They settle into the red plastic chairs before ordering two full breakfasts, a welcome treat after such a tiresome night.

Cook grabs a copy of the local paper from the counter and flicks through it as they wait for their food to arrive. The main story on the front page is on the fire at Robin House and death of one of its residents. A small column also mentions the attack on Shania, appealing for witnesses to come forward.

The Suffolk Times

13 November 2008

Fire Death on Hartsmere Estate

By Phil Wattle

A fire that was deliberately started at a flat on the Hartsmere Estate on Saturday has resulted in the death of one of its' residents. The fire was on the first floor of Robin House, causing the whole building to be evacuated and was the cause of the death of Lewis Smith.

Attack on Girl

By Leah Hart

A teenage girl was attacked on the stairway of Robin House last Wednesday afternoon. Deben Quay Police are appealing for witnesses to come forward who might have seen the attack.

Fifteen minutes later a tired looking waitress with dark smudges beneath her puffy eyes, brings over their food order. The newspaper is discarded so that their greasy food can be devoured and only picked up again once both men have finished eating. Morgan reads through the articles, whilst intermittently swigging down the dregs of a strong black coffee. There is little information in the paper on the two events but even so, it helps to give another avenue for witnesses to come forward.

Once their bellies are full and energy levels replenished, the two men walk back to the station to collect a car before driving back to Hartsmere estate, where they plan to have one last go at trying to persuade Jade to open up to them.

When they reach Jade's flat, they are surprised to find Shania banging on the front door, her tiny fists clenched with rage. Jade is either not at home or ignoring her friend, who turns to shouting through the letterbox in frustration. When she hears footsteps approaching from behind, Jade turns around to see the two detectives standing at the top of the stairs. Immediately she stops thumping on the door and stomps off down the stairs, glaring at Morgan as she passes by him.

The detectives wait until they hear the outer door to the building slam shut before they too knock on Jade's door, much more gently than the previous visitor. This time the door opens, revealing the anxious teenager behind.

'I'm sorry if this is a bad time Jade, but we really need to talk to you,' Morgan says, wiping his shoes on the front door mat.

Jade leads them through to the front living room. Jade's mum Sarah, is in the adjoining kitchen, dishing out chips and fish-fingers onto three plates.

Sarah's eyes roll when she sees Morgan and Cook. 'Not you lot again. Why can't you just leave her alone, she don't know nothing.'

'Is that why she's refusing to talk to Shania?' Cook responds.

'She don't know nothing, just leave her alone,' Sarah repeats as she passes a plate of food to her eldest daughter.

Morgan detects the strong odour of alcohol on Sarah's breath as she roughly pushes her way past him to reach the small table next to the window. He is almost deafened by Jade shouting for her sister to join them for lunch. It is obvious that the girl is not going to talk to them, especially not in front of her overbearing mother who is waiting impatiently for them to leave so that they can eat. The level stare is enough of a hint, so Cook and Morgan retrace their steps back to the front door.

Just as they are leaving the flat, Cooks mobile rings, the tones of Chopin echoing through the sterile walkway. He delves into the inner pocket of his coat and retrieves the vibrating phone. 'DCI Cook,' he says formally.

'Hallo it's Tom from SOCO. We've had some results through that I thought you'd like to know about. We didn't find any DNA evidence from Lewis Smiths flat that belonged to either of your suspects but the rag that used for the Molotov cocktail turns out to be a pair of boxer shorts that originated from a high street discount chain. The petrol soaked into the material will need to be checked against local petrol stations and if we're lucky we might even find some CCTV footage of who bought it.'

'That's good, we've got something else now we can look into. What about the rape case?'

'Not much luck with that one unfortunately. There was no foreign DNA in the samples taken from Shania Smart. There isn't much point testing the stairwell where she was raped as it's a favourite location for junkies apparently.'

Cook detests times like these. Another plea for witnesses could be made, but he knows that in such a tight-knit community, which also has a deep distrust of the police, that they are unlikely to come forward. Even if someone does, it is probable that they will retract their statement again before the court case. It has happened so often now that the CPS are reluctant to even bother with the expense of bringing cases to court from the Hartsmere estate. It is such a frustrating situation for all of them and unlikely to change any time soon.

Jade has not left the flat for two days. Not only is she avoiding Shania but also Marlon Turner and his gang. Every time there is a knock on the door her heart pounds, wondering which one of them it might be. She knows that Marlon will come for her eventually and her head hurts from trying to decide what she should do for the best. She wishes her mum was like those in the movies and would stay at home and cook proper meals and talk to her, instead of going to the pub every day and getting pissed, then coming back home to shout at her for not cleaning, or shopping or whatever it was she was supposed to have done. It is her sister though who she pities the most. Jade is at least old enough to understand why their mum is the way she is. Darcy only sees that her mother prefers to spend more time away from her then with her.

When the knock on the door does come, Jade is surprised to see it is Callum Woods, not Marlon at the door.

'Hi Jade, we haven't seen you for a while so I thought I'd drop in and see if you are ok?' Callum says, standing on the doorstep, his gangly hands pushed into the pockets of his jeans.

'I'm ok,' Jade replies suspiciously, not wishing to say too much in case Marlon and his friends are standing around the corner listening to their conversation.

'Can I come in then?' Callum asks, placing his right hand on the door and gently pushing it open.

Jade walks off into the living room, where Darcy is sitting on the floor in front of the TV.

'Why haven't we seen you about?'

'I haven't been feeling well,' Jade replies, sitting down at the far end of the sofa close to Darcy, who is singing along to the theme tune of her favourite programme that has just started.

Callum sits down at the other end of the couch and leans forward, clasping his fingers together into an arch. 'Marlon's getting worried you, especially when we saw Shania come around here and the police as well.'

'I didn't talk to Shania. I haven't talked to no one,' Jade says quickly.

'Good. You know that you'd get the blame for it all, don't you?'

Jade begins picking at her fingernails.

'Those stupid policemen tried to blame us for the fire that killed that old git,' Callum says callously, taking a cigarette out from his coat pocket and lighting it. He offers one to Jade who shakes her head then sucks deeply on the stick, breathing in the poisonous fumes. 'They can't prove nothing though, they haven't got any evidence have they.'

Jade's cheeks whiten as she begins to understand the purpose of Callum's unexpected visit. 'You don't need to worry about me, I don't tell those policemen anything,' she says defiantly, sticking her chin up in the air.

'Good, we'll see you about then, we've all missed you, you know.'

'Sure,' Jade says, hoping that Callum will leave soon. Darcy is beginning to show an interest in their conversation and the last thing she wants is for her little sister to get caught up in this mess.

'Better go then, Marlon's waiting for me,' Callum says, stubbing the cigarette out onto a plate that has been left discarded on the floor. He crouches down to ruffle Darcy's hair before turning to smile at Jade.

Jade is frozen to the sofa as she listens to Callum's footsteps clipping up the hallway, then out of the flat and down the concrete stairs towards the main door to the building. She waits until she hears the bang of the door shutting, before moving to the corner of the front window. She watches Callum as he strides across the path towards the playground, where Marlon and the others are waiting. Even from this distance she can see them laughing as they look up in her direction. For the second time that week, Jade wishes that she is dead.

Cook, Morgan and Phil Wattle are gallantly fighting their way through the gale force winds that are howling through the bare trees, in order to reach their local drinking establishment before the sun disappears over the horizon. The image of nestling down into their favourite chairs situated next to the open fire, which crackles comfortingly in one corner of the Eels Foot, is spurring them on against the bracing wind that could cut through even the thickest of coats.

The pub is almost empty, which is unsurprising given the atrocious weather conditions. The trio do not mind though as the near solitude allows them more privacy than usual to chat freely without any concern of being overheard. With drinks purchased and seats chosen, the three men quickly focus their attention on the reason for their meeting.

Phil Wattle retrieves a letter from his briefcase, which he places on the table between the three pints. 'I got it in the morning post. It's been postmarked in Deben Quay.'

The letter has few distinguishing features; a plain white envelope containing a single page that has been torn from a spiral notebook. The page itself contains only one sentence, which has been written in a childish scrawl and states: *Marlon Turner is a rapist.*

Morgan peers over the note with interest, 'I wonder why it's been sent to you?'

'No idea,' Wattle replies, taking large gulp of his beer.

'I'll drop it off at the forensic lab, you never know, it might have fingerprints or DNA on it,' Cook says.

'Maybe, though it could just be a crank, they always come out of the woodwork when we put in an article asking for witnesses.'

'Let's be positive Phil, it could also be someone whose too scared to come forward.' Morgan nestles back into his chair, which is nearest to the open. He stares into the mesmerising flames that flicker and crackle as they devour a large log. Not so long ago he had sat here with a different journalist from the local paper, drinking beer and talking about the latest case. This time of the year always brings back to him memories of Caroline. He takes a deep breath and pushes away the memory then focuses on finishing his pint whilst waiting for the others to do the same.

When all three pint glasses are empty, the three men pull on their coats again and prepare themselves for heading back out into the bitter wind. Outside the entrance to the Eels Foot, the leaves that have fallen from the sycamore trees that line the nearby road, swirl in front of them like snowflakes. Morgan has always found this time of year depressing, with the nights growing longer, the days colder and the vegetation withering away to die, just like the previous November, when a vivacious, beautiful and talent woman had died.

Morgan keeps his thoughts to himself as they walk away from the warmth of the pub and back out into the night. All three of them knew Caroline, but no one will speak of her, not after what she did. It seems as if only Morgan is able to still think of her with some ounce of fondness.

The trio walk together in silence until they reach the top of Morgan's road where they must part company; Cook will collect up his car and drop the letter off at the forensics lab before going home; Wattle will head straight for his small, terraced house, where a bottle of whisky awaits him.

From the top of the road, Morgan can see his living room is still lit up, lights blazing in the otherwise dark road. As he draws nearer to the house, he can see through a chink in the kitsch floral curtains that Celia is sitting on the sofa. Bailey is curled up on Celias lap, looking at ease and clearly feeling very settled in his new home.

148

Morgan is in no doubt that it will not be long before the dog makes his way into their bedroom at night, especially as he is still howling and whining at regular intervals.

Morgan wonders if Celia has managed to take the puppy to the vet yet for his vaccinations. The sooner he can start going out on walks the better as Bailey's pent up energy is systematically destroying their once well-kept home. Never having previously owned a dog, Morgan had not realised the destructiveness of such a small animal.

As soon as Celia hears her husband's key turn in the front door lock, she abandons the puppy to the floor and leaps up to switch on the oven. Celia has been eagerly waiting for Morgan to return so that she can tell him the good news that at long last she has found a part-time job. She has been out of work since the town's tearoom, where she had worked for many years, was destroyed by a fire. The few hours she has now found in the chocolate shop located in the centre of town, will do little to help pay the bills but will give her more contact with the outside world, which she desperately craves. Her weekly yoga classes gives her some interest outside of the home but she needs more then she currently has, hence the reason for purchasing the dog. Perhaps they could also rent an allotment when Bailey is old enough to settle down in the sun and has stopped digging up their plants.

After the comforting food has been eaten, Morgan showers and changes before climbing into the cold bed. He sleeps unusually well, only waking once in the night after experiencing a strange dream that involved something furry with a wet nose lying in between him and Celia.

Chapter 15

The sun is just starting to rise behind the desolate Sparrow House when the boy stumbles across the body. He is out delivering newspapers to the few residents in Magpie House who are interested enough about their society to read the local news, when he spots something unfamiliar lying on the ground in the play area. At first, he assumes the woman is drunk; lying in a hazy stupor at the far end of the children's play area, her arms and legs splayed out in opposite directions. Curiosity draws him closer and from his new position he sees that her miniscule denim skirt has been pushed up, her thin, black top is askew, revealing a black lacy bra underneath. A bruise is clearly visible on her right cheek; her right eye, which is open, is distorted by swollen tissue. Further down her body, small bruises can be seen on her upper thighs, one shoe lies beside her foot.

   The boy shuffles nearer, bending over the woman to take a closer look. It is only then that he notices a small pool of blood that has seeped out from an unseen head wound and congealed on the underside of her skull, matting her hair together into a clump. It is at this point that the boy realises the woman is dead. He runs as fast as he can, his heart straining against his rib cage, to Magpie House, where he begins screaming to

151

anyone who is awake and willing to respond to his cries for help.

The first officer to reach the Hartsmere estate is PC Barnes, who, after working on the estate for over twenty years, has grown used to being called out to all manner of incidents - this one though is unusual even by his standards. It takes only a matter of seconds for him to identify the deceased.

Morgan is driving to the police station, fingers drumming to the music blaring out of his CD player, when his mobile rings. He puts the phone onto speakerphone to hear the news that a body has been found on the Hartsmere estate. Quickly he makes a U-turn in the middle of the busy high street and heads back along the main road towards the estate.

When he arrives, Morgan finds that the estate has already learnt of the news, which has spread rapidly through the tight-knit community. He pulls up near Blackbird Terrace and watches for a moment, as a steady stream of resident's head towards the centre of the estate. Nearby in a parked ambulance, a paramedic is comforting PC Barnes. Morgan feels a jolt of curiosity, coupled with a pang of dread of what he might see next – if an experienced beat officer has been shocked by the scene, then he can only suppose that he is in for a nasty surprise as well.

Morgan opens the boot of his car to extract a pair of white overalls and shoe covers, which he pulls over his jeans and trainers. After slamming the boot firmly shut again and checking that the car doors are locked, Morgan hurries towards the centre of the estate. A group of onlookers have gathered outside Magpie House and Morgan meanders through them, gently moving them from his path. He stoops under the police cordon that has been around the perimeter of the playground, where his attention is immediately drawn to the large white tent that has been erected over one section of the children's playground.

Morgan spots Cook talking to Dr Bootle outside the tent. As he approaches, he can hear Cook and Dr Bootle discussing the case.

'What are your first thoughts then?' Cook asks the pathologist.

'Well, she's got an injury to the back of the head, that much is obvious, but whether she fell and hit her head or if she was hit from behind, I won't know for certain until I take a closer look at the wound. It also looks as if she's been sexually assaulted, with a little luck we might get some samples of sperm.'

'Can you tell how long she has been dead?'

'Her body temperature is 29 degrees Celsius, so she could have died six to eight hours ago. It's cold outside though and she's not wearing a lot of clothing so she could have died earlier. If I were to guess though I'd estimate that she died between midnight and two o'clock this morning. I'll be able to give you a better idea later when I've checked the body for the levels of rigor mortis and lividity.'

Cook notices that Morgan is striding towards them and beckons for him to approach. The senior detective moves to one side to allow Morgan through the small entrance into the tent. Inside, a photographer is busy snapping pictures of the cadaver from different angles, taking care not to step on any potential evidence that the scene of crime officers are collecting from the surrounding area.

'We know who she is,' Cook says quietly as he steps up beside Morgan.

Morgan raises an eyebrow, intrigued, especially as he has already been informed that no identification was found on the body.

'Her name's Trudy Barnes. PC Barnes wife,' Cook explains with a grimace.

'Sweet Jesus, no wonder he's being treated by a paramedic. I just thought he was a bit shocked after seeing the body,' Morgan exclaims. 'Was she raped?'

'It looks that way, although knowing our luck the bastard will have worn a condom. We'll have to wait for the post-mortem to get a clearer idea of how she died. Given that she was on the estate and dressed like that though I also think we should request a tox screen as well, see if she'd been taking any drugs.'

The sound of someone entering the tent halts the conversation. Morgan turns to see Dr

Bootle's assistant Harry arrive, ready to help prepare the body for transit to the morgue. Morgan watches with fascination as Harry carefully wraps the woman's hands to preserve any evidence there might be underneath her fingernails. The woman's body is then carefully lifted onto a plastic bag and zipped up. Harry and one of the SOCO lift the body bag to waist height then begin the difficult task of manoeuvring her out of the tent. Once outside, she is placed on a stretcher and wheeled in the direction of the private ambulance that is already waiting at the edge of the estate.

Morgan steps outside the tent to watch the procession; his eyes transfixed by the body bag as it winds its way through the crowd. He follows it's movements until it is out of sight then ducks back inside the tent to continue watching the forensic team collecting and bagging evidence; a shoe, three discarded cigarette ends and two empty bottles of cider have been found on the ground next to the roundabout. These key pieces of evidence will be taken to the forensics lab, six miles from the morgue at Hemley Hospital. Morgan cannot help but bristle with irritation that vital evidence will end up being split over several locations, making it more difficult to protect them from potential contamination and misplacement but alas there is no way around the Governments cost-cutting exercise in centralising forensic services.

The newspaper boy who was unlucky enough to be in the wrong place at the wrong time, is talking to an officer outside Magpie House. Even from a distance, Morgan can see the young lad's hands shaking as he recounts his movements of that morning. As soon as his preliminary statement is complete and the satchel of newspapers that were hastily discarded earlier on the grass verge outside the block of flats has been retrieved, the boy runs up the path towards Blackbird Terrace, keen to get away from the horrific scene.

Morgan's gaze drifts up towards Magpie House, his eyes searching the windows above him until his sees what he is looking for - a small, lone figure watching from the shadows. As soon as Jade notices that she is being watched, she withdraws from the window. The thin pink curtains are quickly pulled across and the light bedroom light switched off.

'Is that Jade up in the flats watching?' Cook asks as he approaches.

'Yes. Do you think she might have seen something?'

'It's possible or maybe she's just as curious about what's going on, just like everyone else on this estate,' Cook replies.

'I think I'll go and talk to her anyway,' Morgan says as he walks off towards the entrance of Magpie House before Cook can protest.

Morgan runs up the stairs and knocks on the front door of the Thompson's flat. Jade must have guessed the identity of her visitor, as the door immediately opens. He follows her into the living room, noticing that Jade's mother and sister are both absent.

'What's happened?' Jade asks, looking up at Morgan, her eyes wide with concern.

'I was hoping you might be able to tell me.'

'I don't know anything,' Jade replies quickly, her gaze shifting to what is happening out of the window.

'Did you see anyone in the playground last night?' Morgan asks as he approaches the window to stand next to the teenager.

'Just the usual people.' Jade continues to look out of the window, fascinated by the scene below.

'What about later on, after you went to bed. Did you hear anything unusual?' Morgan asks.

'I heard some laughing and shouting, nothing different from what I normally hear.'

'No screaming, anything like that?'

'I don't think so but the flat above us had their music on really loud. They must've been having a party.'

'What about your mum, could she have heard anything?'

Jade laughs, her eyes relaxing into a smile. It is the first time Morgan has seen Jade smile and he notices how pretty she is when she is not scowling.

'I reckon she was at the party upstairs,' Jade explains. 'I never heard her come back so it must have been a late one. Darcy had a sleep over at a friend's house last night - a really nice house on the Walton estate. Sort of place I wish I could live.'

'So, you were here alone then?'

Jade realises too late that she has said too much. 'No, no I mean mum popped out but she was here with me, I weren't on my own, she knows that's not allowed.'

Morgan stands to the right of Jade and looks out through the large metal-framed window. 'You've got a good view from here, especially of the play area.'

'I don't look out much,' Jade replies too quickly.

'Well, if you remember anything, even if it seems silly and you don't think it's relevant, please call me.' Morgan retrieves a card from his wallet and passes it to Jade, who takes it before returning to staring out of the window. Morgan watches as the muscles in her face tighten and he wonders if she is thinking about another recent incident not far from where she lives, one that involved Marlon Turner and Shania Smart.

'How's Shania?' Jade asks, eventually breaking the silence.

'Haven't you seen her yet? I don't want to sound like I'm lecturing you but I'm sure she could do with a friend right now.'

'I can't. Marlon would kill me if he found out that I'd been talking to her,' she says, her bottom lip trembling.

'Why would he do that Jade? She's supposed to be your best friend, isn't she?'

Before Jade can respond, the front door slams shut. Morgan watches as Jades mother removes her top and skirt in the corridor before staggering into the bathroom. She does not even notice the detective's presence, let alone her daughters. Morgan doubts that she even realises a woman died in front of her flat during the night.

Jade quietly suggests that Morgan leaves before her mother finds him in the flat – she is clearly not in a fit state for questioning and could be volatile when drunk. Not wanting to make Jades day any worse by angering her mother, Morgan traipses heavily back down the stairs and out into the emerging daylight. He steps outside just as the sun is breaking through the threatening clouds then goes in search of Cook, who is busy co-ordinating a team of officers, some of whom have already begun interviewing bystanders. Other officers are being tasked with knocking at each of the flats in Magpie House, to search for any potential witnesses. Marlon Turner and his gang have also appeared and are standing at the edge of the playground next to the police cordon. Morgan can feel Marlon's eyes burn into him as he walks across the playground towards Cook. He waits for Cook to finish instructing the officers before relaying to him his conversation with Jade.

'Let's go and find out more about that party shall we?'

'Will do boss,' Morgan says cheekily. It will take some time for the results from forensics and the postmortem to come back, so in the meantime, they will just have to rely on good old-fashioned police work.

It takes less than an hour to find the flat where the party was held the previous night. Morgan knocks on the door of the flat that is located directly above Jade Thompsons and waits for someone to appear. When the door eventually opens, it is obvious from the dishevelled appearance of the occupiers, that they have all been asleep and are perhaps still ignorant of the drama that has unfolded outside. They do not seem to be surprised however to find two police officers standing outside their front door.

'Who was it then, complaining about our music again?' The older male sighs as he leans against the door frame.

'So, you did have a party here last night?' Cook asks.

'Yeah, so what, no crime against enjoying yourself is there?' Says the younger male who is standing further back along the corridor.

'What are your names?' Morgan asks as he tries to peer into the hallway. There is a pungent aroma of cannabis and he wonders how the two men would react if they decided to search the place.

'Why don't you just tell us what you want so we can go back to sleep?' The older male says, yawning loudly.

'We're investigating a serious incident that occurred in the playground last night and need to know if anyone at your party saw anything,' Morgan says evenly.

'Ah right,' the older male says, looking slightly relieved. 'I'm Charlie, and this is my younger brother Martin.'

'How many people were here last night?' Morgan asks.

'About ten, I think,' Charlie responds, screwing up his face as his addled brain tries to recall the events of the previous night.

'Can you give me a list of their names?' Cook asks, still holding the front door open. 'As I said before, we're only interested in the incident that occurred last night, not what you've been smoking.'

The muscles in Charlie's face instantly relaxes. He motions to his brother to fetch a pen and pad of paper that is lying next to the telephone on the floor of the hallway. 'What's happened then?' Charlie says, seemingly waking up enough to have process the information has just heard.

'A woman's body was found in the playground this morning,' Cook responds.

A look of utter shock appears on the two men's faces. They were perhaps expecting the incident to be another rape, or a mugging, rather than something as serious as a death. Charlie tears off a sheet of paper from the notepad and hastily scribbles down the names that he can remember of people who attended the party. When the list is complete, he passes it to Morgan.

Morgan checks through the list, his eyes resting on Zoe Thompsons and Susie Smarts names. He knows he should not be surprised to find that both women were at the party but somewhat irrationally, he feels disappointed by it. Morgan passes the piece of paper to Cook and indicates with his finger to the two names of interest on the list.

Having extracted phone numbers for most of the party goers, Cook and Morgan make their way back down the stairs to the flat below. A uniformed officer is standing outside the door of number fifty-seven, attempting to talk to Zoe Thompson, who is wearing a worn cerise dressing gown and slouching bleary eyed against the door frame. She looks up as Cook and Morgan approach, her face wrinkling in puzzlement at their presence.

Cook dismisses the officer who has been trying unsuccessfully to find out where Zoe Thompson was the previous night, so that he can move on to the next flat.

'Where were you last night?' Cook asks, plunging his hands into the pockets of his overcoat.

'At a party,' Zoe Thompson replies sheepishly, ignoring the look of contempt on Morgan's face.

'What time did you get there and leave?' Cook continues.

'What's going on, Jade said something about the police being in the playground?'

'The body of a woman was found this morning. We're trying to talk to anyone who was in the area last night in case they saw something,' Morgan explains.

Zoe Thompson suddenly looks much more awake than she did a moment ago. She shuffles back into the hallway then presses herself against the wall to allow the two men into the flat.

'I'd better go and get dressed,' she says, moving into the first room on the right.

The two detectives continue down the hallway into the living room, which is eerily quiet now that both children are at school and pre-school. Five minutes later, Zoe Thompson appears again, wrapping a pale blue cardigan around her thin shoulders as she stumbles into the living room.

Morgan notices that she has managed to run a comb through her long auburn hair and that her skinny jeans flatter her slim figure. He wonders how much weed she smoked the previous night or what else she might have got up to. As Morgan stares at the young woman, he hopes that perhaps she will start to grow up soon and put her children's welfare first. A more likely scenario is that the two girls will morph into younger versions of their mother as soon as they are old enough to do so.

Cook is also lost in thought but he is thinking about the young woman who was found dead that morning. He wonders how he would cope if it had been his wife. He looks up as Zoe Thompson draws closer, his eyes following her as she stumbles past the sofa towards the kitchen area. The sound of the kettle being switched on cuts through the quietness, followed by the clinking of mugs being pulled out from an overhead cupboard.

The two detectives watch as Zoe shakily holds out a mug towards them to ask if they would also like a drink. Despite Morgans reluctance to drink out of the stained mugs, he smiles, grateful for the short respite from the bitter cold outside. Winter is definitely on its way now, the broken, fallen leaves are becoming crisp underfoot and a slight frost is beginning to form early morning. Despite the strong sunshine that has now managed to fight its way through the dense clouds, it is by far the coldest day they have experienced for many months and a sombre reminder of the months ahead.

When the three coffees have been made, Zoe returns to the living area and sets the mugs down heavily onto a placemat in the centre of a table. She passes a mug to each of the men before settling down into the armchair, drawing her legs up beneath her as she clutches tightly onto the hot liquid between her hands. Her actions are reminiscent of her daughter, who also sits that way.

'The party I went to last night was upstairs,' Zoe says as she blows over the top of the mug to cool the steaming drink.

'We know, we've already spoken to the men who live in the flat,' Cook admits, trying not to show the contempt that he feels for the largely absent mother.

'Jade's old enough to look after herself and Darcy was at a friend's,' Zoe says defensively, as if guessing Cook's thoughts.

'We're not interested in that at the moment. What time did you go to the party?' Cook asks, taking a sip from his mug.

'It must have been about eleven,' Zoe says, her attention returning to the mug of coffee, which has now cooled enough to drink more quickly.

'Who else was there?' Morgan puts his empty cup down onto the windowsill, surprised that he has finished before the other two, who are still drinking theirs.

Zoe reels off a few names that match those on the list the two men have already been given.

'Did you go anywhere else, or see anyone hanging around when you left?' Cook asked as he too, puts down the now empty mug.

'Sorry, it's all a bit hazy. I don't think I did. Have you asked Jade? She likes staring out her bedroom window at night, she doesn't think I know, but I hear her creeping about sometimes when she can't sleep.'

'I spoke to her briefly before she went to school,' Morgan responds, biting back a retort that it should have been Jades mother who was at the flat seeing her daughter off to school and not a police detective. 'How well do you know Susie Smart?'

Zoe looks at Morgan with interest, curious as to why he is asking that particular question. 'I've known Suze for years, we went to school together, just like our daughters.'

'Did you see her last night?'

'Yeah, she was there. We didn't really speak though, sometimes we like to do our own thing, talk to other people if you know what I mean.'

Cook nods, he understands full well how friendships can wan and strengthen. 'It's a pity that Jade and Shania have fallen out. Do you know why?'

'You know what teenage girls are like, it was probably over a boy.'

Cook looks sideways at Morgan before turning his attention back to Zoe. 'You know that

Shania was raped last week? Do you think it could be something to do with that?'

'Might be. I don't think Shania's been back at school since so perhaps Jade hasn't seen her. If you've got nothing else to ask then I really need to go back to bed,' she says, standing up to show the two men out of the flat.

The two detectives are about to leave when Zoe Thompson suddenly asks what most people would have thought to ask when a policeman first knocked on their front door.

'What's happened then, how did that woman die?'

'We're not sure yet but it looks as if she was raped and beaten,' Cook replies.

'Who was she? Was she from around here?'

'Her name was Trudy Barnes,' Cook says, carefully watching the young woman's reaction.

Zoe Thompsons cheeks pale and she mumbles something inaudible that sounded like 'she felt sick'. Before either detective can ask Zoe to repeat what she said, the front door closes.

'Well, that was interesting, I guess she knew Trudy then,' Morgan says. 'We'd better go back to the flat upstairs and find out if Trudy Barnes was at the party as well and if she was, why wasn't her name on the list.'

Chapter 16

When the two detectives reach the flat above Zoe Thompsons, they find the front door is wide open and the occupants are no longer there. Morgan picks his way through the empty flat, it is obvious that the two men have gone and most probably, will not return.

'We'd better go back downstairs and talk to Zoe Thompson again,' Cook says, as they make their way back down the concrete stairs.

This time it takes several minutes for Zoe Thompson to open the door. When she sees who is on the other side of the door, she throws her hands up in exasperation.

'You knew Trudy Barnes, didn't you?' Cook says abruptly, growing tired of the wall of silence that always seems to surround the estate.

Zoe Thompson looks down at the ground and then nods.

'Was she at the party last night?' Morgan asks.

'I think so. She might have been, there were a lot of people there.'

'The two men in the flat upstairs, do they rent or are they squatting?' Cook asks, flexing his knee which has begun to ache from an old running injury that often flares up in cold weather.

'I don't know, they haven't been there long,' Zoe says, a look of guilt flashing across her face.

'Do you know their names?' Cook asks.

'I only know them as Charlie and Martin. They're brothers you know, even though they don't look alike.'

'They don't seem to be there now,' Cook continues, 'If you see them again can you let me know as we need to find out if Trudy Barnes was at that party and if so, who she was with.'

Zoe Thompson nods, looking even more subdued than she had been earlier that morning. Morgan is surprised by the effect that Trudy Barnes death has had on her, leaving him wondering if she knew the woman well.

'How did you know Trudy?' Morgan asks, pulling his coat around him more tightly. The concrete stairwell is damp and he is starting to feel chilly.

'I didn't really, just saw her in the pub now and again and sometimes at parties. We didn't really speak much, I can't tell you a lot about her.'

'Did you know that her husband is a police officer?' Cook asks.

Zoe shakes her head, 'No, I doubt she would've been hanging out with us for very long if anyone knew that. No wonder you lot are looking so worried about finding out who did her in.'

'We always take unexplained deaths seriously,' Cook says tersely, just as the door slams shut again - the conversation is clearly over.

'I need to get back to the crime scene,' Cook mutters as they make their way towards the stairs. 'Can you go and see Susie Smart and find out what she can remember from last night.'

Morgan follows Cook down the stairs and out towards the main entrance of the building. He always feels a strange sense of relief when leaving the tense atmosphere of the estate buildings. Pushing open the heavy fire-resistant door, Morgan takes a deep breath then steps back onto the path and into the ensuing chaos beyond.

The crowd of onlookers has largely dissipated and been replaced by a smaller group of journalists, who are eagerly watching the proceedings, hoping to glean as much information as they can before the official press release.

Morgan watches as Cook marches over to the awaiting group to talk to Phil Wattle, then turns to find Fallow, who is pacing up and down outside the evidence tent, trying to keep warm.

'We need to go and talk to Susie Smart,' Morgan says as he approaches Fallow.

The young officer stands still, his normally pale cheeks flushed by the chill in the air. 'Sure, anything to get out of this cold,' he grumbles.

Morgan snorts, 'Wait until its winter. Right now, it's like summer in comparison.'

As they make their way slowly back through the crowd of onlookers towards Blackbird Terrace, Morgan notices the absence of Marlon Turner and his gang, who have disappeared from the spot where they were earlier. He wonders if they too were feeling the cold, or perhaps they had seen enough.

The Smarts lives in the marginally better part of the estate, leaving Morgan wondering how they managed to acquire a larger home then that of the Thompsons. Even though this part of the estate is newer, Morgan notices the paintwork on the wooden cladding at the front of the building is stained and peeling. Two of the lower storey windows have been broken and boarded up, the remainder are covered with metal grills. Blackbird Terrace may well be the best block on the estate thinks Morgan, but he is relieved that he does not have to live there.

The two men walk around to the rear of the building and take the stairs up to the middle floor, bypassing a young woman who is trying to control her two children who are fighting at the top of the stairwell. Morgan hurries past them towards number ten, leaving Fallow to decide if he too will ignore them, or if he feels the need to intervene.

The door to number ten opens quickly, responding to the sharp rap on the wooden frame. Susie Smart is surprised to see Morgan standing on her doorstep. 'She's not here, she gone back to school.'

'Actually, it's you I want to speak to Susie. Can I come in?'

The door reluctantly opens a little further and Morgan follows Susie to the far end of the flat. He waits for her to sit down on the sofa before taking a seat at the other end.

'I don't know if you've heard, but a woman's body was found this morning in the playground next to Robin House,' Morgan says. 'We know there was a party in Robin House last night and believe you may have been there?'

'I went for a while, just for about an hour or so,' Susie says, picking at the loose skin around the edges of her fingernails.

Morgan shifts uncomfortably in his seat, which offers no support for his lower back that has sunken down onto the hard springs below.

'Did you see anyone hanging around the playground when you were there, or perhaps anyone hanging about in Robin House? Did you see anyone at all who seemed odd or suspicious?'

'I don't think so but I can't say I look anywhere else except where I'm going. It don't do you no good to look at things that don't concern you around here,' Susie replies.

'Ok, so what time did you go to the party and leave again?' Morgan pulls out a notebook from his jacket pocket. He locates a biro and begins taking notes.

'It must have been about ten when I got there and I was probably back by eleven thirty. I don't like to leave Shania on her own for too long, especially with what happened to her.'

'How is she now? You said she's gone back to school?'

'Yeah, first day back today. She was dreading it, poor love, all those kids staring at her and gossiping. She needs to toughen up a bit that girl, she's too sensitive.'

Morgan tries to imagine how hard it must be for the teenager, especially with a parent who seems to be completely lacking in empathy.

'Do you know a woman called Trudy Barnes?' Morgan asks, bringing the conversation around to the real reason for his visit.

Before Susie can reply, their conversation is interrupted by Fallow knocking on the door. The young detective has finally given up trying to assist the woman on the stairs and decided it would be more useful if he caught up with Morgan. Susie Smart takes the opportunity to usher the policemen out of her flat, leaving Morgan in no doubt that she will be straight on the phone to Zoe Thompson.

Shania has been dreading going back to school, especially as she still hasn't heard from Jade. She guesses her so called best friend no longer wants to be seen with her. Maybe she doesn't want to talk about what happened, or maybe she knows who attacked her and doesn't want to get involved. She'd heard that Jade wasn't seeing

Marlon Turner any longer, so what is stopping them from being friends again?

Shania does not see Jade until lunchtime. The school canteen is the last place that she wants to be, with the other kids talking about her, pointing her out as they whisper loudly. It is free food though and her mum won't give her much to eat tonight, so she doesn't have much choice. Shania chooses cottage pie and peas, then makes her way towards the back of the cavernous room, where she finds a seat on one of the long tables.

It is then that she sees Jade, sitting with Callum Woods, a few tables away from her. Jade looks the other way when she spies Shania staring at her. Shania watches the couple as they eat. It looks as if Jade is uncomfortable with the conversation she is having with Callum. She wonders if her ex best friend is being warned off from talking to her.

Shania remains in her seat long after her food has been eaten. She waits for the bell to ring for the next class, then waits until everyone else has left before she too heads out of the canteen. Keeping her head down as she walks, Shania preys silently that she will not bump into Jade or Callum. She knows she cannot avoid them forever but she does not know what she will do when the time comes for her to face them. Perhaps after school she will go to the library and catch up on some of the reading she has missed out on over the last few days. Her mum will not notice her absence and it will give Jade and Callum time to leave the school premises before she does. It was such a relief to hear that Marlon Turner was expelled for smoking in the toilets. She could not have faced coming back to school if he had been here as well.

Chapter 17

The postmortem on Trudy Barnes body has been scheduled for just after lunch, much to Morgans relief as he seldom feels like eating after seeing a corpse being cut open. In a rare moment of protracted kindness, Morgan decides to bring Fallow with him to the mortuary, so that he too can experience the delights of a postmortem. To enable the novice detective to gain the most from his experience, Morgan has gained special permission for them to watch from inside the mortuary suite itself, instead of from the viewing gallery where visitors normally sit to observe the proceedings.

By the time Fallow and Morgan arrive, having been delayed by their visit to Blackbird Terrace, Dr Bootle has already begun to examine the exterior of the body. Harry, the mortuary assistant, who is standing next to the pathologist, with a digital camera in one hand, awaiting instructions. Harry spots the two detectives arrive through the stainless-steel doors and motions for them to find a place near to the mortuary table where they will not be in the way.

'Hallo, do you two want to stand over there?' Harry says cheerfully. 'We're almost ready to make a start. As you can see the woman's clothes have already been removed and sent off to the forensics lab.'

'What about her handbag?' Morgan asks.

'It didn't contain much - a few pound coins, a packet of Silk Cut and a box of matches. It's gone to forensics though to check for fibres etc.,' Harry replies before turning his attention to the Dr Bootle, who is waiting to begin.

Dr Bootle speaks aloud as he works, 'The body is of a Caucasian female, approximately five foot three in height, weight is eight stone two pounds and her age was thirty-nine. Her shoulder-length hair and has been dyed a dull plum colour but the roots are chestnut.'

The pathologist waits for Harry to take some blood samples and record the woman's internal temperature before continuing with the examination. 'As you can see, rigor has already spread downwards from her head, reaching her toes,' Dr Bootle explains, indicating to the respective parts of the body as he speaks. 'This suggests she has been dead for approximately eight to twelve hours. Can you see the lividity on the underside of the body?'

Morgan nods, trying to avoid looking too closely at the now partially dissected body.

'This tells us that she probably died in the position she was found in. We'll take some tissue samples to check that lividity is fixed, which will confirm that the body was not moved postmortem,' Dr Bootle explains.

Morgan reluctantly looks at the corpse, unable to avoid it any longer. He is surprised at how youthful her face is, despite the grey pallor of death. The dark blue bruising to the tissues around her eye seem to be even more prominent now due to the contrast in colour with her unblemished skin. There is a small cut on her right cheek, which could have been made by someone who was wearing a ring back-handing her. The woman's nose is slightly reddened and that the inside of the nostrils inflamed, indicating that she was a long-term cocaine user.

Dr Bootle continues to examine the outside of the upper body. 'Can you see there are finger marks on her upper arms?' The pathologist turns to look at the two detectives, whilst holding up one of the arms so that they can see the bruises for themselves.

Dr Bootle continues to examine the body, 'Do you see the bruising to her upper thighs and vaginal region? Harry please can you measure the bruises on the inside of her upper thighs and take swabs of the vaginal fluid to test for semen and the presence any other substances such as latex.'

Harry works diligently, carrying out the pathologist's instructions then photographing the areas identified. A relaxed stillness has descended on the mortuary suite, as the two men continue their work swiftly and efficiently, each perfectly in tune with the other.

'Do you see these injuries to her foot? Her right foot was missing a shoe and she has abrasions across the heel and the big toe,' Dr Bootle says as he points to the appendage. 'These injuries could have been caused by the woman moving across the hard surface of the playground after the shoe was lost. The question is, did she move herself or was she dragged?'

The body is then turned over to look at the head wound. The pathologist carefully parts the congealed hair to reveal a small raw wound, the surrounding tissues having been crushed by a blunt trauma. Dr Bootle takes a closer look at edges of the broken tissue, searching for any substances that might have been caught in the wound.

'If she had fallen on the hard surface of the playground or against the roundabout or swing, traces of paint or tarmac could be found in the wound,' Dr Bootle explains. 'Traces of other substances such as splinters of wood may indicate that she was hit by an object such as a baseball bat.'

Morgan tentatively moves closer to the table whilst trying not to breathe in the noxious odours. He motions for Fallow to do the same so that he too can get a better look at the wound. Even to their untrained eyes, the two detectives can clearly see the presence of grit on the outside of the wound.

Further inside the crushed tissue, Dr Bootle points out a green flaky substance that could be paint. Harry carefully removes samples of the flakes and deposits them into a tube, which he then seals and labels. The sample will be sent to a separate forensic unit that specialises in carbon materials.

Morgan hopes that the forensic team have had the sense to check the roundabout and swing for any blood when they combed the playground after the discovery of the body. He makes a mental note however to check on this, just in case it has been missed.

Dr Bootle concludes his examination of the outside of the body by noting the bruising to the upper back and shoulders and a small scrape on the back of the buttocks. Harry steps forward to assist the pathologist in turning the cadaver back over again.

Morgan steels himself as he realises that the easy part has been done. Now their resolve will be sorely tested as the pathologist makes a large incision down her body to open up the cavity. Morgan braces himself for the assault on his senses that he knows will quickly follow.

Dr Bootle deftly cracks open the thoracoabdominal cavity, the sudden loud noise of the Stryker saw jolting Morgan from his thoughts. It is immediately obvious that the young woman was a smoker; her lungs blackened by years of abuse, delicate pink tissues stained from the inhalation of tar and noxious chemicals.

'Can you see her liver is swollen and scarred – it's likely that she had the beginnings of cirrhosis, probably caused by persistent alcohol abuse,' says Dr Bootle.

Morgan takes a step back as Dr Bootle removes the organs and passes them to Harry, who weighs them and takes samples before placing them carefully back inside the cavity. Before closing up the body cavity, Dr Bootle also notes that there is nothing in the stomach, indicating that the last meal Trudy had eaten was at least several hours before her death.

'Was she alive when she got the head wound?' Fallow asks.

Dr Bootle moves back to the site of the head injury. 'Can you see that blood and serum have accumulated in the wound? This confirms she was alive when the injury occurred.'

Harry takes an x-ray of the head to check for any structural damage to the skull, before moving to one side to allow Dr Bootle to open up the skull. Fallow blanches and stumbles away from the body. For one second, Morgan thinks that the rookie is going to vomit but the young man manages to control his revulsion long enough for the moment to pass.

As soon as the incision is made, a large pool of blood is released, spilling down onto the mortuary floor. Once the flow had subsided, it reveals swollen bruised brain tissue underneath.

'So, there we have it, this lady had a blunt head trauma, which resulted in a skull fracture, causing an intracranial subdural bleed at the back of the skull,' Dr Bootle concludes.

Harry steps forward with the x-ray that he processed while Dr Bootle was examining the head wound. He hands the film to the pathologist, who holds it up to the overhead strip light.

'Do you see this simple linear fracture at the back of the skull?' Dr Bootle says to no one in particular. 'This type of injury is likely to have been caused by a fall rather than a more aggressive force, such as a blow to the back of the head.'

'So, it could be an accidental death?' Morgan asks, squinting to try to make sense of the x-ray.

'It's possible,' Dr Bootle replies before continuing on with his work. With Harry's help, he takes some tissue samples from the area surrounding the trauma. When the last task has been completed, Dr Bootle deftly removes his gloves and protective clothing and waltzes out of the mortuary suite.

Morgan and Fallow hurry to catch up with the pathologist, who is surprisingly nimble for his physique. They locate Dr Bootle in his office, where he has opened a fresh bottle of mineral water and filled two glasses for his guests. Fallow, who is still looking particularly pale, sips the water gratefully.

'As I said earlier, it's clear that the cause of death is due to the blunt trauma to the back of the head but I can't say for definite how she received it. It could be that she was hit across the face, stumbled backwards and hit her head on something. I did find some green paint in the wound so that may have come from the swings or roundabout. It also looks like we have some sperm, so hopefully we can find a match for it,' Dr Bootle says gruffly.

'She wasn't murdered then?' Morgan asks, before he takes a sip of the cool clear liquid - the antiseptic smell of hospitals always makes his throat feel dry.

'Not necessarily, although she has got bruising to her face and thighs. We could be looking at manslaughter or an accident, either way it's up to you to find out. I would suggest however that you start by re-checking the playground as I'm not confident SOCO would have checked the swings or the roundabout as they were some distance from the body.'

'How did she get over to the other side of the playground?' Fallow asks, beginning to recover a little from the traumatic experience.

'The scrape on one of her heels could indicate that she was pulled across the tarmac, which might explain the bruising to her upper arm, or she might have pushed herself over that way, it's difficult to tell. I'll have to leave this one with you though as I have got another three postmortems to get through today,' Dr Bootle says, making it clear that it is time for his guests to leave.

As soon as the exterior door slams shut behind them, Morgan gratefully inhales a few deep lungful's of the cold fresh air. He leans against the brick wall of the mortuary for a moment, clearing his nostrils of the sterile stench of the hospital, before heading back to the car with Fallow still in tow.

'I think we should head back to the Hartsmere estate and take another look at the playground,' Morgan says as he climbs into the car.

Fallow nods then quickly clamber's into the car, relieved to be leaving behind his first postmortem even if it does mean having to suffer Morgans erratic driving all the way back to the estate again.

Chapter 18

This time of year does nothing to improve Morgans mood as the ever-present damp seems to penetrate through to his skin, however many layers of clothing he wears. It is moments like these that makes him wish he were in a snug, cosy office, sat in front of a hot radiator, nose close to a computer monitor. The fantasy never lasts long enough to actually take a proper hold though and prompt him to change from the career that he had always dreamt of doing as a young boy. The only real niggle he has right now is that Cook has been promoted over him, leaving no way for him to move up the career ladder without changing to another team.

Morgan pushes the thought aside as he and Fallow reach the outskirts of the estate and find a parking space. As the two detectives walk towards the playground, they see little evidence of the drama that had unfolded earlier that morning. The only clue that something untoward recently occurred, is from the as yet undamaged police tape that surrounds the perimeter of the playground - something that is by no means an unusual occurrence on this estate. As the forensic team have completed their search of the playground and the surrounding area, the protective white tent that covered one end of the playground has been removed. Even the journalists have left, leaving only a few estate residents still milling about, gossiping about the day's events.

Morgan ducks under the police tape and carefully makes his way across the crime scene. The body was found in the far corner of the playground, close to a large overgrown Hebe. It seems likely though from the pathologist's findings, that Trudy did not sustain the fatal injury at the spot where she was found. Morgan wanders across the play area towards the swings, keeping his eyes peeled for any traces of blood as he walks over the tarmac. There is no obvious sign of disturbance so he moves onto the oversized roundabout, which is gently swinging back and forth in the wind.

Morgan grabs hold of one of the horizontal arms of the roundabout then kneels down to inspect it more closely. Pulling the aging structure slowly towards him, he inspects the outside of the metal edge on the footplate. His heart thumps when he spots what looks likely to be dried blood on the edge of the rim and he reaches inside his jacket pocket for his mobile phone.

Dr Bootle arrives on the Hartsmere estate in a little under twenty minutes. Normally this would be a job left for the scene of crime officers but he liked to take any possible opportunity to interfere and the fact that SOCO missed this vital evidence, has given the pathologist the excuse that he needed to get out of the mortuary for a couple of hours.

The elderly pathologist directs Harry to photograph the evidence before he carefully scrapes up a sample of the rust-coloured stain and surrounding green paint for analysis. Pulling out a fingerprint kit from his bag, Dr Bootle passes it to Harry and directs him to dust for fingerprints around the stain. If Trudy had been incapacitated from hitting her head on the roundabout, then someone must have moved her and if someone moved her, then there might just be fingerprints on the roundabout to prove it.

Morgan watches as Dr Bootle crouches down and tilts his head to one side, trying to peer underneath the structure. It is possible that if someone had been standing close to the roundabout, perhaps leaning over it, they may have left footprints in the gravel beneath the equipment. If there are any footprints connected to the death of Trudy Barnes, then this could be the only sensible place to find them.

It takes less than a second for Dr Bootle to spot a partial footprint in the loose stones; the tip of a large boot can just be made out imprinted into the dusty layer beneath the grit.

'What is it?' Fallow asks.

'A partial footprint,' Harry explains as he pulls out a camera and begins to photograph it.

Morgan peers over the Harrys hunched shoulders and watches him make a casting of the footprint. If they are in luck and the footprint is connected to Trudy's death, it could tell them not only the approximate height of the suspect but also provide a positive identification if they can find the matching boot. He watches as Harry also takes some samples of the surrounding gravel and tarmac, carefully placing them into plastic evidence jars and labelling them.

Morgan wonders what else SOCO might have missed that morning and decides to follow the direction Trudy Barnes may have moved in from the roundabout to the shrub where she was found. Given the large volume of blood that had seeped out from Trudy's head wound and is now congealed underneath the Hebe, Morgan supposes it would be logical to conclude that the woman had died here rather than at the roundabout. What of course they do not know is if the rape and her death are in any way connected. It is possible she fell onto the roundabout, then dragged herself across the playground or she was moved by someone to the edge of the playground out of sight. It could have been here that she was raped? Perhaps her attacker thought she was already dead? There are so many unanswered questions milling around Morgans brain. What they need now are some reliable witnesses and so far, no one has come forward.

Phil Wattle is sitting in the incident room, drinking what appears to be a large mug of coffee but is in fact laced with a tot of good quality whisky. The editor of the local newspaper is grateful for his symbiotic relationship with DCI Cook. Not only does it mean that he receives first scoop on a story but he often gets to do so from the comfort of a warm office.

Wattle would not normally have expected an editor with as many years experience as himself to still be chasing up stories, but they are short staffed at the moment, having lost one of their best reporters the previous year. Wattle knows that at some point he will have to find a replacement but for now he just cannot bear the thought of another stranger joining his tight-knit team.

The editor of The Suffolk Times slicks back his greasy, thinning hair, relaxing further into the back of the chair whilst periodically sipping the warming liquid. Cook is eagerly chatting about his latest case and Wattle waits for an appropriate moment to steer the conversation back towards the reason for his visit.

'We had another one of those notes yesterday,' Wattle says, grimacing as he burns his tongue on the bitter liquid.

Cook raises an eyebrow and waits for Wattle to continue.

'It's similar to the last one. Kids I reckon by the look of the handwriting, either that or someone who's not too bright.' Wattle retrieves the note from his briefcase, which he sealed in an unused plastic sandwich bag once he realised it's significance when opening the morning post. He passes it to Cook, who carefully checks both sides of the paper before turning his attention to the text, which reads '*Marlon Turner did it.*'

'It is indeed similar to the previous one but if it were written by the same person, there won't be any fingerprints, just like the other one,' Cook says wistfully, turning over the piece of paper. 'I'll ask Morgan to have a word with a couple of young girls on the Hartsmere estate, see if they can shed any light on it.' Shania Smart and Jade Thompson will both be out of school soon and it will be a good opportunity for Morgan to catch up with the two girls.

Chapter 19

Jade left school sometime after lunch according to her class tutor. She attended biology class immediately prior to lunch but must have disappeared afterwards, failing to reappear for the early afternoon registration.

After a little searching, Morgan finds the teenager sitting on a bench outside the parade of shops on the Hartsmere estate. She is wearing a blue padded jacket and is swinging her legs back and forth, scuffing her black patent shoes against the paving slabs.

'Hello again,' Morgan says cheerfully as he approaches the bench.

Jade looks up but after seeing who it is, continues swinging her legs back and forth.

'Have you been writing notes to the local newspaper?'

'What you talking about, what notes?' Jade says, looking around her, not wanting to be seen talking to the police.

'Someone's been sending notes to The Suffolk Times about Marlon Turner.'

'Well, it weren't me,' she says, looking defiantly at Morgan, her bottom lip wobbling with determination.

'Do you think it might have been Shania?'

Jade stares at Morgan for a moment. 'How would I know, I don't speak to her anymore.'

'Was she at school today?'

'Might have been, don't mean I saw her though.'

'Do you know where she is now?' Morgan persists.

Jade looks at the ground and begins kicking at the concrete post beneath the bench. 'She might've gone to the library. I reckon she got some stick from the other kids, you know what they're like.'

Morgan nods, remembering all too well what it felt like to be the outcast at school. 'Thanks Jade. If you do remember anything from last night, then please phone me.'

Morgan makes his way on foot to Hartsmere School, which is a ten minute walk from the estate. The school was constructed at the same time as the rest of the estate but is in a much better state of repair than the buildings where the residents live. The main building, which dominates the centre of the school grounds, is three stories high and peppered by a large number of corroding metal windows. The structure towers over football pitches and a netball court, where an after-school club is busy practising for their next match. Newer additions to the school have been linked to the main building by long corridors, connecting the new science labs, library and assembly hall to the main entrance hall.

As the main entrance to the school is shut, Morgan presses the buzzer located on the right side of the massive wrought iron gates. A dejected voice coming from the intercom, directs him to a smaller side entrance, where a janitor is idly polishing the floor of the long corridors.

Morgan walks along the corridor to the library, which is situated at the far end of the school. There are only two other pupils in the room, one of whom helpfully directs the detective to where Shania is sitting on the top mezzanine floor. From the top step of the stairs, Morgan can see the teen's nose is firmly fixed in a Harry Potter book.

Morgan approaches the girl slowly so as not to startle her but even so, Shania jumps when she realises that someone is coming towards her. Her face relaxes into a tentative smile when she recognises the figure on the dimly lit mezzanine.

'Jade thought you might be here,' Morgan says quietly.

'What do you want now? I still can't remember anything from the other day.'

Morgan ignores the statement and instead sits down on the chair next to Shania. 'A woman was found dead in the playground this morning. Have you heard anything about it?'

'No,' she says quietly. 'What happened?'

'It looks as if she was attacked by someone. Her name was Trudy, Trudy Barnes. Her husband is your local police officer.'

'Oh my god. How weird is that.'

'We think she might've been at a party in Magpie House last night. Jade's mum was there with yours. Did you hear your mum go out?'

'Yeah, she went out about ten and got back really late, I think it was about three.'

'Has your mum ever mentioned Trudy Barnes to you?'

'I don't think so, though she don't talk about her friends much. Maybe if I saw a photo of her, I might recognise her?'

Morgan pulls a grainy black and white photograph out from his inner coat pocket, which he picked up from the police station on the way to the estate. He passes the photo to Shania who looks up at him in surprise.

'Yeah, I knew her, she was always in the pub with my mum. I didn't think she was very nice. I shouldn't say that though should I, as she's dead and all that.'

'That's ok Shania, we want to know the truth about Trudy. We need to find out as much as possible about her so that we can work out how she died.'

The teenager nods but still retains a guilt-ridden expression on her face.

Morgan stands up to leave, then remembers to ask Shania about the note. 'I don't suppose you've been sending notes to the local newspaper?'

'What kind of notes?' Shania asks.

'They accuse Marlon Turner of being a rapist.'

Shania's cheeks redden as she looks up at Morgan with large dopey eyes. 'It weren't me,' she replies quickly, picking up a text book from the nearby table. 'I need to get back to my homework, I've got a lot to catch up on because of missing school last week.'

Morgan leaves the mezzanine level, allowing the comforting silence of the library to envelope him momentarily before he heads back outside into the fading sunshine. Fallow, who was waiting in the car, has brought the vehicle around to the front of the school.

'Her mother lied about how long she was at that party for and about knowing Trudy Barnes,' Morgan explains to Fallow as he pulls open the car door. 'The question is why. Let's leave the car here, I think we need to go and talk to Susie Smart again.'

There is no answer at Susie Smarts flat, so they decide to try the Punch and Judy. Despite the early hour, the young mother is already in the pub, sitting on a bar stool, gossiping with two men who are ordering pints of beer for them all. One of the men turns around to stare at the two strangers who have just walked through the door. Susie Smart, intrigued by what has attracted her companion's attention away from her, also turns around. She groans loudly when she recognises the visitors, the smile rapidly disappearing from her face.

'What do you want now, can't I get any peace from you lot?' She shouts across the room. Her two drinking companions, instantly recognising the men as being police detectives, pick up their pints and move towards the back of the pub.

'Why did you lie to us?' Morgan asks as he approaches the bar.

'About what?' Susie snaps, drinking deeply from the glass of rich walnut-coloured liquid.

'About knowing Trudy Barnes and about what time you left the party last night,' continues Morgan.

'I didn't lie to you, I said I knew Trudy.'

'But you didn't say that you knew her well or that she used to drink in here with you.'

Susie Smart pushes her lips out into a pout and flutters her eyes at Morgan, which has no effect on him whatsoever. 'So, what time did you leave the party then?'

'I told you, it was about eleven,' Susie says sullenly, returning her attention to the now almost empty glass on the bar in front of her.

'But you didn't go straight home, did you. Where did you go?

Silence falls as Susie contemplates her answer. 'I went round to someone's flat, all right.'
'Whose?' Morgan asks, leaning one hand on the edge of the polished bar.

'None of your business, a fella', that's all you need to know'.

'And was Trudy at the party?' Morgan persists.

'She arrived just as I left.' Susie picks up her empty pint glass and looks sulkily at it, as if willing it to refill itself.

'Was she drunk?'

'Maybe a bit, I don't know. It's difficult to tell when someone's on charlie.'

'She'd taken cocaine?'

'Yeah, of course, it was a party weren't it. Trudy would take anything to enjoy herself.'

'So where did she get the drugs?' Morgan leans more heavily on the bar, his face closing in on Susie's.

'I wouldn't know anything about that,' Susie says, motioning to the barman to refill her glass as she reluctantly pulls out her purse from her handbag, having conceded that no one else would be buying her a drink at this moment. 'She wasn't on her own though, if you get my meaning.'

'We need to know everything Susie, her death could be connected to it.'

'I don't know nothing else, why can't you all just leave me alone.' Susie turns to look at the other side of the room. The conversation is over.

Morgan and Fallow leave the pub and make their way back to the car. Fallow waits until they are out of earshot of anyone lurking nearby before asking if they should talk to Colin Barnes.

'I think we should wait for the toxicology reports to come back first, we need to know what she took before we go and tell her husband that she was a junkie,' Morgan snaps, irritated yet again by the enthusiasm of the younger officer.

The two men meander their way through the evening traffic in silence, both deep in thought. Morgan knows that they will need to talk to Cook before questioning PC Barnes, it is a delicate situation and they need to tread carefully.

Morgan drops Fallow off at his flat before continuing on through the dwindling traffic towards home. Hearing the front door open, Bailey begins to whine from somewhere behind the kitchen door, where Celia placed him earlier that evening before she went to her yoga class. When he opens the kitchen door, he is instantly greeted by the overwhelming stench of canine faeces. Morgan promptly places the puppy outside so that he can clear up the mess and put down fresh newspaper. As soon as Bailey comes back into the house, he squats on the newspaper, soaking the vinyl floor beneath it yet again with fresh urine. Morgan sighs loudly then clears up the mess once again, trying not to feel irritated at the young pup.

By the time Morgan has heated up and drunk a mug of hot chocolate, the puppy has tired of his company and returned to his basket. Morgan is also starting to feel sleepy so without waiting for Celia to return, he heads straight upstairs where he hopes that for once he might get an uninterrupted night's sleep. It is a short-lived expectation as even before Morgan has had time to shower and change into his pyjamas, the sound of Bailey's whining penetrates throughout the house.

Chapter 20

Cook is not pleased when he hears of Morgan and Fallow's idea to interview PC Colin Barnes and makes his feelings abundantly clear during the team's morning briefing. The last thing he needs is for PC Barnes to make a complaint, which will no doubt lead to an internal investigation given that this particular officer is well known as being 'old school' and will not take kindly to being interviewed. Cook has not yet had enough time to prove to Chief Superintendent Bennett that he is capable of running a high-profile team and he is not about to risk jeopardising his career. He does however have to inwardly admit that the interview is going to be necessary at some point, especially as they are fast running out of other leads. No witnesses have come forward to admit seeing Trudy the night she died and the two brothers who held the party in Magpie House are still missing. Their disappearance may be entirely coincidental and probably drug-related but Cook does not like coincidences and loose ends such as these, niggle at him.

Cook has received some good news though in that the miniscule paint samples found in Trudy's head wound matched those taken from the edge of the roundabout, where spots of dried blood had stained the metal structure. It is a pity that the area around the playground has been laid with tarmac. If the surface had not been so hard and impenetrable, they might have seen the marks made by Trudy's feet as she moved across the playground, which would have indicated whether she had been dragged or if she had shuffled her way towards the edge of the playground.

It is clear though that at some point, Trudy Barnes suffered bruising to her arms and her vaginal area, though it is impossible at the moment to ascertain if this is connected to her death. They do not even know if Trudy Barnes was deliberately killed or if it was the result of an accident and without witnesses, they have no way of knowing if she was alone when she died.

Cook runs his fingers through his thick, curly hair, pondering on the best course of action to take. The solution immediately comes to him - he should be the one who talks to Colin Barnes. However much Cook respects Morgan as a detective, he is painfully aware of his friend's limitations; tactfulness and patience are two of them. Earlier that morning Cook received the postmortem report for Trudy Barnes, so this would be an ideal opportunity to talking to Colin Barnes.

Colin Barnes lives on the Flixton estate, which is considerably more up-market then neighbouring Hartsmere. There are far fewer council houses on the estate, which is dominated by privately rented accommodation. The dwellings largely consist of

Victorian and Edwardian semi-detached houses that have been converted into spacious flats to increase both occupancy and rental rates. At the centre of the estate is a small park, which is a far cry from the pitiful playground aimed to service the needs of residents in the tower blocks on the Hartsmere estate.

The Barnes' live in a 1930's semi, close to the northern entrance to the park. Their front bay window overlooks a small pond just inside the park railings, where they can watch children idly feeding the residing ducks, coots and moorhens. Cook climbs up the steep steps to the front door. He pauses for a moment to take a few deep breaths, trying to quell the nagging discomfort that he feels in the pit of his stomach at having to visit a work colleague's home, especially in these circumstances. Cook lift's up the heavy brass door knocker and allows it to clang against the front door, the sound echoing through the hallway beyond. As he waits patiently for the door to open, Cook pushes aside the small voice inside him that hopes the door will not be opened.

Just as he is about to give up and leave, a shadow appears behind the stained-glass door. Cook's stomach sinks when the door opens to reveal a stooping dishevelled occupant, eyes red-rimmed from lack of sleep and cheeks reddened by too much alcohol.

'Sorry to disturb you Colin but I need to speak to you about Trudy, you know how it is with these things,' Cook says apologetically.

Colin Barnes nods, opening the door a fraction wider to allow Cook into the house. Cook wipes his feet on the door mat before following Barnes down the hallway, turning left into the front living room. Colin turns off the TV set that is nestled in the bay window and settles down into a leather chair, motioning for Cook to take a seat on the cream sofa nearest to the door.

'Have you found out what happened yet, how Trudy died?' Colin Barnes asks, his face sporting a few more creases than had been visible earlier that week.

'We're working on it Colin, you know that it can be a slow process. We've had the postmortem report back though and it looks as if Trudy hit her head on the roundabout, which caused a massive bleed to her brain. What we don't know is if her death was an accident or not. She did have other bruising that suggests she could have been assaulted.'

Colin Barnes shifts forward in his seat, clasping his hands in front of him as he rocks back and forth on the edge of the chair.

'Can I ask when you last saw your wife?'

'It must have been about teatime. She'd cooked fish and chips. We were supposed to be going to the cinema as I had to night off but she'd already made other plans.'

'That must have been disappointing for you?'

Colin Barnes nods, his eyes focusing on the carpet beneath his feet as he tries to recall the events of that evening. 'She gave me my dinner then just left. She was all dressed up and wouldn't tell me where she was going.'

'What did you do next?'

'What do you mean?' Colin Barnes' head snaps up to stare at Cook, his face hardening.

'I meant after Trudy left the house. What did you do then?'

'Oh I see. I went for a walk, to clear my head then came back home and watched some TV. She didn't come home so I thought she must've been staying with a friend.'

'You weren't worried when she didn't come home?'

'No. She often stayed with her girlfriends when she'd been out with them. She didn't like getting a taxi home by herself, especially when I'm working and the house is empty.'

But the house was not empty though, thought Cook as he waited for Colin Barnes to continue. An uncomfortable silence descended on the room, neither man knowing quite what to say to the other.

'There is one more thing I need to ask you but it's a little delicate,' Cook says, clearing his throat.

Colin Barnes stares at Cook, his eyes boring into him.

'We need to take a DNA sample from you?' Cook says quickly, as if trying to lessen the impact of his words.

'Ok, I guess so,' Colin Barnes replies, wrinkling his forehead in puzzlement.

'We also need to know when you last had sex with your wife.'

Colin Barnes frowns as he ponders on the question. 'The day before she died. Why do you need to know that?'

'We found some semen inside her,' Cook grimaces, not needing to explain any further the implications of the finding to a fellow police officer. 'Would you be able to come to the station tomorrow morning?'

Colin Barnes places his head in his hands and begins to sob. Cook waits for the moment to pass, not wanting to leave him in such a state. He looks up at the clock perched on top of the TV, counting the minutes as they tick by. After what seems like hours but is only seconds, Colin Barnes stands up, his eyes brimming with fresh tears and slopes off into the hallway. Cook wonders if he should follow, or perhaps go into the kitchen and make a cup of tea.

To Cooks surprise, Colin returns a few minutes later with two steaming mugs of coffee. He hands a mug to Cook, who is perched on the edge of his seat. Cook takes the cup from Colin before leaning back into the soft cushions that adorn the sofa. The coffee is strong and dark, much too bitter for his taste, but it is important to establish a rapport with Colin Barnes, especially if, as he suspects, there will be further difficult topics they will need to discuss. This sort of situation is never clear cut but Cook is beginning to wonder if there is more to Trudy's death then they had first thought. There certainly seems to have been some tension within the Barnes household.

Chapter 21

By the time Cook has returned to the station, Fallow, being efficient as ever, has already arranged for a press conference. Cook feels an unfamiliar pang, which he interprets as a sense of achievement at the ongoing development of the youngest member of his team. He hopes that Fallows' positive progress will help to appease Bennett when he finds out how few leads they currently have on any of his team's investigations.

Cook is a little surprised to see that a local television crew has arrived at the station, deepening his sense of pride for his protégé. This will give them the ideal opportunity to put out an appeal for anyone who might have seen Trudy the night she died.

Phil Wattle is not present amongst the group of journalists, having gone to Shropshire for a few days to visit his sister who lives in Telford. Cook misses seeing a friendly face in the sea of eagerly awaiting journalists but quickly shrugs off the thought to focus on the task ahead. It does not matter how many times he does these press conferences, he still feels a flutter of nerves when speaking to an audience.

Half an hour later, a statement has been given and the press have largely dissipated again. Cook heads up the stairs to grab the opportunity to catch up with his team and discuss any progress they have made during his absence that morning.

By early evening the incident room is buzzing. The phones have been ringing continuously since the television appeal went out on the six o'clock news, with the urgent request for further information being prioritised by the local news presenters.

Fallow has been tasked with the important job of deciphering the genuine calls from the mass of false and useless information they always receive after such an appeal. The result is that there are only a handful of calls that warrant a follow up response from Morgan, who is beginning to tire and sorely regretting his eagerness to volunteer for the task.

The first call on Morgans list is to a Mrs Bishop, a resident of Magpie House. The middle-aged woman takes great delight in having the opportunity to complain about the loud music that was blaring out from the party the night Trudy died. Morgan grits his teeth as he listens to the endless whinging and whining about the selfishness of todays youngsters. As soon as he has the information that he needs - the time the party started and finished - Morgan waits for a break in the tirade and brings the call to a close.

The second call is infinitely more interesting. Another resident from Magpie House just happened to be looking out of their window at about 11.30 PM on the night Trudy died and had seen a man and a woman arguing near the playground. Joshua Stewart had not recognised either of the couple and reluctantly admitted that it had been too dark to be able to positively identify either them, however it was still a new lead for them to follow up.

Morgans next call is to one of the residents of Robin House who had seen Marlon Turners' gang hanging around the playground but could not recall what time they had left.

By the time Morgan has made the last phone call it is getting close to ten o'clock and he decides to call it a night. Slowly he makes his way back home, driving as carefully as his tired brain will allow him. As Morgan crawls into bed, even the copious amount of strong coffee he has drunk throughout the evening cannot keep him from sinking down into the soft mattress and falling into a deep slumber.

When Morgan wakes up the next morning, the sun is already peeping through the curtains. He scrambles out of bed and swears loudly at Celia, who has forgotten to set the alarm clock. Then he storms into the bathroom and turns on shower, the warm water refreshing him as it trickles over his tired body.

Celia has already put some bread in the toaster and made a pot of tea by the time her husband is washed and dressed. Bailey, having also been allowed to sleep in late, has unhelpfully urinated onto the kitchen floor just in time for Morgan to walk through the puddle. Morgan returns upstairs again to change his wet socks, muttering a few swear words as he leaps up the steps two at a time. Ignoring his wife's offer of breakfast, he sneers at Bailey then strides off out the front door, slamming it forcefully behind him. Morgan can tell already that it is going to be one of those days.

The office is already fully occupied when Morgan arrives, having stopped off first to purchase a bacon and egg roll and a mug of coffee from the staff canteen. He catches up with the news from last night after he left, whilst munching greedily on the greasy sandwich. When his breakfast has been eaten, Morgan sits down on the nearest chair, pondering on whether he should try to speak to Marlon Turner again. He is still staring out of the fourth floor window, when Cook drops a report onto his desk, jolting him from his thoughts. It is the results of the samples taken from the petrol stations closest to the Hartsmere estate.

'They found a match, excuse the pun, for the petrol used to set fire to Lewis Smith's flat,' Cook says.

Morgan looks up at Cook, raises an eyebrow and waits for him to continue.

'It's just outside the Hartsmere estate, I need you to go down there and see if they have any till receipts or even better any CCTV footage. Take Fallow with you, he could do with an outing after staying here for most of the night.'

Morgan rolls his eyes at the news of Fallows diligence, then collects his coat from the stand, where he deposited it only forty minutes earlier. He locates Fallow in the canteen, where he is tucking into a cooked breakfast accompanied by a cup of sweetened tea.

The senior detective sits down on the chair opposite Fallow and begins loudly drumming his fingers on the table. Fallow seemingly does not notice and continues to mop up the last remnants of fried egg, whilst Morgan updates him with the latest development.

'We need to go to a petrol station near the Hartsmere estate,' explains Morgan. 'We've got a match for the petrol used at Lewis Smiths flat. Things are starting to look up.'

'That's great news, I'm ready whenever you are.'

Morgan drains the rest of his coffee, leaving the polystyrene cup on the table and heads towards the back door of the station to the car park beyond. He unlocks the door of the pool car and climbs into the driver's side before Fallow can protest. The last thing Morgan needs is to endure Fallows over-cautious driving. He pulls out of the car park and begins to weave his way through the rush hour traffic, pushing through the heavy flow of short-tempered drivers and onwards, towards the Hartsmere estate.

The petrol station is located on the main road just before the estate and is surprisingly quiet, with only three customers waiting to pay for their fuel, morning newspapers and packets of crisps.

Morgan pushes his way through to the front of the queue. 'I need to see whoever is in charge,' he barks, pulling out his ID card.

The cashier glances at the card and smiling nervously, unlocks the side door. 'Come through, the supervisors in the back office,' the cashier says, pointing towards a half-closed door.

Behind the customer service desk, Terry Green is diligently sorting through paperwork. He looks somewhat surprised by the presence of two strangers in his office until Morgan explains the purpose of their visit.

'Yes, I remember now. Someone came to take a sample of the petrol. What can I do for you this time?' Terry Green says, putting down the pile of invoices he has been sifting through.

'The sample we took from here matched the petrol used to set fire to a flat on the Hartsmere estate. Do you still have till receipts and CCTV footage from last weekend?' Morgan asks.

Terry Green reaches across the desk to open one of the drawers in the enormous filing cabinet that dominates one corner of the room. He pulls out a box of receipts that are waiting to be processed and sifts through them until he finds the ones for the previous Friday and Saturday. With the pile narrowed down, Terry Green then scans through the paperwork, looking for anyone who purchased a can of petrol. He quickly finds what he is searching for – a cash purchase made on the Saturday afternoon.

Morgan groans at the news, his shoulders slumping with disappointment that there is no paper trail for whoever bought the can of petrol. 'I don't suppose you still have the CCTV footage for that afternoon?'

'We should have, let's take a look.' Terry Green pulls out a DVD from the pile on his desk and begins searching through the CCTV footage from the Saturday afternoon. He flicks through the images until he reaches 3.05 pm, the time stamped on the till receipt. The CCTV footage clearly shows the image of a young black male holding a can of petrol, a group of his friends lingering outside on the petrol forecourt.

When Morgan first became a police officer, he had often been surprised by the stupidity of criminals who took unnecessary, ill-thought risks. He hadn't expected Marlon Turner to be quite so reckless, especially when he could have easily coerced one of his minions to buy the petrol. Morgan wonders if the gang leader had wanted to take the opportunity to show off, to set an example to his followers. His overinflated ego is going to finally convict him. It is time to arrest Marlon Turner for the death of Lewis Smith.

Chapter 22

Colin Barnes arrives at Deben Quay police station a little after eleven o'clock. He passes through the building, barely noticing the platitudes made by his fellow officers as he makes his way to the custody suite. The duty doctor, who arrived early morning to check on a drunk inmate who was vomiting profusely in one of the holding cells, is now waiting in the treatment room to take a swab of Colin Barnes cheek cells. Cook watches over the proceedings to ensure that everything is done by the book. He cannot afford for any mistakes to be made with this one.

Cook waits until the medic has finished labelling the swab sample before informing Colin Barnes that the results of the blood tests that were taken at the postmortem have come back. Colin Barnes wrinkles his forehead in puzzlement as Cook explains to him what the pathologist found.

'She wouldn't, she'd never do anything like that,' Colin Barnes says, his lower lip trembling.

'There's no doubt about it I'm afraid, we found cocaine in Trudy's blood samples.'

Colin Barnes swallows anxiously, his Adams apple bobbing up and down. 'I don't know anything about her taking any drugs.'

'We think she'd been taking them for some time given the damage to her nasal tissue. Are you sure you don't know who any of her friends are?'

'I think one was called Susan but I'm not sure about any of the others.'

'Ok, thanks for your help Colin, we'll be in touch when we have more news,' Cook replies, moving to the door to leave.

It looks as if they will have to speak to Susie Smart again.

Marlon Turner is arrested late afternoon, having been finally located in his flat, where he was sleeping off the previous night's indulgence. His arrogance and unwitting self-belief prevented him from running - he has every confidence that the police will not have any evidence against him. This time though, he is wrong.

After having his fingerprints and photographs processed, Marlon is led to an interview room where Cook and Morgan are already eagerly waiting.

Morgan sips a hot cup of coffee as he watches Marlon settle into the chair opposite him. The young man has a smug expression on his face as he leans back into his chair, gently rocking it to and fro.

'Do you want a solicitor?' Cook asks.

'Nah, what for, you ain't got nothing on me,' Marlon says.

'Is that so,' Morgan replies, trying not to smirk.

'Yeah, that's right.'

214

'We want to talk to you about the death of Lewis Smith,' Cook interjects before the two alpha males have a chance to rear up at each other.

'I told you last time, I had nothing to do with that old gits death.' Marlon stops rocking his chair back and forth and instead folds his arms across his body whilst staring intently at the two detectives.

'Why did you buy a can of petrol from Hartsmere Road petrol station the day Lewis Smith died?' Cook asks.

'I haven't bought any petrol.'

'We have you on CCTV Marlon, we know it was you,' Morgan says, leaning forward closer to the suspect.

'It was for my lawn mower.'

'C'mon be serious, there's hardly any grass on the Hartsmere estate, let alone near your flat,' Morgan snorts.

'What you going to do man, charge me for buying some petrol?'

'That's exactly what we're going to do. The petrol you bought matched the samples of petrol taken from Lewis Smiths flat,' Cook replies. 'Marlon Turner, we are formally arresting you for the murder of Lewis Smith.'

Jade is idly watching the six o'clock news when Marlon Turner's face flashes up on the television screen. Pumping up the volume, she just catches the newsreader saying that a man has been arrested for the murder of Lewis Smith. Jade's chest tightens as the newsreader says the name that she has been hoping to hear.

The first thing Jade does is to switch on her mobile to text Shania. Whilst she waits for a response, she flicks through the TV channels, looking for any further news bulletins that might give her further information.

It is two hours before her phone bleeps, with a message that contains a brief but courteous reply from Shania. Jade knows she shouldn't be surprised really, the way she treated Shania has been shameful, hateful even. She wonders if Shania will ever forgive her, or if she can forgive herself. Perhaps she should go to her flat and take Shania a bar of her favourite chocolate? Maybe she could even stay for a drink and chat the way they used to, gossiping about the girls at school, laughing at the stupidity of boys their own age.

Jade leaves the flat before she can change her mind and ambles along the path to the supermarket. The shop does not close until late, allowing the locals plenty of opportunity to stock up on supplies of alcohol and cigarettes. Jade walks around to the front of the shop and picks up two bars of chocolate and two cans of cola from the refrigerated unit before joining the back of the queue. The teenage girl behind the counter stares at her as she counts out the loose change she took from the dining table. Jade is so wrapped up in trying to decide what to say to

Shania that she does not notice she is being watched as she leaves the shop.

Jades heart pounds as she forces her wobbly legs up the stairs to the first floor. She knocks gently on the front door of Shania's flat and waits for it to open. The door opens briefly then closes again.

'Please Shania, open the door, I know I've been a bad friend and I'm sorry. I was scared but its ok now, Marlon's been locked up,' Jade shouts through the letterbox, which she is holding open with her small hand.

The door tentatively opens again and Jade squeezes through into the hallway.

By the time Jade leaves Shania's flat it is dark. She zips up her jacket as she hurries down the stairs and out the main entrance door of Blackbird Terrace then skips along the path towards Robin House. She is so much happier now that they have made up and she is even looking forward to going back to school tomorrow. With her thoughts focussing on her friend, Jade does not notice the group of lads who are waiting in the shadows of Robin House. She does not hear Callum Woods creep up behind her as she is turning the key in the lock and opening the front door to her flat.

'Where have you been then Jade?' Callum spits, roughly pushing the teen into the hallway.

'I just went to the shops,' Jade stammers, trying not to sound as scared as she feels.

'Don't lie to me Jade, we saw you go to Shania's. You didn't really think you would get away with it, did you?'

'I just went to drop some off homework, Mrs Sharp asked me to.'

'Don't lie,' Callum shouts, slapping Jade across her cheek.

Jade's legs give way and she drops to the ground, holding her stinging cheek in her right hand. 'I'm sorry,' she whispers, not daring to look at Callum.

'You thought it would be safe because Marlon's locked up, is that right?' Callum says calmly. He reaches down to grab hold of Jades hand. 'Well, I'm in charge now Jade, so I guess that makes you my new girlfriend.'

Jade closes her eyes, biting at her lower lip as she tries to hold back the tears that have formed.

Callum opens the door nearest to them, pulling Jade with him into the bathroom. 'You know what to do,' he says, unzipping his jeans, 'and I don't just want a blow job, it takes more to satisfy me then it does Marlon Turner.'

Shania stands transfixed to the spot as she looks out of the living room window, watching as Jade hurries up the path towards home. Unlike her friend, Shania has seen the lads walking in the shadows towards Robin House. She watches as they hide in the darkness, waiting for Jade to return. She knows what will happen next. It is no more than Jade deserves.

Shania's thoughts are interrupted by another knock on her door. This time she finds Morgan on the other side.

'Hi Shania, I'm sorry to disturb you so late but I'm looking for your mum,' Morgan says.

'She's not here, she must be down the pub,' Shania replies quickly, wishing that the police officer would go away again so that she can return to the window.

'Ok thanks, I'll look for her there,' Morgan says, slightly concerned by the teenager's disconnectedness. He wonders if something else has happened since the last time he spoke to her.

Shania says goodbye then closes the door again, shutting Morgan outside. As she starts to walk back up the hallway, she hears voices coming from the other side of the front door. Recognising one of the voices to be her mums, she opens the door again.

'You should be in bed,' Susie Smart says, stumbling through the doorway and wincing when she catches her right elbow on the edge of the door.

Shania sighs, shuts the front door and patters into the kitchen, where she flicks on the kettle. She pulls two mugs out from the cupboard and a glass for herself. With the coffees made, Shania fills her glass with water from the tap before making her excuses to leave. The teenager slinks off towards her bedroom, shutting the door quietly behind her.

Shania creeps across the room without turning on any lights. She moves to the window, so that she can peer out through the gap between the thin curtains. From here she can see the wide, paved path that bisects the estate and stretches up to the tower blocks at the far end. In the distance, she can just about make out a group of teenagers standing near the playground, which is still cordoned off by yellow tape that is flapping in the wind. Even from this distance Shania knows who they are and what they have now done.

Chapter 23

Morgan is finding it increasingly difficult to talk to Susie Smart, who appears to be even more drunk than she had been when she first walked into the flat. Morgan glares at her, as she rambles on and on about her evening in the pub, wondering if there is any point in him having this conversation with her whilst she is so inebriated.

'How well did you know Trudy Barnes?' Morgan asks hopefully, whilst holding few expectations of obtaining a sensible answer.

'I told you,' Susie slurs, 'I knew her from going to the pub.' Susie totters over to the sofa and throws herself onto the soft cushions, her coffee splashing across the grubby seat covers and onto her wrists. Clumsily she wipes up the worst of the spilt droplets onto her jeans, adding yet more stains to the faded material.

'Well, her husband seems to think that the two of you were good friends,' Morgan persists.

'She didn't have any friends, she looked after herself,' Susie replies, sipping from the steaming mug.

'What do you mean by that?' Morgan asks before he too takes a sip of the bitter liquid.

'She did whatever she wanted, didn't care who she hurt.' Susie looks up at Morgan, her head bobbing about as she tries to focus.

'Did she hurt you?' Morgan asks as he tentatively sits down at the other end of the sofa.

'Doesn't matter now does it,' she mutters. Susie finishes drinking the rest of her coffee, then pulls herself up from the sofa and stumbles over to the fridge, where she pulls out a can of cheap lager. She holds one up to Morgan, who shakes his head in response.

Morgan watches as Susie pulls on the metal ring to open the can and slurps its contents. 'In my experience, women mostly argue over men, was that what happened?' Morgan asks, his eyes following Susie as she stumbles back across the room. Her eyes narrow, before she turns her head away from him. 'Was she seeing someone else? Someone you liked?'

'That cow would have anyone, especially if they had any gear. She was a right tart and I'm not surprised she was done in. If you ask me, it was her husband, he must have known what she was up to.'

'Who was she seeing before she died?' Morgan asks, a little more forcefully than he intended, tiring of the charade.

'I don't know. She'd gone off Simon, that's who I was with that night,' she slurs.

'What about Zoe Thompson, has she got a boyfriend?'

Susie throws her head back and laughs. 'Nah, she's not that fussed about men. Jade's father used to hit her about. Trudy was probably with someone though, she usually is, especially if she's had a few.'

Morgan wonders if Susie also usually ended up going home with someone after a few drinks but decides not to antagonise the woman by pressing her on the subject.

'That's all I can tell you. I left the party early and went back to Simons flat,' Susie says. 'Trudy was still there when I left, flirting with a couple of blokes I hadn't seen before. Maybe she went off with them. Maybe Zoe remembers seeing her?' Susie turns to look at Morgan, trying to deflect the attention away from her.

'I'll ask her again, she wasn't too forthcoming last time I spoke to her,' Morgan replies.

Susie hiccups a couple of times. 'No one wants to get involved do they, especially after what happened to Lewis Smith. Who's to say it weren't those kids that killed her. Look what they did to my Shania.'

'You know who raped your daughter?' Morgan cannot believe what he is hearing, that Shania's own mothers refuses to help the police catch her daughters rapist.

'Doesn't everyone? That don't mean anyone's going to testify against them though.'

Susie slumps back onto the sofa and closes her eyes, the can of beer slowly falling from her fingers, eventually dropping onto the floor. She begins to softly snore, leaving Morgan with little choice but to leave and head for home. Interviewing Jade's mother can wait until the morning.

It is still early when Morgan returns to the Hartsmere estate the following morning. A light mist is drifting over the grassy area behind the tower blocks, making Morgan shiver as he strides towards Robin House.

To his surprise, Zoe Thompson is already dressed and feeding her youngest daughter. Despite it being so early, Jade has already left for school, perhaps out of habit, to avoid her mother who would normally be hungover at this time of the day. Morgan casually walks over to the table where Darcy is crunching on the chocolatey contents in her breakfast bowl. He smiles at the youngster as she noisily eats, spraying droplets of food over the scratched, pine table.

'I need you to tell me the truth about Trudy Barnes,' Morgan says, turning his attention back to Zoe. 'Susie Smart's already told me what she can remember from the night of the party, so you might as well tell me the rest. We need to find out what happened to Trudy Barnes and right now you're the only one who can help.'

'I don't want to end up like Lewis Smith,' Zoe says quietly, watching her youngest daughter slurp a glass of milk. 'Anyway, I don't know that much really. I saw her arrive and a while later I saw her flirting with some men who looked young enough to be her sons. I didn't see her again after that so she must have left.'

Zoe pulls a cigarette out of a packet that is lying next to her daughter's cereal. She lights the end of the stick, taking in deep lungful's of the poisonous fumes, then picks up an ashtray from the windowsill and flicks the loose ash into it before it can drop onto the floor.

'You don't know if she left the party on her own or not?' Morgan asks.

'Nope sorry. I'd be surprised if she left on her own though, she was well gone when I saw her and I don't reckon she'd had just booze either. Bit of a junkie that one but then aren't most people around here.'

'How did Trudy end up socialising with people on the estate?'

Zoe laughs, 'What you mean is us common, rough lot, as opposed to where you live. I suppose you've never got pissed before?'

'Sorry, I didn't mean it to come out like that.'

'I know what you meant,' Zoe says, taking a deep drag on her cigarette. 'She grew up here, went to school with me and Susie. She was one of the lucky ones though, she escaped from here. She still came back though from time to time, especially when she'd had enough of her husband. He's a weird one, something a bit odd about him, I can't quite put my finger on.'

'You're not a fan of Colin Barnes then?'

Darcy finishes drinking her milk and clambers down from the table. She totters over to her mother, clinging onto her thin legs and tugging at her jeans. Zoe stubs out the cigarette and places the astray on the table before pushing the child towards the sofa. She switches on the television and flicks through the channels until she finds her daughter's favourite programme.

'I only met him a couple of times and that's only been when he's been on the estate. I never met him when he was with Trudy though, she wouldn't have allowed that. She didn't want anyone to know that her husband is a copper.'

'I imagine she didn't. He met Susie though?'

'Did he?' Zoe sounds surprised. 'Well I never, maybe she bumped into them in town? I can't imagine Trudy would've wanted them to meet.'

Zoe walks over to a nearby chair and grabs hold of a small, scarlet coat, which she holds out to Darcy. 'I've got to get this one off the nursery now,' Zoe explains as she helps her daughter into the coat.

Morgan waits for Zoe to find her shoes, before making his way out of the flat. He walks with them towards the edge of the estate where they part company. He watches as the young girl holds tightly onto her mother's hand as she skips along the path towards the nursery. Morgan cannot help but feel a pang of sadness that he will never watch his own wife replay such a scene.

The incident room is unusually quiet. Fallow and Cook have already left to interview one of the residents in Robin House who phoned in response to the appeal. Morgan takes the opportunity to catch up on paperwork - he needs to write up detailed notes from his conversations with both Susie Smart and Zoe Thompson. By lunchtime he has barely managed to scrape the surface of the pile of paperwork and now his stomach is rumbling, forcing him to take a break.

Morgan has already arranged to meet Cook for lunch at The Crown, which is popular with the other officers as it is only a short walk from the police station. For once it is not raining and Morgan enjoys ambling along the cobble street towards the town centre. Less than ten minutes later, he has reached the mustard colour exterior of the seventeenth century pub. He pushes open the heavy wooden door, automatically stooping to avoid hitting the low beams.

Cook is talking to Phil Wattle at the bar. The two men appear to be chatting intensely as they wait for their pints to settle. When Cook spots Morgan approach, he orders another pint of the guest bitter, which he knows his friend will like.

Morgan pulls out a menu from the stand at the corner of the bar and reads through the list, eventually settling on a cheeseburger and chips, which Celia would wholly disapprove of. He orders the food before joining Cook and Wattle, who have now moved to a small table at the far end of the pub. He pulls up a creaky wooden chair from a neighbouring table and places it next to the log fire, which is spitting and crackling, the comforting noises soothing his tired mind.

'Phil's been chatting to someone he thought we'd be interested in,' Cook says, filling Morgan in on the latest development.

'Yeah, a guy by the name of Charlie phoned me a couple of days ago, said he had a story for me. I met him last night and he said he was with Trudy Barnes the night she died,' Wattle explains.

'The bloke from the party?" Morgan asks, as much to himself as to anyone else.

'That's right. His brother Martin was also in the pub and joined in the conversation. It turns out that not only were they hosting the party but they also both had sex with Trudy Barnes.'

'Have you got their address by any chance?' Cook asks, drinking deeply from his pint.

'I'm afraid not but I have arranged to meet them tonight to pay them for their story.'

'Nice one Phil, we need to have a chat with them. I don't suppose they said anything else of interest?' Morgan says as he also sips his pint of bitter.

'Just that Trudy was well known for her drug problem and for being loose. She apparently liked to pay for her drugs in kind.'

Their conversation is interrupted by the waiter putting food on their table. Morgan immediately smothers his chips with black pepper and tomato ketchup before picking up the enormous burger, which barely fits into his mouth. Wattle and Cook have both ordered beef and ale casserole, which they tuck into. The three men eat in silence, enjoying the stillness of the almost empty pub, a rarity at this time of the day, especially given the establishment's excellent reputation for food.

'I'll arrest Martin and Charlie tonight,' Cook says quietly to Morgan, who is polishing off the remainder of his chips. 'I think you could do with a night off. Why don't you take Celia out somewhere?' He says, giving his friend a gentle warning that he needs to pay more attention to his wife.

'Thanks, I'll do that,' Morgan replies, wiping his mouth on a napkin.

'Good idea, you don't want to end up with a repetition of last year,' Wattle chips in as he chews his last piece of tender beef. 'We all know what happened then.'

'Celia doesn't,' Morgan snaps. He turns to face the fire, the heat from the flames reddening his cheeks as he fights to calm himself.

'Sorry, I just don't want you to end up like me, a sad lonely old man. I did the same thing you know, had an affair with someone I worked with. My wife found out though and couldn't forgive me,' Wattle explains.

'She left you because you're always at work,' Cook chuckles, trying to lighten the mood of the conversation.

Morgan offers to buy another round of drinks, indicating that the moment of discord has now passed. He notices the older man's hand shaking as he lifts up his pint glass. Morgan wonders if Wattle is a little too fond of drinking or if he could be ill?

'Better not thanks, it's going to be a long day and I need to keep a clear head,' Wattle says, before continuing to discuss with Cook the arrangements for that evening. The two men decide on the time Cook will arrive at the pub where Wattle is meeting the brothers.

Morgan listens to their plans, quietly seething over their previous conversation. He drains the rest of his pint glass before excusing himself from the group, informing them that he wants to go back to the Hartsmere estate and talk to Shania again. Now that Marlon Turner is in custody, she might feel confident enough to tell him who it was who raped her. They know it was Marlon but with no forensic evidence and no witnesses, there is little more they can do.

Chapter 24

Morgan spots Shania's slight frame ambling along the path towards the estate, her school bag dragging on the pavement. As he had expected, the teenager is alone. He feels a pang of empathy with her as he remembers how difficult he had found it at school. He slows the car to a walking pace then winds down the window on the passenger side, calling out to the schoolgirl. Shania reluctantly pushes her hood away from her eyes to see who is calling her. The relief on her face is clear when she recognises the figure in the car.

'Do you want a lift back to the estate?' Morgan asks. 'I'm now going there.'

For a moment Shania seems undecided. She looks around to see if anyone else is watching, then pulls open the car door. 'Sure, might as well,' she says, throwing her school bag into the foot well and climbing into the front seat.

Morgan waits for Shania to clip on her seatbelt before pulling out into the road.

'Is it me you want to talk to?' Shania asks as she rummages around in her school bag and pulls out a battered packet of cigarettes.

'Sorry but you can't smoke in here,' Morgan says, wondering when the teen had started smoking.

Shania sighs loudly then puts the packet back into her bag.

'I take it you've heard that Marlon Turner is in custody?'

Shania nods, chewing on her bottom lip.

'Well, I wondered if that would make a difference to your statement, from when you were attacked I mean,' Morgan says tentatively.

Shania shrugs her shoulders, turning her head away from him to watch the streets passing by from out of the side window.

'He's going to be kept in custody until the trial you know. He can't hurt you now,' Morgan continues.

'The others are still out there though, aren't they,' Shania says, turning back to face him. 'Why didn't you arrest them as well?'

'We haven't got any evidence that they were involved. He will be convicted Shania, he won't get anyway with it this time, I promise.'

'It won't help. Jade gave him an alibi didn't she, for when I was attacked. It'd be my word against hers.'

'Maybe she'll change her mind now?' Morgan says as he pulls into the bus stop nearest to Blackbird Terrace.

'Thanks for the lift,' Shania says, opening the car door.

'Think about it, will you?' Morgan shouts after the teen, as she slams the door shut. He exhales slowly, wondering if he should run after her. The decision is made for him, as a bus pulls up behind him, beeping it's horn loudly. Morgan quickly pulls out of the bus stop and drives on towards the main road that leads back out of the estate. He will follow the Cook's advice and go home to spend some time with his wife.

By the time he has driven home, Morgan has decided that he should take Celia out for dinner, something he rarely does. As he pulls up in front of his house, he can see Bailey behind the obscured glass, scratching at the porch door. Morgan feels an odd sense of pride that the dog has already learnt to recognise the sound of his car.

By the time he unlocks the front door, the dog is barking frantically, leaping up and down at him as he tries to remove his coat and boots. The over-excited puppy cannot wait any longer for attention and begins trying to climb up his owner's legs. Morgan gently pushes the puppy down, which only serves to move the dog onto the task of chewing his shoes. It is then that he discovers the puppy has been so excited to see him, that he has peed up his trousers. Bailey picks up the boot that Morgan has just removed and runs off towards the kitchen, enticing Morgan to chase him.

Just at that moment, Celia comes downstairs to see what the commotion is and is surprised to discover her husband lying prone on the lounge floor holding a slightly chewed boot in the air with Bailey standing on his chest.

'Hello love, Tom let me off early so I thought I'd take you out for dinner.'

'That would be nice, but what about Bailey? He cries when I just go to the shop.'

'How about a takeaway then? We could watch a film afterwards?'

Morgan lifts the puppy from his torso and returns the soggy boot to the shoe rack in the porch. He grabs a ball that is lying on the windowsill and begins to tease the dog with it, throwing it to and fro, just out of reach of the dog. Bailey barks in frustration and eventually slinks off towards Celia.

'A takeaway would be nice,' Celia says, picking up the puppy. 'You haven't forgotten that he's going to the vets tomorrow have you? He needs his second vaccinations.'

'Of course not dear, what time was it again?'

'Nine o'clock. I can get a taxi if you're busy,' Celia says, trying not to laugh at Morgan who has very obviously forgotten.

'If you don't mind, it's just that Tom gave me this evening off, so I'll need to go in early to interview a suspect whose being arrested tonight.'

'That's ok. Is it something to do with that poor woman who died?' Celia asks as she puts the puppy down on the floor. She picks up another toy and throws it towards Bailey.

'Yes, hopefully it's the breakthrough we need.' Morgan clambers up from the floor and sits down on the sofa, relaxing into the soft cushions. He smiles as he watches his wife playing with

Bailey. Cook is right he does need to spend more time with Celia.

Celia phones for a takeaway whilst Morgan takes a shower, changing into a pair of jeans and a jumper and dropping his urine-stained trousers into the laundry basket. By the time he has returned downstairs the food has already been delivered, fragrant aromas wafting throughout the house. Celia has even opened a bottle of wine, which is rare as her father had been far too fond of alcohol and she normally avoided drinking it herself.

Bailey settles into an opportune position under the table, awaiting any small morsels that might accidently drop to the floor. Morgan does not want to imagine the affect a chicken jalfrezi might have on the stomach of a young dog and hopes he will never have to find out.

When the meal has been eaten, Celia clears away the dishes from the table, scraping the remnants of the food into the bin, before stacking the plates neatly in the dishwasher. Morgan finishes drinking the rest of his glass of wine then ambles through to the lounge to find a suitable film for them to watch. He does not usually share the same taste as he wife but for once he does not feel like watching anything scary or bloody, so opts for a romantic comedy that he knows Celia will like. With the film chosen, he switches off the main light and settles onto the sofa. By the time Celia returns with cups of tea, Bailey has already settled onto Morgans lap and begins softly snoring as the film's opening credits roll up.

DCI Cook is having a far less relaxing evening than his friend. He arrived at the Falcon at the arranged time to find no sign of Martin or Charlie and Wattle drinking what Cook assumes to be his third pint, judging by the number empty glasses that are lined up on the bar beside him.

Cook orders half a pint of lager and finds a small table in the corner, tucked away from the main bar area but still close enough to see anyone walk through the main entrance. He settles onto a stool, far enough away from Wattle so it does not look like the two men know each other, but close enough to be able to see anything that might unfold. Once he is in place, Cook relaxes a little, feeling confident that the plan will come off. What Cook has not realised however is that the pub also has a back door, and that it is this second entrance that is used by most of the regular drinkers. And it is for this reason, that the detective completely fails to notice when Charlie and Martin arrive, until they are already deep in conversation with Wattle.

Cook reaches for his phone, which is already out on the table and messages one of the officers who are waiting outside. He gives a description of the two men and tells the officers about the back door that leads out into a small car park. Cook waits until he has received confirmation that there are officers now outside

236

both doors to the pub, before striding across the room to where Wattle is sitting.

'Hello Charlie,' Cook says cheerfully as he approaches.

Charlie looks at Cook in curiosity, wondering if he knows the man.

'I can see you don't know who I am, so let me introduce myself,' Cook says, pulling out his ID card from the back pocket of his jeans.

Charlie groans, immediately realising that they have been set up and given that he is trapped between Cook and Wattle, there is no place for him to run. His younger brother though is near to the door. Martin grabs his coat and flings open the door, letting it bang against the wall as he runs out of the pub. Cook watches, trying not to chuckle, knowing that the young man will only get as far as the three officers who are waiting outside.

'I suppose this is something to do with you?' Charlie spits at Wattle.

'No, it isn't. You don't seriously think I'd treat a valued customer in this way?' Wattle replies, slightly annoyed at the possibility that he might now gain a reputation of being a police informant.

'We need to talk to you and your brother about the party you held in Magpie House the night Trudy Barnes died,' Cook explains.

'I already told someone about it,' Charlie says angrily, slumping dejectedly onto a stool.

'We don't believe that you've told us everything, so I'm afraid we're going to need you to come down to the station with us. Just for an informal chat you understand.'

Cook takes a step back, motioning for Charlie to move towards the door. 'Don't worry, your brother will be joining you as well so you won't get too lonely in your cell,' Cook chuckles as he follows Charlie out of the door.

Cook decides to leave the two men alone for a few hours in one of the holding cells, located in the basement of the station. Experience has taught him that making a suspect wait to find out what they are being accused of increases their anxiety levels and therefore the probability that they will co-operate. It is a useful tactic as it provides a short insight into what it is like to be kept in prison, especially useful if they are not seasoned criminals. Once Charlie and Martin have been processed and their fingerprints etc taken, Cook will be able to check on the criminal record database and see what exactly he is dealing with.

Charlie is first to be taken to the interview room, leaving his younger brother alone in the cell. The holding cells always feel different at night, every sound seems louder in the oppressive darkness. Even the stench of urine and unwashed bodies that has seeped into the plastic covered mattress after years of usage, somehow seems even more pungent in the dark.

The solitude of a darkened cell challenges even the toughest of criminals, especially if they also happen to have subjected themselves to years of drug-induced paranoia.

Cook thinks that Charlie seems slightly less cocky, less sure of himself then he had been earlier in the evening. A few hours in the cells has given him the opportunity to rack his pitiful, shrunken brain for an explanation as to why he is now in this current predicament. Cook sits down and motions for Charlie to do the same.

'Why am I here then?' Charlie asks, slouching into the hard plastic chair.

'We have reason to believe that you knew Trudy Barnes, is that right?' Cook asks, sipping a strong black coffee from a polystyrene cup.

'Yeah, I knew her, so did most of the blokes on the Hartsmere estate, if you know what I mean.'

'You knew her well?' Cook asks, ignoring the implication that Trudy Barnes was not a faithful wife.

'Well enough, I guess,' Charlie says, his eyes narrowing as he tries to work out where this line of questioning is going to take them.

'Did you have a sexual relationship with her?'

'It wasn't like that. She shagged a lot of men, especially if she wanted something back.'

'Drugs you mean?'

'I don't know nothing about drugs,' Charlie says, folding his arms in front of his chest.

Cook shifts forward in his seat to pick up a folder from the table. 'Well your police record says otherwise,' he says, waving the documents in the air. 'You have convictions for possessing and selling marijuana, amphetamines and ecstasy. So, I'm guessing that nowadays you also deal in cocaine?'

'What makes you think that?' Charlie says, scratching the new growth that is appearing on his chin.

'Because Trudy Barnes had cocaine in her system and we have witnesses who will swear that you were the one who supplied it to her. In fact, we also know that she had sex with you and your brother the night she died as payment for the coke,' Cook explains, drumming his fingers on the table. 'So, you'd better start co-operating with us pretty quick Charlie, otherwise you'll be in serious trouble.'

Charlie stares at the desk then begins to pick at the corner of the table.

'We need to know what happened the night Trudy Barnes died.'

'I didn't touch her honest. She was fine when she left the flat, real happy in fact. I might have given her a little something to help the party along but that's it, I swear.'

'What time did Trudy leave the flat?'

'It must have been about 12.30, maybe a bit later. I didn't really keep any eye in the time.'

'Did she leave with anyone?' Cook asks, chewing the end of his biro.

'I think she was with that friend of hers, the one with that lives in the flat below ours. The one that hates men if you know what I mean. If you ask me, they were a bit more then friends.'

'Do you mean Zoe Thompson?' Cook stops chewing the end of his pen and leans in closer towards Charlie.

'Yeah, that's her. Now can I go or are you going to charge me with something?'

Cook stares at him. 'I'm not going to charge you, for now in any case. Just don't disappear again.'

The sense of relief is obvious on Charlie's face as the interview is terminated and he is taken out to the custody sergeant who will handle the paperwork for his release.

As he passes the front desk on his way to retrieve Martin from the cells, Cook notices a young woman who has just been brought into the station. She is clearly very drunk and having difficulty in standing up straight as she tries to speak coherently to the custody sergeant. The young woman is well known to Deben Quay police station, having been picked up on numerous occasions for being drunk or for fighting at the Punch and Judy. It is Zoe Thompson.

Chapter 25

By the time Morgan arrives at the police station, Zoe Thompson has sobered up enough to be deemed fit for interview. Cook has left to go home for a few hours rest, leaving Morgan with the unenviable task of talking to Zoe again.

Morgan braces himself for what is bound to be a frustrating interview, he just hopes that the woman is slightly more cooperative than usual. He pours out two drinks from the coffee machine near the reception desk and carries them down to the holding cells. The cells are quiet now that Charlie and Martin have been released, the terse silence only being interrupted by someone snoring in the end room, sleeping off the previous night's overindulgence in booze.

A night in the cells has done nothing to sweeten Zoe's usual spiky demeanour, nor her breath, which reeks of cigarettes and alcohol. The pungent aroma hits Morgan as soon as he opens the cell door.

Zoe is sitting slumped over the bench, her head bowed downwards. When the door opens, she looks up, surprised to see Morgan. He sits down on the bench and hands Zoe one of the coffees, setting the other down on the bench beside him.

'What are you doing here? Come to give me a telling me off?'

'Actually, I need to talk to you about Trudy Barnes,' Morgan replies, folding his arms across his chest. 'You didn't quite tell me the truth the other day, did you?'

Zoe bites her lower lip, her pupils widening. 'I don't suppose you have any painkillers on you?'

'Sorry but we can't give anything like that without checking with the doctor first,' Morgan says. The way Zoe rolls her eyes reminds him of Jade. 'When was the last time you saw Trudy Barnes?'

'It was at the party, I already told you'.

'I have a witness who says that she left with you,' Morgan continues.

Zoe takes a sip of her coffee, wincing as the scalding liquid burns her tongue. 'Got any sugar?'

'I'll get you some after you answer my questions.'

Zoe sighs, glaring at him defiantly. She folds her arms across her body, a mirror image of Morgans own body language.

'Well?'

Zoe exhales loudly, putting her coffee down onto her knees. 'She walked me back down the stairs as I was a bit worse for wear, that's what friends do.'

'I heard that you were more than just friends, that you were in fact lovers. Is that why she never introduced you to her husband?'

'It might have been. She wasn't ashamed or anything, she was just scared that her husband would find out.'

'How long had you been having a relationship with Trudy?' Morgan asks, setting his empty cup down onto his lap.

'A few months. We only saw each other occasionally, mostly when we bumped into each other at parties and in the pub. She was a sweet person really, just had a lot of problems, her husband being one of them.'

'What do you mean?' Morgan asks, intrigued by her comment.

Zoe shrugs her shoulders. 'She never said exactly but I got the feeling he liked getting his own way.'

'In what way?'

'I don't know for sure but I got the feeling she was a bit scared of him, that he would go off on one if she didn't do what he wanted, when he wanted it.'

'Did that include sex?'

Zoe snorts, 'they didn't have that sort of relationship.'

'Did Susie Smart know about your relationship?'

'God no, she would've found that funny.'

Morgan raises his eyebrows, waiting for Zoe to continue.

'I was rather fond of the lads when I was younger'.

'I also heard that you had problems with your husband, is that true?' Morgan asks.

Zoe looks down at her legs and begins picking at a loose thread on her jeans that is close to a large stain. It is clearly a topic Zoe does not want to talk about, so Morgan brings the conversation back to the reason why he is questioning her. 'What time did Trudy leave your flat?'

'I'm not sure exactly, I reckon it was about one. Jade might know. She's always got her ear to the door, listening in. She's nosy that one, something that's going to get herself into a lot of trouble one of these days.'

The thought has crossed Morgan's mind more than once, only he wonders if she already is in trouble. 'What about after she left the flat, did you see Trudy leave the building?'

'Nah, I went straight to bed. As I said, I'd had a bit too much to drink that night.'

Morgan nods, imagining her to be in a similar state to the one she was in last night when she was brought into the station. The custody sergeant gave him a brief but graphic description of Zoes behaviour. She was arrested for making a nuisance of herself at the Punch and Judy, shouting abuse at some of the customers and arguing with a friend.

Morgan motions for Zoe to follow him out into the dimly lit corridor and down towards the custody sergeant's desk. Ten minutes later, with the paperwork signed and belongings returned,

Zoe is released, accompanied by a stern warning about the adverse effects of alcohol.

Morgan shows the young woman out through the rear door of the station. As soon as they are outside, Zoe pulls out a packet of Marlboros from her handbag and lights a cigarette.

'Do you want a lift back to the estate? I'm going back there if you do,' Morgan offers.

Zoe ponders over the offer for a moment before nodding gratefully. Despite her severe hangover, she has still managed to compute that she does not have enough money for a bus fare home and she does not relish the idea of a long walk back to the Hartsmere estate feeling as nauseous as she does.

Zoe grinds her cigarette into the concrete path then follows Morgan to his car. As Zoe pulls open the front passenger door, it hits it against the neighbouring car. Morgan winces before glancing in the direction of the CCTV camera to see if it is pointing their way. He cannot bear to see if any damage has been caused and decides to hope for the best and pretend he has not noticed the accident.

The rush hour traffic has by now mostly dissipated, leaving only a few vehicles on the road. The journey, which should have taken at the most fifteen minutes, is however hampered by the presence of a bus, which keeps stopping in front of them frequently and in such awkward places that it makes it impossible for Morgan to overtake. Just as he is starting to feel the irritation bubbling up inside him, they reach the outskirts of the estate where the road widens into a dual carriageway.

Morgan parks at the far end of the estate, having found a space on the road in between the double yellow lines. He clicks the button on the remote several times, checking that the car is properly locked, a habit that enormously annoys Celia.

Zoe pulls out another cigarette and cups her hands around it, trying to light it in the rain that has begun to fall. With the cigarette lit, they walk up the path that leads through the estate and onwards to Magpie House.

Their path takes them past the dilapidated building opposite the Thompsons flat, which looks even more menacing in the drizzly greyness of the morning. Every time he sees Sparrow House, Morgan wonders when it will be demolished and what will be built in its place. The concrete structure has certainly seen better days but then so has the other buildings on the estate and they have not been ear-marked for demolition. Perhaps they too will be pulled down in time and the residents re-housed elsewhere. It is a pattern that is being echoed across the country and Morgan is fully aware that it is not just due to the state of the buildings and cost of their maintenance. It is also because the design of these older estates has given rise to behavioural problems that are not being seen on newer developments, with more green space and fewer residents crammed in. Whoever designed these soulless estates had obviously not thought through the implications of housing such large numbers of poverty-stricken families in such a dreary, stark place.

As the rain starts to fall harder, Morgan pulls up the collar of his coat around him more tightly and increases pace, hurrying to get inside before the dark clouds unleash a torrent. He notices Zoe Thompson's thin shoulders through her worn denim jacket and immediately feels a pang of pity that the young woman is living in such obvious poverty.

As they approach Robin House, Morgan spots Jade sitting on the low wall that wraps around the side of the building. The teenager is swinging her legs back and forth, scuffing the bottom of her trainers on the concrete path beneath, seemingly irreverent to the rain.

Morgan waits until Zoe has disappeared into the building before heading around to the back of the building, where he can see Jade still sitting next to the fenced off area where the plastic rubbish bins are housed.

'Hello Jade, I was hoping to speak to you,' Morgan says overly cheerfully as he approaches.

The teenager looks up, the motion of her legs coming to an abrupt halt. She looks at Morgan before pulling out a piece of gum from her pocket. Unwrapping the packet, Jade discards the paper on the ground before pushing the soft stick into her mouth. Morgan watches as the girls' jaw moves rhythmically, chewing noisily on the gum.

'I've just brought your mum back from the police station,' Morgan says. 'She'd had a bit too much to drink last night and was annoying some of the customers in the Punch and Judy.'

Jade nods, her small fingers picking at the brickwork on the overhang of the wall she is sitting on.

'Your mum said that you're normally really observant and you like to keep an eye on what's going on around here,' Morgan says. 'Were you awake the night Trudy died? The night your mum came back from the party upstairs?'

Jade nods, her jaws chewing faster.

'Did you hear your mum bring a friend home?' Morgan asks gently, hoping that Jade might understand the implication.

'I'm not stupid you know, I knew what was going on with mum and that woman.'

'Do you know what time they got back to yours?' Morgan asks, feeling slightly uncomfortable at the topic of conversation.

Jade stops chewing and screws up her face in concentration. 'It was about 12.30. She left again about half an hour later. I heard them talking loudly outside the front door. Mum sounded cross.'

'Could you hear what they were saying?'

'Not really, something about a bloke. It didn't sound like they were really arguing though, they weren't shouting at each other.'

'Did your mum come straight back into the flat after her friend left?'

'I don't know. I went to the bedroom window and I didn't hear her come back in. I didn't see mum outside though so she must've come back straight away.'

'What about her friend, did you see her leave?'

'Yeah, she walked towards the playground. After that I went to bed as I was really tired.' Jade jumps down from the wall and straightens her jeans. 'I'd better go and get mum something to eat,' she says, walking off towards the main entrance to the building.

Morgan cannot believe how close Jade had been to seeing what happened to Trudy Barnes. Perhaps he should talk to Zoe Thompson again, he decides, walking back around the building to the front. She clearly hasn't told him everything that happened. Perhaps the two women had been quarrelling over Martin and Charlie and what had occurred earlier that evening at the party.

Morgan's thoughts are interrupted by his mobile ringing. To his surprise it is Celia. At first, she is too upset to make much sense. Morgan soothes his wife as best he can, before asking her to repeat herself.

'It's Bailey, he's gone missing from the back garden,' Celia wails.

'What do you mean, gone missing? How could he have got out of the garden?'

'I don't know. The doorbell rang and when I went back outside, he'd gone.'

'Who was at the door?' Morgan asks, immediately suspicious.

'Just someone selling stuff, cleaning products.'

Morgan groaned. It is obvious what has happened. 'I'm coming back now,' he says, ending the call and running back to his car.

Chapter 26

Morgan finds Celia sitting on their front doorstep, tears streaming down her cheeks. He rushes over to comfort his wife, who seems even more distressed than she had been on the phone.

'Tell me again what happened,' he says, more forcefully then intended.

'It's not my fault. I thought he'd be safe in the back garden but when I got back from answering the door the back gate was open and he'd gone. What if someone's stolen him?'

'I'm going to drive around and see if I can find him. Can you remember what the bloke looked like, what car he was driving?'

Celia looks at Morgan as if he is mad, 'Well of course not, I didn't take any notice.'

'Please tell me that you got him insured?'

'Yes of course, I'm not that stupid.' Celia says, marching back into the house and slamming the front door behind her.

Morgan phones Cook to tell him what has happened then gets back into the car to drive around the roads nearest to their home. It is possible, though unlikely, that Bailey has escaped and that the distraction of the sales person at the door is just coincidence.

Morgan drives around for an hour or so, looking up and down each of the roads. Eventually, he has to admit to himself that the exercise is pointless and he might as well go back home.

Whilst her husband has been out looking for Bailey, Celia has begun contacting local rescue centres and veterinary practices, in case the dog has been found by someone and brought in. She chastises herself yet again for her failure as a new dog owner to keep the puppy safe, especially as he is not yet fully protected by his vaccinations, having only received the final injections the previous morning. At least though he is microchipped and insured – something else she will need to look into sorting out. Celia cannot bear the thought that someone might have stolen him and instead concentrates on the belief that he has run away and will soon be found. For now though, there is nothing more she can do but wait for news.

Morgan is driving back home when it occurs to him that perhaps he should check out the breeder who sold Bailey to them. Celia's account of the man did not fill him with confidence and it is just possible that the whole episode has been a scam. He screeches to a halt in the driveway and runs into the house to obtain the address from his wife, without bothering to explain why he needs it. When Morgan is back in the car, he phones Cook to see if he's free to come with him – he has a feeling that he might need some help.

A few minutes later, both men are travelling back to the estate where Bailey was bought.

'What do you think then?' Morgan asks, having relayed his fears to his friend.

'It's possible it's a scam, you do hear about those sort of things happening. Why don't we park a distance away and take a walk around the place first, see if we can see anything from the back of the house?"

Morgan agrees and quickly volunteers to fight his way through the overgrown path that runs along the back of Mr Holt's house. Leaving Cook to mind the car, he pushes his way through the stinging nettles and overgrown ferns, which almost completely cover the access path that runs parallel behind the row of 1970's semis. About half-way down the path, Morgan locates the breeders house, which is easily identifiable from the chorus of yapping coming from both within the house and from the enormous wooden dog kennel in the ill-kept garden. From his position next to the dilapidated fence, Morgan can see through the thin, patterned curtains that partially cover the patio doors.

Whilst he waits for Morgan to return, Cook phones Fallow to ask him to search through their databases for any information on the breeder. It does not take long to discover that Mr Holt has been interviewed by Trading Standards on a number of occasions for buying and selling dogs in suspicious circumstances. However, with no concrete proof, the case was dropped late last year. It is possible that Bailey has come from a puppy farm or even been stolen to order, or as Morgan suggested, that Mr Holt is involved in some kind of scam. Cook's stomach sinks as he decides that he should be the one to talk to Mr Holt to avoid any possibility of his friend blundering in on an ongoing investigation.

Cook decides that he will pose as a potential buyer to gain access to the house. Even through the closed front door, Cook can detect a strong odour of urine and faeces. He rings the doorbell and is surprised when it is opened almost immediately. A fetid aroma hits Cook squarely in the nostrils as soon as the door is opened by an overweight, middle-aged man who has clearly not seen the inside of a bath for some time.

'Yeah, what do you want?' The man says, pulling down his t-shirt, which has ridden up over his protruding belly.

'Sorry to disturb you but a mate of mine bought a puppy from you recently and I wondered if you had any more for sale? The wife's been going on about having one so I thought I'd get one to keep her sweet.'

'Yeah, I have. Come in and take a look, see if there's any your wife might like,' Mr Holt says, opening the door wider to allow Cook through to the hallway. 'What sort of dog are you looking for?'

'Nothing too big, something small and cute looking.'

Mr Holt chuckles, 'Got just the one for you.' He picks up a small dog that is crying in a pen in the corner of the room, which looks like it is a cross between a West Highland terrier and a Poodle.

'What sort is it?' Cook asks.

'It's a Poodle, a pedigree at that. You're lucky as I've only got one left.'

'Have you got anything a bit bigger, I might feel a bit silly walking something that size?' Cook says, his eyes combing through the squalid room to see if Bailey could be there.

'Not at the moment. Give me your phone number and I'll let you know when I do.'

Cook writes down his mobile number and hands it to Mr Holt before making his excuses to leave. Bailey is not there.

Morgan is already waiting for Cook in the car by the time he returns, drumming his fingers on the steering wheel, wondering where his friend has disappeared to. Cook quickly fills him in on the situation, making it clear that there isn't sufficient cause to search the property, leaving Morgan with no choice to but accept that this is not an avenue they can pursue. For now, there is little more they can do but wait and hope that the puppy is found.

The two men travel in silence, neither knowing what to say to one another. Morgan drops Cook off at home and drives on towards his house. He is dreading the look on Celia's face when he admits that he has failed to find Bailey. Even he is a little upset, he had started to become fond of the dog.

As Morgan turns into his road, he spots Celia standing in the porch, waving frantically.

'He's been found!' Celia shouts across the driveway as Morgan steps out of the car.

'Where is he?' Morgan asks, relieved at the news.

'He's at the vets on Morton Road. Someone found him running around the quayside and caught him. The vet found the microchip and phoned us about five minutes ago. He must have managed to open the catch on the back gate after all.'

Morgan chuckled, 'Well I guess he should be clever, being my dog.'

Celia's drawn face is suddenly transformed by her smile, her shoulders relaxing as she takes hold of Morgan's hand and leads him back to the car.

Half an hour later, Bailey is back on the sofa, having eaten a whole tin of dog food and two treats that Celia insisted on giving to him to help him recover from his ordeal. On their way home from the vets, Morgan stopped off at a DIY stored to buy a padlock for the back gate. He just hopes that the dog does not discover how to jump fences as well as unbolting gates.

Chapter 27

Jade is bored. She has spent the afternoon playing with Darcey, whilst her mum sleeps off the previous night's indulgence. She has grown tired of watching her sister placing jigsaw pieces into the second-hand puzzle someone gave to them. Jade pulls herself up from the sofa and begins looking through the cupboards, searching for anything that they can eat. The kitchen is empty - her mum has forgotten to go shopping again.

It is just as well that Jade knows where her mum keeps the emergency money – she saw her taking money from it one night when she had run out of her dole money and needed more fags. Jade's heart thumps as she lifts up the lid on the grotesque onion-shaped pot that lives on the windowsill in the living room. She has no idea if there is any money left in there and even less of an idea what to do if it is empty. Jade peers into the pot, her pulse relaxing as she spies what she is hoping to see. There is less in there than the last time she looked – clearly there has been more than one emergency that has required her mum to dip into her savings. Jade has no doubt that those emergencies involved the purchase of nicotine and alcohol. Carefully the teen counts out five pound coins from the pot then pulls on a jumper and laces up her trainers.

As soon as she sees that her older sister is going to leave the flat, Darcey starts pulling at the bottom of Jade's jeans, wanting to know where she is going and if she can go too. Jade gently picks up her sister and plonks her onto the sofa then flicks through the TV channels to find something for her to watch. She will not be out for long and in any case, their mum is in the flat even if she is dead to the world.

Pushing aside her feelings of guilt at leaving her sister, Jade locates her only jacket, which is far too thin for this time of year. Maybe when her mum is feeling better, they can go shopping and get her a new one. Her mum has been ill for as long as she can remember. She remembers once when mum was feeling ok, that they went to the park and fed the ducks. The memory seems a very long time ago now.

Daylight is beginning to fade and Jade hates being alone in the dark, especially if she is outside on the estate. It isn't the type of place that you really want to be, especially at night but she needs to buy something for them to eat.

It starts to drizzle as Jade walks through the estate, raindrops clearly visible in the light from the streetlamps that line the path. The short walk to the supermarket used to be something that Jade enjoyed doing. She would cheerfully say hello to anyone who would stop to chat to her. Nowadays, she dared not look at anyone, let alone speak. She just hopes that she can reach the shops and back again without bumping into Callum Woods.

The small supermarket is busy with local residents who are either too tired or too lazy to catch a bus to one of the larger shops outside of the estate. Jade picks up a basket and walks down one of the aisles, totting up in her head anything she wants to buy. She has just enough money for some bread, milk and a pizza for their tea, leaving just a few pence to buy Darcey some sweets. When she was younger her mum would buy her a whole box of sweets on a Saturday night, giving them to her after tea as they settled down to watch a film. Those evenings seem a long time ago now. It is even longer since she had a father in her life. She barely remembers the tall, mousy-haired man who slept in her mother's bed. She guesses that she is lucky though, Darcey has never had a father at all. At least she did meet hers. Sometimes when she can't sleep, she looks out of her bedroom window at the stars, wondering if her dad is doing the same thing. Wondering if he remembers that he has a daughter. She does not even know if he is still alive.

By the time Jade leaves the shop it is pitch black, as daylight has descended into night. She walks quickly past Robin House and the playground where the woman died. She knows that her mum had been fond of Trudy and was upset when she found out that she was dead.

Despite what she said to Morgan, Jade does not really understand what had gone on between the two women. She thought it had been strange that the woman slept in her mother's room when she could have stayed on their sofa, especially as it was one that pulled out into a bed. Mum had bought it in case they ever had any friends over to stay, not that they did, they were too embarrassed to do so even though everyone knows what her mum is like. Maybe that's why she was such good friends with Shania. Her mum is just the same.

Shania is also bored. Unlike Jade however, she does not have a younger sister to keep her company and her mum is not at home – she has gone to the Punch and Judy. It is typical for a Saturday evening but until recently, Shania had Jade to spend time with, giggling over the boys at school and talking about what they want to be when they were grown-up.

Even though it is dark and she still has not forgotten what happened to her, Shania decides that she must get out of the flat and go for a walk. She trips down the steps and out of Blackbird Terrace to step out into the fresh air. Shania is glad that she thought to bring her umbrella with her, as the soft pelts begin to rain down harder the further she walks away from the flat.

There are quite a few people about, which makes Shania feel a bit safer even though they are strangers. In any case, Marlon Turner is locked up and cannot hurt her now. She walks towards the playground and stops by the police cordon to take a look. Standing on her toes, Shania strains her neck forward, trying to catch a glimpse of where the woman died the other night. She knows that Trudy was a friend of her mums but Shania did not know her well enough to be bothered by her death. At her age, death is something a long way off that happens to someone else.

Hearing footsteps on the path behind her, Shania turns around to see who it is.

'Hello Shania, I thought that was you. How are you?'

'I'm ok thanks Callum. Where are the others?' Shania replies, unsure if she should be glad to see him or not.

Callum laughs, 'I'm not with them all the time you know. I bet you're glad now that Marlon's in prison.'

Shania tips her head to one side and looks at him with narrowing eyes. 'Why do you say that?'

'C'mon, we all know what happened to you and who it was. I'm sorry that I wasn't there to stop them.'

'Thanks,' Shania says, her cheeks flushing a deep crimson. She had hoped that people would have forgotten by now what happened to her, especially with Trudy being found dead giving them something else to gossip about.

'I'm getting wet standing here, why don't we go and shelter under Robin House?'

Shania nods and walks towards Callum, raising her umbrella higher so that he can also shelter underneath it.

'How's it been at school?'

'It's been ok.'

'I bet it's been a bit awkward with the other kids not knowing what to say to you?'

'I suppose so,' Shania admits, not wishing to be reminded of school at the weekend.

They walk towards the rubbish bins and stand underneath the overhang from the flats above, pressing their backs against the cold bricks.

'You know I've always liked you, don't you?' Callum asks, his hand reaching out for hers.

'I thought you liked Jade?'

'Nah, she's Marlon's girl. How about we do something together one evening, maybe go and watch a film or something?'

Shania does not respond, unsure of what to say.

'Look, I know that you've had a rough time of it, I won't pressure you.' Callum moves closer towards Shania, taking hold of her hand that is wet and cold from clasping onto the umbrella handle.

'Ok,' Shania says softly, wondering how she can leave before Callum tries to kiss her.

She's always fancied Callum but she's not sure she is ready for anyone to touch her yet.

As if reading Shania's thoughts, Callum pulls away from her again and walks off towards the back of Robin House. 'I'll see you soon then,' he says, turning back to smile at Shania.

Shania watches as he climbs up the grassy bank and disappears, swallowed up by the darkness.

The shopping is heavy and hurts as it swings against Jade's thin legs, as she makes her way back along the path towards Magpie House. Jade bends her head down, trying to protect herself from the worst of the rain, which is lashing against her face. She glances up to see where she is going, stopping in surprise when she sees Shania standing near the rubbish bins outside Robin House. It is only when she has walked further towards the building, that she can see Shania is not alone. Beside the teen is Callum Woods.

Jade stands in the rain, rooted to the spot, unable to move until she sees Callum move out of sight around the back of the building. She waits for a moment to make sure that he has gone before striding angrily across the path towards Shania, who is still staring after him.

'What you doing, talking to him?' Jade shouts to her friend.

Shania turns around, puzzled as to who is shouting at her. She is taken aback when she sees who it is, she certainly was not expecting to see her ex-best friend. 'None of your business.'

'Don't go there Shania, he's trouble you know.'

'He's ok and anyway what do you know about it?' Shania challenges.

Jade stands still, wanting to tell her friend what Callum has done to her but she is too ashamed, especially when it was her fault that Shania was raped. She stares open mouthed at Shania, trying to get the words out but she can't.

Shania storms past her and hurries up the path, leaving Jade still standing in the rain. Her thin coat gives her little protection from the damp chill that is seeping through to her clothes. The cold eventually stirs her from the stupor she has fallen into. Shania picks up the carrier bags that she dropped a few moments earlier, then slowly makes her way back to the flat.

Zoe Thompson wakes up just as Jade is putting a pizza into the oven. 'You're a good girl,' she says, kissing Jade on the top of her head.

Jade is too shocked to reply - it has been a long time since her mother has shown her any affection. She pulls three plates out from a cupboard and opens a tin of beans to go with the pizza. Her hands are still shaking a little from her encounter with Shania. With her appetite now lost at the thought of her ex best friend, Jade puts a larger share of the meal onto her mother's plate before taking them through to the living room.

Zoe Thompson is sitting on the sofa smoking a cigarette, an open can of cheap lager on the table beside her. She smiles gratefully as Jade passes her a plate of food, before turning away to look out of the window. Jade wonders if her mother feels any shame that her daughter is the one looking after her, when it should be the other way around.

Chapter 28

Shania is seething. How dare Jade try to warn her off Callum, it is none of her business who she goes out with. Jade is just jealous now that Marlon is in prison and she no longer has any status on the estate. Shania turns on her mobile, trying to decide if she should text Callum tonight or leave it a bit longer. She does not want to appear too keen, but then again, she is so annoyed with Jade that she wants to see Callum again just to spite her.

Shania's thoughts are interrupted by a loud beeping coming from her phone, informing her that a new text message has been received. The message is from Callum, asking her to meet him on Sunday. Shania hurriedly replies that she is free that day and can meet him after tea. She feels a sharp pang of disappointment that she will be spending yet another Saturday evening stuck in the tiny flat on her own. With her earlier burst of anger having now dissipated, Shania wonders what Jade is doing and if she too is spending the evening alone.

It is going to be another lonely night for Jade, who has been left in charge of her little sister again as her mum is going to a party with Susie Smart. The thought of Shania makes her stomach knot up and a sickly feeling rises up in her throat. She can't believe that the girl who is supposed to be so brainy could be so dense when it comes to boys. It's obvious what Callum wants. She should know, the same thing happened to her when she got together with Marlon and look how that ended. She's just grateful that she did not get in any deeper with the gang, especially as she's heard rumours at school that they were caught sniffing solvents in the gardeners shed.

However much her best friend infuriates her, Jade does not want her to get involved with all that. She knows all too well where it could lead, her mum has told her often enough how she dated her father when she was at school, reminiscing about the time when they were caught at smoking in the alley behind the school and how they stole bottles of vodka and cider from the corner shop to drink in a nearby park. By the time they had left school, Zoe Thompson was five months pregnant and Jades father had moved onto more dangerous past times. When he was released from prison two years later, Zoe Thompson had welcomed him back with open arms, little realising the affect that prison could have on someone so young and impressionable. His personality had changed beyond recognition. Gone was the carefree impish lad who she fell in love with, replaced by a hardened junkie who had little time or energy to focus on anything other than his habit. Even so, Zoe had still married him.

Jade has seen the simple snaps that were taken after the ceremony at a local registry office; a pub meal afterwards with their friends had

268

sufficed to celebrate the union. It had not lasted of course. His behaviour had become increasingly erratic, more volatile, until her mother could stand no more of it and had kicked him out of the flat. That was the last they saw of him. Jade knows that it's likely her father is dead and is not certain that she really cares.

The afternoon drama has inspired Cook to investigate Mr Holt further and it only takes a few phone calls to establish that Trading Standards are indeed still interested in the breeder. They are also very interested in receiving Cook's amount of the condition of the house and by early evening, two Trading Standards Officers, one RSPCA inspector and a police constable, have descended on the quiet residential cul-de-sac. An hour later, Mr Holts house has been searched, documentation relating to the provenance of the animals in the property seized and Mr Holt taken to the council offices to be interviewed. The RSPCA, having witnessed the grim conditions the animals were living in, duly removed all the animals from the property.

During a search of the house, the police constable found a ladies' purse and a pink mobile phone stuffed at the back of a cupboard in the hallway - not the type of items they would have associated with a middle-aged man. The items, having been bagged and brought back to the police station for further investigation, soon revealed their real owner; Trudy Barnes.

Cook hurries to the council offices to escort Mr Holt back to the police station, where he will be formally interviewed. The journey does not take long, with most of the residents of Deben Quay either settled in their homes for the night or having already made their way to the pubs and restaurants.

Cook turns up the radio to fill the uncomfortable silence. As he listens to the soothing sound of classical music, he can feel his stress levels reducing as they drive closer to the police station. He pulls up into one of the empty spaces in front of the building, clearly marked for visitors, then escorts Mr Holt into the building so that he can be booked in at the front desk. Whilst Mr Holt is having his fingerprints and photos taken, Cook takes the opportunity to grab a cup of coffee from the vending machine on the ground floor. He winces as he sips the watery liquid but soon appreciates the shot of caffeine, which hits him just as Mr Holt is ready to be interviewed. Cook leads the suspect to an interview room where Fallow is already waiting to observe the proceedings.

'Do you know why you are here Mr Holt?' Cook asks as they sit down.

'Not really? Something to do with me selling dogs?' Mr Holt replies, looking nonchalant about the whole situation.

'Nope, that was why you were interviewed by Trading Standards. The reason why we are talking to you is because one of our officers found a purse and mobile phone in your house that does not belong to you.' Cook holds up the two items, which are sealed in clear plastic evidence bags.

'Oh them. I bought them off a fella in a pub, I thought they might make a nice present for my niece,' Mr Holt explains.

'Do you know where they came from?' Cook asks.

'No, I don't ask silly things like that.'

'So, you realise that they're stolen then?'

'I guessed they might be,' Mr Holt confesses. 'Can't really say otherwise can I?'

'Do you also realise that this purse and phone were owned by a young woman who is now dead?'

Mr Holt's eyes widen, he shakes his head slowly. 'No, I didn't,' he says quietly. 'It wasn't that one who was in the papers was it?'

'Trudy Barnes - she was found dead on the Hartsmere Estate. We're investigating her death so need to know how you acquired her purse and mobile phone.'

'I didn't know they were hers, honest. I bought them off two blokes in a pub.'

'Have you got names for the two men?' Cook asks, a thought popping into his mind as to who they could be.

'I don't know them, never seen them in the Kings Arms before but I heard they are called Charlie and Martin,' Mr Holt replies.

Cook glances at Fallow, who is diligently watching the story unfold in front of them. He cannot tell if the youngster recognises the significance of the information or not.

Cook smiles at Mr Holt. 'Thank you Mr Holt, you've been very helpful. We will need to charge you with handling stolen goods but once you've been charged you will be free to go.'

Mr Holt swallows hard, looking a lot less confident than he had been earlier. As soon as he has been formally charged, Fallow is tasked with escorting Mr Holt back home and with dropping Cook off en route. It has been several days since Cook has been home in the evening and he is desperate to read bedtime stories to his children.

Just as the trio reach the car, Cooks mobile rings - it is forensics team with the DNA results for Trudy Barnes – both of the samples given by both Martin and Charlie match the semen samples taken from Trudy's body.

The Hartsmere estate is eerily quiet, especially for a Saturday night, with one exception - directly above the Thompsons' flat another party is has started up. Music pulsates through the floor, vibrating through the concrete structure, keeping Jade's sister from sleeping. Jade sighs, she has no doubt her mum will be at the party. It is so unfair, just for once, couldn't her mum stay at home with them on a Saturday night? It has been so long since they all watched Saturday night TV together, even longer since they had been read bedtime stories. A thought occurs to Jade, if there was no party for her mum to go to then perhaps she would stay in with her and Darcey instead. Jade flicks through the mound of toys on her bedroom carpet until she finds what she is searching for; a card with a mobile phone number on it. Jade hesitates for a moment, unsure if she should really do this, then she reaches out for her mobile phone.

It is Morgans night off, but as ever, his work phone is switched on and to hand. A number that he does not recognise, flashes up on his screen. Curious, he presses the connect button and is surprised to hear Jades voice.

'Hello Mr detective, I thought you might like to know that those two blokes are having another party upstairs again. My sister can't sleep, they're making so much noise.'

Morgan pulls himself up and reaches for the remote control to turn down the volume of the TV. 'Thanks for letting me know Jade, we'll send someone out to sort it out. Try and get some sleep now.'

Morgan ends the call and redials to connect to Cook, who has now reached home. Cook fills Morgan in with the latest developments and Morgan in turn, informs Cook that at this precise moment, he knows the exact location of Charlie and Martin. The pieces of the jigsaw puzzle are all starting to fall into place.

Even by Deben Quays drug squad's standards, this particular Saturday evening is proving to be extremely busy. The party in Magpie House is in full flow by the time they arrive, the familiar aroma of cannabis floating down the stairwell as they approach the door to Martin and Charlies flat. Cook has tagged along as well, keen to ensure that the operation goes smoothly and any vital evidence is secured. He is determined that he will not let these two young men get away with anything else.

It takes several hours to process the crowd of party goers, all of whom are under the influence of at least one illegal substance or another. Cook accompanies Martin and Charlie back to the station, where they are booked in and taken straight to the cells so that they can sober up before being interviewed. Now they have the evidence, the two men can be formally charged with rape, as well as theft, selling stolen goods and possession of drugs.

Morgan arrives a little after ten PM, bringing with him a flask of coffee and a Tupperware box full of cakes that Celia made that afternoon. Cook grins when he sees the container, having experienced Celia's excellent cooking on many occasions. It is just what they need - it is going to be a long night.

As soon as the duty doctor has deemed Charlie and Martin fit to interview, the two detectives hurry down to the rooms, keen to get the interviews over.

'Let's start off with the drug charges, shall we?' Cook says as he sits down opposite Charlie.

Charlie stares at the wall, seemingly unable to comprehend how serious the situation is, or perhaps he is only too aware of the consequences of his actions and is choosing not to think about it.

'Ok, so you were found this evening with both cannabis and cocaine in your possession.' Cook says, staring at Charlie.

Charlie nods, 'Yeah, can't really deny it can I seeing as they were found on me.'

'And you understand that you will be charged with possession and the intent to supply these drugs?'

'No way! I didn't say nothing about selling them. They were just for me.'

'Ok well, we will be talking to the others at the party, so let's see what they say about it,' Cook says. 'Let's move onto the other reasons why you are here.'

Charlie looks up at Cook in puzzlement, 'What do you mean?'

'I mean the sale of stolen goods to a Mr Holt in the Kings Arms pub. In particular, a purse and mobile phone.'

'I don't know nothing about that,' Charlie snorts.

'We have a witness who can confirm that these items were sold by you to Mr Holt.'

'Ok but that doesn't mean they were stolen,' Charlie sniggers.

'It does if the items happen to belong to Trudy Barnes, who as you know, is dead.'

Charlie closes his eyes and takes in a deep breath. 'Ok, you got me there as well. She left them in our flat the night she died. And yes I did sell them, but I didn't steal them, she left them behind. Finder's keepers and all that.'

'That's still classed as stealing Charlie, they weren't your property to sell.'

Charlie sighs deeply, crossing his arms in front of him. The evening is very rapidly turning from bad to worse.

'So, let's move on shall we, to the night Trudy died. You see, the postmortem proved that Trudy was raped.'

'I don't know nothing about that,' Charlie says quickly, the colour draining from his cheeks.

'No? Well, you and your brother had sex with Trudy the night she died and we have the DNA evidence to prove it. How did she die Charlie? Were you and your brother there?'

'No!' Charlie shouts. 'It was nothing to do with us I swear!'

'Why don't you tell me what happened that night then?' Cook goads.

'We didn't hurt her I swear, well nothing that she didn't mind us doing. She liked it rough, you see.'

Cook nods his head, 'Go on.'

'We both had sex with her at the party then she left with some bird. I swear she was alive when we last saw her.'

'What if I don't believe you Charlie, what if the DNA evidence we have is enough to convict you of Trudy Barnes murder?'

'It wasn't me, honest,' Charlie whispers, slumping forward, his head in his hands. 'I think I'd better see a solicitor before I say any more.'

Cook reaches over to pause the recorder, the interview will have to be suspended until a solicitor is found.

In the adjoining room, Morgan is having a similar conversation with Martin. It does not take long to obtain a confession to the sale of the stole goods, nor the fact that both brothers had sex with Trudy the night she died. Martin's account corroborates his brother's, that Trudy liked rough sex, though he did also admit that Trudy was in quite a state that night, intoxicated with both alcohol and cocaine and was barely conscious, let alone in a fit state to give informed consent. The two brothers are settled back into their cells for the night, awaiting a solicitor to witness them making formal statements. It is probably the closest they will get to the truth, Morgan deduces as he drives home again, eager to enjoy the rest of his Saturday night with his wife.

Chapter 29

Morgan has been asleep for less than two hours when he is awoken by the sounds of a mobile phone ringing; trouble is brewing on the Hartsmere estate. He scrambles out of bed, hitting his knee on the bedside table as he pulls on the thick socks that were discarded only a little while earlier.

The sound of Morgan swearing at his now injured knee, wakes Celia who opens her eyes, blearily looks at Morgan, then closes them again. Morgan watches as his wife rolls onto her side, pulling the duvet up underneath her chin as always.

By the time Morgan has pulled on his jeans and jumper and collected his jacket from the porch, Fallow is already waiting outside in the car.

'What's happening?' Morgan asks as he climbs into the front seat.

Fallow waits until Morgan has fastened his seatbelt before pulling out of the driveway. 'Apparently there's some kind of riot on the estate. We think it might be something to do with Marlon Turners gang and another gang who live on the estate.'

'Bloody hell, we're turning into Americans,' Morgan says cheekily, silently willing the young detective to drive faster.

'Bennett has instructed us to stay out of the way until it's calmed down but he thought we should be there given we're already working on three cases on the estate.'

'Fat lot of good we're doing with them,' Morgan snorts.

Fallow looks a little disappointed at his mentor's attitude. 'We got Marlon Turner, didn't we?'

'Only for Lewis Smiths death, what about Shania and all those other girls he's abused and victimised. What about Trudy Barnes, we're no closer to finding out what happened to her. Hell, at the moment we don't even know if her death was accidental or not.'

Morgan folds his arms and turns his head to look out of the car window, taking in the passing houses as they speed past the quiet community who are largely asleep. Fallow takes the hint and drives on in silence.

Zoe Thompson has just left the Punch and Judy when the trouble begins. Luckily for her, she decided to visit the pub instead of going to Charlie and Martins party - she didn't fancy going there again, not after last time. The thought of being in the same place she had last seen Trudy was too much to bear and a decision that unbeknown to her, saved her from being arrested.

Zoe hurries along the walkway as quickly as she dares, tottering about on her high heels, desperate to reach the safety of her flat before it all kicks off. She can sense that the atmosphere is even more tense than usual. She has lived on the estate long enough to know when something is about to happen.

Zoe pushes the key into the door lock, still breathless from the effort of trying not to slip as she swayed up the concrete staircase. Pushing open the door, she stumbles down the hallway and into the living room, which is encased in darkness.

'Blimey, what you doing here sitting in the dark? You scared me half to death!' Zoe says when she spots the small figure that is barely visible in front of the window.

'Just watching out the window, something's going on, I can feel it.'

'I know what you mean. The estate gives me the creeps at night, especially when those lads are hanging around.'

Jade turns to look at her mother. 'Which lads?'

'The ones who live at the other end of the estate. Who knows what they're doing here, causing trouble I reckon.'

Zoe turns on the cold water tap and fills two glasses, handing one to Jade. 'I'm off to bed. Don't stay up too late.'

Jade nods, having no intention of moving from her spot by the window. She wonders if she should warn Shania, just in case she has gone out to meet up with Callum. She pulls out her mobile phone from the front pocket of her jeans and quickly types a message, presses send then sits back on the sofa to wait for a reply.

The roads nearest to the estate are already blocked by police vans, fire engines and ambulances by the time the two detectives arrive. Fallow pulls the car over next to an ambulance, where a paramedic is tending to a police officer who has a large cut on his face that is bleeding profusely. As soon as the officer sees Morgan and Fallow, he motions for them to approach.

'I'd turn around and leave if I were you, there's a bloody riot going on if you hadn't already heard.'

Morgan pulls out his ID card and shows it to the officer. 'What's happening then?'

'It looks like a couple gangs are fighting over the estate. They started out fighting outside the shops, then one of them pulled a gun out and took over Blackbird Terrace.'

'Do we know who they are?' Fallow asks.

'Not yet, we think they're local lads.'

The conversation abruptly ends as the paramedic steps in front of the injured office to tend to his cheek, which is oozing blood onto the lapels of his jacket.

In the distance, Morgan can hear shouting. He walks towards the parade of shops in the direction of the noise. As he turns the corner onto the paved walkway, he sees spots of blood on the ground, intermingled with debris from the vandalised shops. In front of him is a line of police officers standing across the path, preventing anyone from entering or leaving the area. Close by, near the Punch and Judy, a group of youths are throwing anything they find - bottles, bricks and burning rags - towards the police line.

Morgan stares transfixed as the thin blue line of officers in riot gear pushes on towards the group of lads, ducking the missiles as they fall around them. Gradually the group moves out of sight behind the pub, where Morgan knows from his own training, they will now be trapped by another line of officers who will have gathered behind them.

Morgan only realises that he has been holding his breath when the rioters have moved out of sight. As a relived silence descends on the area that only moments before was a battleground, Morgan brings his attention back to the parade of shops. Coming from behind the retail outlets, thick black smoke is billowing out from a window in Blackbird Terrace. Morgans stomach churns; Shania.

Hearing footsteps behind him, Morgan turns to see Fallow jogging to catch up with him.

'Blackbird Terrace is on fire,' Fallow says breathlessly as he stops beside Morgan.

'I can see that,' Morgan replies sharply, turning his back on the young officer.

The air is acrid and heavy, the smell of burning synthetic materials wafting over each time the wind blows in their direction, bringing with it a flurry of charred flakes that snow down upon them. Morgan hopes that is all that is burning and wishes he could work out which window belongs to the Smart's flat.

Morgan is jolted from his thoughts by Fallow, who is tugging at his sleeve. A figure has appeared from Blackbird Terrace and is walking towards them, carrying what looks like a body. Morgan pushes his way through the line of officers to reach the young woman, who is struggling with the heavy load and collapses in front of him.

'Someone get a paramedic,' Morgan shouts over the din of the fire, which is eating its way through the building in front of him. He scoops up the unconscious figure and passes her to Fallow before turning back to the young girl who is now curled up on the pavement, gasping for breath. Tears begin to wash away the blackened soot, leaving pink streaks across her youthful face. It is Jade.

Morgan looks back towards the other figure, who is now being carried off towards an ambulance. He can of course see now that it is Shania. Morgan helps Jade to sit up and drink some bottled water, then he sits down beside her on the pavement, whilst they wait for the paramedics to return. When the paramedics eventually reappear, Morgan tightly holds onto the teen's hand as an oxygen mask is placed over her swollen mouth.

'We need to get her to hospital,' the paramedic says, gently moving Morgan out of the way so that they can lift Jade into an awaiting wheelchair.

Morgan steps to one side, his eyes fixed on Jade, a sense of pride washing over him as she is carefully wrapped up in a crimson blanket, still struggling to breathe through her damaged lungs. For once the girl has done the right thing.

Morgan and Fallow follow the ambulance to Hemley Hospital. The chaotic scene they have left behind them soon becomes a distant memory the further they travel away from the estate. Their focus now is on Jade and Shania.

As they are parking in the hospital car park, an announcement comes over the radio that the police now have control over the estate - the riot is over. Several arrests have been made and a number of casualties are now on their way to the hospital. The fire crews have been issued with the task of ensuring that there are no further flames in Blackbird Terrace, leaving the police officers to account for those who are still missing and identifying those whose bodies have already been found.

Morgan sinks into a hard plastic chair in the reception area, waiting for Fallow to return with something that loosely resembles coffee. He watches as a myriad of faces hurry past him, their features a blur. All Morgan can see is Jade carrying her friend out of a burning building. He

284

wonders if they will both survive and if they do, how the events of today might change their lives. When he arrived at the hospital, the doctors had been uncertain if Shania would pull through, the burns to her face and hands being so extensive. Jade's future though looks more hopeful, having suffered only minor burns and smoke damage to her lungs from breathing in the toxic fumes.

As Morgan looks up to take hold of the coffee that Fallow is offering to him, he catches sight of a stretcher rushing past him, a familiar face lying on the trolley. Morgan pushes Fallow to one side, leaps up and runs down the corridor, calling after the paramedics who are racing ahead of him towards the operating theatre. He catches up with them just in time to see the trolley disappear through the double doors into the anaesthetic room. Forbidden to enter, there is nothing more he can do but pace up and down outside, waiting for someone to appear.

Chapter 30

An hour passes before Morgan is rewarded with the news that surgeons have been able to repair Callum Wood's injuries. The lad was stabbed three times in the abdomen and suffered some superficial burns to his hands. Although still very weak, he is now conscious and Morgan is allowed to speak to him for a few minutes.

Morgan is shown through to the intensive care ward, which is located in close proximity to the operating theatre. He spots Shania lying in the first bed on the right as he enters the room. She is sleeping, having been heavily sedated to allow her damaged body time to recover from her horrific burns. He passes by her bed towards the closed curtain where Callum is lying.

Morgan is surprised at how pale the boy is, how feeble he has become as he struggles to sit upright. A nurse brushes past him to assist Callum, plumping up a pillow behind him for support.

'What happened?' he asks Morgan.

'I was hoping you might be able to tell me that. You know that you're in serious trouble, don't you?'

'How's Shania? I tried to get her out of the flat but I couldn't breathe.'

'Lucky for her Jade was there then. She got her out.' Morgan walks around the bed to the window and opens the blinds a couple of inches so that he can watch the sun begin to rise over the hospital car park. 'She's been burnt quite badly you know, she's had to be sedated,' he says, looking in the direction of the bed that Shania is occupying.

Callum swallows, his eyes searching the area where Morgan is looking. In the corner, the motionless outline of a teenager is being tended to by a nurse. Morgan follows Callum's gaze. 'Yes, that's her. They're going to move her to a specialist burns unit soon but first they need to stabilise her breathing as her lungs and windpipe were damaged by the smoke.'

Callum nods, sinking back down into the pillows. 'It wasn't my fault you know.'

'What wasn't?'

'Any of it. I had nothing to do with Shania being attacked.'

'Who did then?'

'Marlon. Jade accused him of fancying Shania, she thought she'd been flirting with him, wanted to steal him from her. He wanted to show Jade that it wasn't true. And show the rest of us how it's done.'

'What about Lewis Smith?'

'I don't know, I wasn't there.'

'Now why don't I believe you?' Morgan says, his patience waning.

'I don't know, honestly.' Callum's gaze moves to the nurse who is heading towards them.

The nurse quietly asks Morgan to leave, protesting that he has been there long enough and Callum needs to rest. Morgan, who is only too pleased to get away from the troublesome teenager, heads straight back down the corridor towards the front entrance of the hospital, where Fallow is still waiting for him to return.

As soon as Fallow sees Morgan approach, he stands up to greet him. 'Jade's awake, we can go and see her.'

'Ok, I'll go. I need you to stay here and wait for news on Shania. Callum Woods is also in intensive care. He reckons that it was Marlon Turner who attacked Shania.'

Fallow sighs, 'I guess we may never know the truth.'

Morgan rolls his eyes, the young detective will never solve cases if he has such a despondent attitude.

The ward is quiet, with just one nurse creeping around the dark corridors. Morgan is shown into a side room where he finds Jade lying in the bed, her mother sitting beside her.

'Can I have a few minutes alone with Jade please?' Morgan asks as he enters the room.

Zoe Thompson scowls. 'I'll just go and get a coffee, I won't be long,' she says to her daughter.

Morgan waits until Zoe has left before gently shutting the door. He sits down on the newly vacated chair, trying not to reveal on his face the pity he is feeling for the young girl.

Jade removes her oxygen mask so that she can speak more easily. 'How's Shania

288

doing?' She asks, her voice raspy as she struggles for breath.

'She's not too good Jade. She's going to be taken to a specialist burns unit soon where she will be able to get the help she needs. Can you tell me what happened last night? Why were you in Blackbird Terrace?'

'I saw what was happening from my bedroom window and I was worried that Shania might be out with Callum and get caught up in it all so I went to take a look.'

'That was very brave of you Jade.'

The teen shrugs her shoulders before replacing her mask again for a few moments, breathing in the oxygen. 'They were all outside the shops when I got there. I saw Callum and the others go towards Blackbird Terrace, I knew where Callum would go. He looked scared and was holding his stomach. I guessed he'd been hurt so would try and hide somewhere. Not much of a leader is he?'

'No, I suppose not.'

'I ran around to the back of the building and hid under the stairs. I got there too late though, one of the other gang members had already followed Callum up to Shania's flat. I saw him set light to something and push it through the letterbox. Callum came running down the stairs but Shania didn't, so I went in there and got her out.'

'I thought you weren't friends with Shania anymore? I guess you two made up?'

Jade looks towards the door, perhaps wishing that her mother would arrive and rescue her from answering the awkward question. 'I'm tired now, I need to go to sleep,' she says, wriggling down into the crisp white bed sheet. Jade pulls the blanket up to her neck, wincing as the movement hurts her burnt fingers.

Realising that Jade is not ready to talk, Morgan leaves the ward to re-join Fallow, who is still waiting in the reception area for any further news on Shania.

Cook is also waiting for news. Bennett has instructed him to assist with interviewing the suspects who were arrested on the Hartsmere estate - they do not yet know the identities of those involved in the riot but they have a very good idea of who they might be.

When the call comes, Cook makes his way down to the front desk where a group of teenagers are waiting to be processed. Cook walks amongst them, checking to see if he recognises any of them. He counts three members of Marlon Turners gang and seven others who he does not recognise, presumably belonging to the other gang. It is going to be a very long night.

Zoe Thompson is surprised to see Susie Smart standing at the reception desk, shouting at the receptionist as she tries to find out where her daughter has been taken. Zoe strides over to her friend and puts a hand on her shoulder, gently squeezing the bony frame.

'Have you come to see Shania?' Susie says.

'No, I didn't know she was here. My Jade's here. Do you know what happened?'

'I was still in the Punch and Judy and heard all the noise outside but they wouldn't let us out, so we had to stay there until it was all over. The police reckon it was that gang who attacked my poor Shania.'

Zoe nods, 'I'd heard that as well. There was a fire at your flat wasn't there?'

'Yeah, poor Shania's in a terrible way and I don't seem to be able to get any help from this lot,' she says, staring at the receptionist who is still flicking through the records on the computer.

'Ms Smart, your daughter has been taken to Harefield Hospital, which is a specialist burns unit. I'll organise a taxi to take you there.'

Susie stares at her, trying to absorb the information into her befuddled brain. 'That means she's bad, don't it?'

The nurse receptionist smiles sympathetically, reaching for the phone to call for a taxi.

'Can't you tell me how bad she is?' Susie asks, frantic for news of her daughter.

The receptionist holds up a hand to calm the woman whilst she speaks to a local taxi firm. After she has replaced the receiver, she asks

Susie softly to wait by the main entrance for the taxi, which will take her to the nearby burns unit.

Zoe watches as Susie settles into one of the hard plastic chairs in the waiting area, before walking onwards towards the all-night café where she can get a coffee.

Morgan spots Susie from where he is sitting in the waiting area of the emergency department. He has never felt very comfortable around distressed women and is reluctant to go over there. Instead, he picks up a discarded newspaper from a nearby chair and begins reading.

Fallow on the other hand is in his element. As soon as he sees Susie he walks over to her and sits down in the vacant seat beside her. Morgan watches from behind his newspaper as Fallow informs Susie of the evening's events as best he understands them.

As soon as the taxi driver appears, Fallow leaps up from his seat and accompanies the shaken woman outside. Morgan watches as Fallow gently pats Susie's back, wondering how someone so young could have learnt such good people skills. Morgans thoughts are abruptly interrupted by a nurse, who informs him that Jades condition has suddenly deteriorated and that she is asking to see him.

Chapter 31

Jade is pale and weak. Her breathing has become even more laboured than when Morgan saw her earlier. Jade tries to smile at Morgan when he enters the room and in turn, the detective tries not to show the deep concern he is feeling at seeing how much worse she has become in such a short space of time.

Jade motions for Morgan to sit down on the chair next to her bed. She takes a few deep breathes before removing her oxygen mask so that she can talk more easily.

'You asked to see me,' Morgan says gently, resting his hand on the bed.

'I need to tell you something,' Jade says before breathing into her oxygen mask again. 'It was all my fault, Shania I mean.'

'What do you mean?'

'It was my fault,' she repeats. 'I told them where she'd be and what time. I said I'd meet her in the playground, then text her to say I would be in Robin House. It's my fault she was raped.' Jade says, her face crumpling. She replaces her mask again and leans back into the pillow, exhausted by the conversation.

Lack of sleep is making Morgan feel confused and he wonders if he has heard Jade correctly. 'You set her up? But why would you do that? She's your best friend?'

Jade removes the mask again. 'She was after Marlon. She'd always liked him.'

'What made you think that?'

'He told me. They were all talking about it, how she was going to be his girl. I told him she wanted to show him that she liked him and that she liked being roughed up. I told him the more the merrier. So, you see it's my fault.'

'Is that why you went to rescue her last night?'

Jade nods, too exhausted to answer. 'Please, you got to tell her to stay away from Callum Woods. He's just as bad as Marlon.'

'What do you mean?'

Jade looks down at the sheets and begins picking at her nails.

'Did he hurt you Jade?' Morgan asks.

Jade nods, tears running down her cheeks.

Morgan reaches across the bed to grab a tissue from the box on the bedside cabinet. 'Why didn't you tell me?'

Jade replaces the mask over her mouth and closes her eyes, the tears still running down her cheeks. Morgan watches as her breathing becomes shallower and the exhausted girl falls into a deep sleep.

Callum Woods is moved onto a surgical ward as soon as he has recovered sufficiently from surgery. His face shows his undisguised annoyance when he spots Morgan approaching his bed.

'We need to talk,' Morgan spits, pulling up a chair and sitting down next to the bed.

'What about, I already told you about last night.'

'How about the night you raped Jade Thompson?'

The noise on the ward slows to a standstill as those in earshot crane to listen in on the conversation.

'Well, I'm waiting.' Morgan says, his foot pumping up and down on the hard floor.

Callum looks up at him and shrugs his shoulders. 'She enjoyed it, what else can I say.'

'You'll be charged for this you know.'

'Prove it, it's her word against mine and I say she was up for it, just like she was up for it with Marlon Turner.'

'Jade's made a statement and is willing to testify against you,' Morgan lies.

Callum's face pales as he realises that this allegation is not going to go away as easily as he had first thought. 'What if I tell you about Lewis Smith?' he asks hopefully. 'I'm surprised Jade didn't tell you herself - she was there after all.'

Morgan leans forward, drawing his face closer to Callum's. 'Go, on.'

'She followed us. The others didn't see her but I did, skulking in the doorway as we went up the stairs to that nosy old gits flat. I saw her standing in the shadows, she must have seen

Marlon pour petrol onto his pants and set fire to them. We couldn't stop laughing, Marlon setting fire to his pants I mean.'

'I wonder why Jade was there?' Morgan said softly, as much to himself than to Callum.

Callum shrugs his shoulders, 'Maybe she wanted to see where it happened, with Shania I mean.'

Morgan looks at the teen in disgust. 'You'll be arrested once you're out of here, let's see if that wipes that smug look off your face.' He pushes back the chair, hitting it against the wall with a bang loud enough to gain the attention of a nurse who is attending one of the other patients. Then Morgan strides out of the ward without looking back, unsure of whom he feels more angry with at this precise moment, Callum Woods, Jade or himself.

Jade does not look any better than she did half-an-hour earlier. Morgan wonders what is delaying Fallow, who has gone in search of Jade's mother. Jade seems surprised when she wakes up to see Morgan there again. She tries to wriggle up the bed, sitting up as much as her tired body will allow.

'I've just been talking to Callum,' Morgan says. 'Why didn't you tell me you saw Marlon set fire to Lewis Smiths flat?'

Jade removes her oxygen mask an inch so that she can speak. 'I didn't want to end up like him did I. Anyway, I got a younger sister you know, it was bad enough what they did to me but Callum promised he would do the same to my sister if I ever blabbed about that night. I didn't have no choice, did I.'

Morgan nods, his anger dissipating a little. He sits down on the end of the bed. 'What about now? Callum Woods will be arrested as soon as he leaves this hospital, you don't need to worry about him anymore.'

'There's always more of them though, isn't there.'

Morgan sighs, knowing that the teen is right. He walks over to the small window, which allows a meagre amount of natural light into the room. 'How did you know they were going to torch Lewis Smiths flat?'

'I saw them from the living room window. They were carrying a petrol can and were walking towards Robin House. It weren't difficult to work out the rest.'

'What about the night Trudy Barnes died. Were you looking out the window that night?'

Jade does not respond. Morgan turns around to look at her and sees that the teens eyes are glinting with fear. 'Come on Jade, you need to help me out here. We need to catch whoever it was who killed Trudy. What did you see that night from your window?'

Jade sighs heavily then begins coughing, her lungs trying to rid themselves of the noxious substances from its' delicate tissues. She takes in a few deep breaths and waits for the cough to settle again. 'It was about 12.30 when Trudy left our flat. She'd had a row with my mum, then I heard her run down the stairs and slam the front door. Mum must've followed her as I saw them near the playground arguing. She didn't do it anything to hurt Trudy though, I know as I watched mum walk back into the building.'

Morgan nods, waiting for Jade to take a few more deep breaths before she is able to continue talking. 'Did you see anyone else outside?' Morgan asks.

'Only that policeman who walks around the estate. I've always thought he was a bit creepy. Me and Shania always hide when we see him, there's something about him, we just don't like.'

'Do you mean Trudy's husband?'

Jade shrugs her shoulders. 'I don't know his name, but he's always hanging around, even when he's not in his uniform.' She slumps back into the bed, too exhausted to talk any further.

Morgan watches as Jade closes her eyes, her breathing becoming shallower. This is the break-through they have been waiting for but somehow it no longer feels like a victory.

At that moment, Fallow returns with Jades mother. As soon as Morgan sees them, he grabs hold of Fallows arms and pulls him back out of the room. 'We need to go back to the station. Colin Barnes was seen with his wife on the estate the night she died.'

Fallow raises his eyebrows but does not respond, not wishing to say anything foolish in front of Morgan. He always seems to annoy his team, no matter how hard he tries to be helpful. It is not how he expected the job to be but he's stuck with it now, he can't let down his family again.

Morgan drives at high speed back through the busy roads of Deben Quay towards the police station. He pulls up outside the front of the building and gets out of the car, leaving Fallow to try to find a parking space in the car park. Morgan runs up the steps, slamming the front door open in his haste to reach Cook, who is still interviewing suspects from the previous night.

Cook, who is exhausted and more than a little frustrated by his lack of progress with the gang members who started the riot, was even less pleased at being torn away from the interview room, snapping at Morgan before he has the chance to explain the reason for the interruption.

Morgan ignores his friend's ill-temper – he knows all too well how the job can get to you. He pulls Cook into an empty room. 'We've found a witness who saw Colin Barnes on the Hartsmere estate the night Trudy died. And even better, she saw them together at the time of Trudy's death.'

Cook's mouth falls open in shock, 'Who's the witness?'

'Jade Thompson.'

Cook rolls his eyes, as he sits down on the edge of a nearby desk.

'I'm sure she's telling the truth. She also saw Marlon Turner and Callum Woods go up to Lewis Smiths flat. Callum has admitted to seeing Marlon push a burning rag through the letterbox.'

'Well I never, any more surprises for me?'

'Callum raped Jade. I don't know when but I think it's unlikely she will press charges especially after what she just told me.'

Cook raises one eyebrow, waiting for Morgan to continue.

'She set up Shania to get raped by Marlon. The silly girl was jealous of her. Callum Woods swears he wasn't there but I have a feeling he was. It was definitely Marlon though who instigated the attack.'

'I doubt we will be able to pursue that one, not without Shania telling us what happened. Good news about the Lewis Smith case though, Marlon's bound to be convicted now. I can't wait to see his face when he hears of the evidence against him.' Cook stands up, his face relaxing at the thought of good news for a change.

'Any luck with the rioters?' Morgan asks.

'Not really, none of them will talk. We had to send a couple of them to hospital to get treated, but I can't see them wanting to press charges, can you?'

Morgan shakes his head - they will never involve the police, any disagreements between gangs are normally settled amongst themselves. They should expect a re-run of the previous night sometime soon and this time they might not be so lucky; someone could end up dead.

Cook makes his way back to the interview room, having first stopped off at the canteen to grab a sandwich and a coffee. For once, Morgan is not hungry. The day's events had left a bad taste in his mouth and as yet, he still has not visited Shania. Having witnessed the effects of fire on the human flesh before, it is not a visit that he is relishing.

Chapter 32

It takes just over an hour to reach Harefield Hospital. Morgan feels a slight flutter of anxiety as he enters the building – he does not know what to expect and just hopes he is able to hide the shock on his face from Shania.

A nurse, who is sat at the reception desk, shows him through to the high dependency unit. The smell hits Morgan before he has even entered the room; a noxious mixture of disinfectant and cooked flesh. He is glad that he has not yet eaten and wonders if he will ever be able to eat barbecued meat again.

Shania's bed is located in the far corner of the room, overlooking a small courtyard garden, which houses a singular bird table. Before Morgan reaches the bed though, his mobile bleeps and he backtracks out of the room and into the corridor again.

'James, it's Tom. I've got some bad news,'

Morgan leans against the corridor wall, his back pressing into the cold sterile structure. 'What's happened?'

'I'm really sorry but Jade died about half-an-hour ago,' Cook says.

Morgan closes his eyes, the room spinning as the world comes crashing down around him. He cannot speak, the shock crushing him.

'Her lungs were just too badly damaged by the smoke,' Cook continues.

'Thanks for letting me know, I'm just about to speak to Shania.'

'Maybe she shouldn't know quite yet,' Cook says gently. 'It's going to take her a long while to recover from her injuries.

Morgan sighs, 'I don't know what to do. I can't lie to her if she asks after Jade.'

'Do whatever you think is best.'

The call ends, leaving Morgan with the unenviable task of either telling a young girl that her best friend who saved her life is dead, or lying to her until she is strong enough to cope with the truth. He decides that he will just wait and see what happens.

Taking a deep breath, Morgan pushes open the door to the ward and strides over to Shania's bed, a smile pasted onto his face. Shania looks worse than he had imagined. One side of her face is covered in plastic to protect the singed flesh beneath. Her hands, which are lying on top of the blankets, have been bandaged, leaving only the fingertips protruding from the encasement. Underneath her right hand is a push button to control the syringe driver that is lying on the bed next to her.

Shania looks up when she sees her visitor approach and beams at the detective. Susie Smart is sitting by her daughter's bedside, trying hard to behave as a caring mother should.

'Hello,' Shania croaks as Morgan reaches her bed. 'Have you come to check up on me?"

'Of course,' Morgan says, pulling up a chair from a neighbouring bed. 'How are you then?'

'Been in the wars as you can see but they're looking after me well in here.' Shania stops talking to take a sip of water, which Susie passes to her from the bedside table. She sucks noisily through the straw, barely able to lift her head up far enough up from the pillow to swallow.

'What happened? I don't really remember anything after Callum knocked on the front door?'

Morgan takes a deep breath. 'It looks like he was followed by the other gang and they set fire to your flat. You've had a very lucky escape.'

'How's Callum, he was stabbed, wasn't he?'

'He's had surgery to repair the damage from the knife wound, it looks like he will be ok.'

'I'm sure I dreamt that Jade was there but she couldn't have been, could she?' Shania looks up at Morgan with doleful eyes, waiting for him to respond.

Morgan stands up and begins to slowly pace up and down beside the bed, his trainers squeaking on the polished floor as he tries to decide how best to tell Shania what has happened.

'What's wrong?' Shania asks, realising that there is something that the detective does not wish to say.

'Jade was there Shania, she saw what was happening out of her window and went to find you. She was worried about you.'

'Where's she now then? I thought she'd visit me?'

'Jade was very brave Shania, she rescued you from the flat, she saved your life.'

'No, it was Callum who got me out.'

'No Shania, it wasn't Callum.' Morgan sits down again next to the bed. 'The thing is, Jade breathed in a lot of smoke which damaged her lungs. I'm really sorry Shania but Jade passed away earlier today.'

Shania stares at the wall opposite her, seemingly no longer listening. 'I want you to go now,' she says. Her eyes clamping firmly shut as tears begin to creep down her pale cheeks.

Morgan is too exhausted to protest and he walks back across the room that he had entered only minutes before.

The drive back home was one of the most painful Morgan ever encountered as he flicked through the radio stations, listening to the dance tunes that he knew Jade had loved. A dense fog has descended upon his life, which it seems will never dissipate.

Bailey is waiting by the front door for his master to return. Morgans shoulders sag with the relief at being home again. He bends down to scoop up the young pup, who enthusiastically licks his chin. He will need to talk to Shania again but for now he just wants to enjoy being alive.

Chapter 33

Cook is having a really bad day. Having procrastinated for as long as he dares, it is time to face reality. He needs to interview Colin Barnes again.

Having first consulted Bennett on how best to handle the case, Cook collects Fallow from the team office, where he is catching up on some paperwork.

It is rush hour in Deben Quay and the sheer volume of traffic hampers their progress, dragging it to a painfully slow pace. Cook can feel his heart pounding as they draw ever closer to Colin Barnes home. No one likes having to interview another officer, especially when it now looks as if he could have been involved in own his wife's death.

The curtains are closed in the living room and there are three curdled bottles of milk on the front doorstep, which is bathed in sunlight from the setting sun. Through the glass panels in the front door, Cook can see a pile of envelopes on the other side. He wonders if it is a reflection on Colin Barnes state of mind as normally a police officer would be wary about leaving a house looking unlived in. He knows of Colin more by reputation then by personal experience and has heard that although Colin is good at his job, he is not well liked amongst fellow officers, a fact that does not seem to unduly bother the forty-three year old.

Cook raps loudly on the door and waits for it to open. When the door does open, the unshaven, dishevelled appearance of the police officer behind it, accompanied by the strong aroma that immediately assaults Cook's nostrils, answers any questions that he might have about Colin Barne's state of mind.

'Can we come in please Colin, we need to talk.'

Colin stares at the two officers for a moment before shuffling back down the hallway. Cook watches the rounded, hunched shoulders disappear through the doorway, before following him into the house, leaving Fallow to shut the door behind them.

Cook picks his way through the myriad of empty beer cans, pizza boxes and discarded clothing, which adorns the patterned lounge carpet. A photograph album is lying on the coffee table, left open at some early pictures of the couple. He sits down in the armchair opposite Colin, who seems to care little at their presence. Cook wonders if anyone is looking after him.

'Colin, I'm sorry to visit you again but we've had some more information about the night your wife died.'

Colin Barnes does not respond but continues to stare at the television, which is switched off.

'Why didn't you tell us you were there that night, on the Hartsmere estate?'

Colin's focus slowly turns to Cook, his eyes boring into him.

'Did you see Trudy? Were you there looking for her?' Cook continues.

'I told you I went for a walk, I must have ended up there,' Colin mumbles.

'Come on Colin, it's time to tell us what happened. Did you see Trudy with Zoe Thompson? Did it make you angry?'

Colin makes a noise that almost sounds like laughter, before returning his attention back to the TV.

'You know that we're going to have to arrest you, don't you?' Cook says, standing up to retrieve his handcuffs from the back pocket of his trousers.

Colin looks at Cook with disdain. 'There's no need for that, I'll tell you what happened shall I? That tart was with her girlfriend, that pussy she's been fucking behind my back. How do you think that made me feel, knowing she was with a woman and on my patch as well. They all knew about it. Laughed at me when I walked my beat, kids taunting me that I couldn't keep my wife satisfied. Have you any idea how that feels?'

Cook shakes his head. 'Why don't you tell us what happened that night?' he says gently.

'It was like you said, I went looking for her on the estate. I knew she'd be there getting whatever it was that made her feel good and paying for it however she can. I saw them arguing outside Magpie House, Trudy stormed off towards the playground and I followed her. She didn't see me until I was right in front of her, too busy worrying about that slag.'

'Go on,' urges Cook.

'She was angry. Zoe had told her it was over, that she didn't want to share her anymore. She was really pissed off to see me, called me names, laughed at me. I just lost it, I hit her and she fell backwards onto the roundabout, I just thought she'd been knocked out,' Colin explained. 'I panicked, so I ran back here and waited for her to come back but she never did. I thought that she'd gone back to that sluts flat and stayed there the night. It was only when I went on duty the next morning and saw her still in the playground that I realised she was dead. She must have woken up and made her own way to the other side of the playground. I swear she was alive when I left her.'

'If you thought she was still alive, why didn't you phone for an ambulance? Why did you rearrange her body and her clothes, making it look like she had been raped?'

Colin snorts and looks at Cook. 'Why do you think, you seem to know everything.'

'I think you wanted us to think that she had been raped so we wouldn't find out that she'd sleeping with whoever supplied her with drugs. You were ashamed of her. Everyone knew who

310

she was and taunted you with it. I think that deep down you wanted her dead.'

'No, I never wanted to kill her,' Colin sighs resignedly.

Silence descends, no one knowing what to say next. Eventually Cook stands up, motioning for Colin to follow. They leave the house and head to the police station where Colin Barnes will be formally charged with manslaughter.

Chapter 34

In the last six months, much has changed on the Hartsmere estate. Morgan Turner is still awaiting trial for the murder of Lewis Smith and Callum Woods has had a short spell in prison for affray, for his part in the riots. As predicted, Callum retracted the confession he made in the hospital to Morgan about having any knowledge of the death of Lewis Smith or of the rapes of Shania and Jade. Without Jades witness account, there is little that can be done to pursue either case and reluctantly they have been left unsolved.

Morgan has been busy working on the case of Mr Holt, Bailey's breeder, who has at last been prosecuted for selling dogs with false pedigree certificates and issued with a large fine, which will hurt Mr Holts wallet, even if only for a short while. With the case now closed and the afternoon not quite over, Morgan decides to go to Blackbird Terrace and visit Shania, who he has not seen since that time in the burns unit when he told her of Jades death. After walking up the familiar steps to the second floor, Morgan feels a mixture of anticipation and excitement at seeing the teen again. To his surprise, Susie Smart opens the door, holding a dish cloth in one hand.

'Hello,' she says cheerfully, 'What brings you here?'

'I just finished working on another case and thought I'd pop in and see Shania.'

'She's at college this afternoon, she goes there three days a week, doing a hairdressing and beauty therapy course.'

Morgan grins, surprised at the news.

'She's had a lot of practice you know, with makeup on her face so she reckoned that she should put it to good use, help others like herself.'

'That's brilliant, I'm really pleased to hear that she's doing well,' Morgan says, a warm glow burning in the pit of his stomach.

'I'll tell her you called then,' Susie says before shutting the door again.

Morgan stares at the closed door for a moment, remembering the last time he was here. There is little evidence of the fire now but the events of that night are still fresh in his mind. He heads back down the urine-stained stairwell, his heart feeling lighter than it has been for a long time. It is warming to know that something good has happened to Shania despite all she has been through. Morgan feels a small flicker of hope that perhaps others on the estate might also escape the infinite cycle of evil, which seems to penetrate through so many of their lives.

ABOUT THE AUTHOR

J. D.Missen was born and raised in a small seaside town in Suffolk - the type of place that is overrun with tourists in the summer months and in the winter, an anticipatory quiet descends. She still lives in the town, with her two children and several pets.

Julie was first inspired to write after studying First World War poetry at school and has had poetry published in several anthologies as well as publishing her own poetry book 'Love, Death and Madness'. This passion for writing also developed into writing fiction and she quickly settled into the crime fiction and psychological thriller genres though she also has an interest in history, particularly modern and local history. J.D.Missen published her debut novel 'Confessions from a

Fractured Mind' in 2024, along with the first Detective Inspector Morgan Mystery 'Secrets From A Misty River'. She has also written two children's books; 'The Little Mole' and 'The Little Spider'.

Printed in Great Britain
by Amazon

62201777R00180